HOW DO YOU SAY GOODBYE

It occured to me that spending time in school with Alex—or Lawrence, for that matter—could get mighty sticky. What if one of them discovered me laughing and holding hands with the other? The thought made me want to ask for a sick pass and leave school immediately.

"So, what's your schedule?" Alex repeated his question.

I looked around to make sure Lawrence wasn't turning the corner.

"What's the matter?" Alex asked. "You know, you're acting kind of weird, Lisa."

I grabbed Alex's hand and pulled him inside the library.

"I didn't want Mr. Blomberg to see me. I told him I was going to be finishing up my report this period—I'm two days late already," I lied.

Alex looked at me and a few very big seconds elapsed before he said, "Are you sure it's Mr. Blomberg you want to avoid right now, Lisa?"

Bantam Sweet Dreams Romances
Ask your bookseller for the books you have missed

How Do You Say Goodbye

Margaret Burman

BANTAM BOOKS
TORONTO · NEW YORK · LONDON · SYDNEY

RL 6, IL age 11 and up

HOW DO YOU SAY GOODBYE
A Bantam Book / July 1982

ISBN 0-553-22517-0

Published simultaneously in the United States and Canada

*Bantam Books are published by Bantam Books, Inc. Its trademark,
consisting of the words "Bantam Books" and the portrayal of a rooster,
is Registered in U.S. Patent and Trademark Office and in other countries.
Marca Registrada. Bantam Books, Inc., 666 Fifth Avenue, New York,
New York 10103.*

PRINTED IN THE UNITED STATES OF AMERICA

0 9 8 7 6 5 4

How Do You Say Goodbye

Chapter One

I guess I'm what you'd call ordinary. Even my name, Lisa Kentwood, is ordinary. Some people say that I'm very pretty because I've got this long strawberry blond hair that falls straight and shiny down to my shoulders, but frankly, I think my looks are just OK. I'm certainly not a knockout like my best friend, Candace.

But I believe if you look hard enough you'll find something special about even the most ordinary person. So I hope you won't think it really weird that in my case the special thing about me is that I bake. I mean, *I* don't think it's weird, even though I am the only fifteen-and-a-half-year-old girl I know who comes home from school in the afternoons and heads straight for the kitchen—not to raid the refrigerator but to bake. And I don't mean those yucky package mixes, either. I mean right-from-scratch, big, shiny chocolate cakes and crunchy pecan pies and three-layer birthday cakes with inscriptions and fancy roses on them.

1

I probably fell in love with baking even before I knew how to light an oven—maybe when I saw my own first big, white, beautiful birthday cake when I was one year old. Now, I consider myself kind of a professional because I sell my cakes. Lately, my reputation has been growing in the neighborhood, and the orders are pouring in.

When I answer the phone at home, I always say, "Hello, Lisa's Creations. May I help you?" Often it's someone ordering my Devilish Chocolate Cake or a special Birthday Beauty three weeks in advance. Of course, sometimes it's Candace calling. She thinks my professional tone is a riot and never misses a chance to tease me.

"Lisa's Creations? Good," she'll say in a phony voice. "Because I'd like to order four thousand cupcakes—iced, of course—for tomorrow morning, promptly at nine. That won't be a problem, will it?"

But first, back to my baking. As I was saying, the orders are pouring in, and sometimes it gets pretty hectic trying to find time for cake orders, schoolwork, and my social life. Last fall I had this nightmare that I delivered a cake to school and my English report to some seven-year-old kid's birthday party. I don't know whether or not you believe that dreams can foretell the future, but that dream was a clear warning that I was going to be getting myself into real trouble.

It all began on a Friday afternoon in October. I was racing to put the finishing touches on a birthday cake that I'd promised to deliver at six o'clock sharp to a new family in the neighborhood, the Wileys. I was in a real panic because I was running late. It was nearly six, the cake wasn't ready, and I had a date at seven-thirty. Lawrence, my boyfriend, and I were double-dating with Candace and her boyfriend, Mike, that night. Then my mother, who's a part-time real estate broker, came home from work with two bags of groceries and had a fit when she had to put the bags down on the floor because every other surface was piled with pans and mixing bowls and pink frosting roses lined up on waxed paper.

"Really, Lisa, this is too much!" my mother fumed. "I promised you I'd make an early dinner tonight so you'd be ready for your date on time. But how can I make dinner with this mess?"

"I know, I know." I groaned. "I guess I did it again."

"That's right," she agreed. "You did it again."

What I'd done again was to say yes instead of no. I was always saying yes: "Yes, sure, I'll fill that order." "Yes, I'll volunteer to read my social studies report first." "Sure, Candace, you can call me tonight to talk about your argument with Mike. It's OK. Really. I'll just wake up early tomorrow morning to study for my math test."

My mother called it a Problem with a capital P. My sister, Ellie, called it a neurotic syndrome. (She's in her first year of college and wants to be a psychologist.) My father called it "just being nice," but I knew it was more than that. I knew it was my biggest fault, but I just couldn't seem to help it. If there was one thing that could make my heart pound in fear, it was that look of disappointment on someone's face or that sound of anger in someone's voice when I had to say no. If there was one thing I hated, it was knowing someone was mad at me. So I said yes, yes, yes to almost anything they wanted.

I told myself it was easier that way. But, of course, it wasn't always easier—sometimes saying yes made things much more difficult.

"Who was it this time?" my mother wanted to know.

"A new family—the Wileys," I told her without meeting her gaze. "I couldn't help it, Mom. Mrs. Wiley called a couple of weeks ago, I think, and asked as a special favor."

My mom was nodding. "Yes, yes, I know them. I sold them the white house on Mayview Lane about two months ago. I'm afraid I even boasted to Mrs. Wiley about your cakes."

"Oh, I guess that's how she heard about me so quickly," I said, piling the bowls and pans in the sink, happy to get off the subject of my "Problem."

Not that I really could forget about it. Not even for a minute. After all, in just a few hours I would be seeing Lawrence, and he was the major example of the trouble I could get myself into whenever I was less than truthful.

I guess I've known Lawrence longer than almost anyone. Even longer than Candace. I met her in the eighth grade, but I've known Lawrence since the fifth. Now we're all sophomores at Creston High in Michigan.

"I don't know why, but you're the only boy I feel comfortable calling up and talking to," I told him at the beginning of the year. "I mean, you're so easy to be with. I never get embarrassed asking to borrow your gray sweater or asking you to help me with my math homework."

What I was really trying to tell him was that I thought of him as kind of like the brother I never had. But he didn't take it that way.

"I'm really glad you feel that way, Lisa," he said seriously and stared at me for such a long, silent moment that for the first time, I began to feel uncomfortable with him.

After that, Lawrence stared at me a lot. I'd catch him silently staring at me while I'd be talking and laughing with a group of kids after school. "Come and join us, Lawrence!" I'd call casually.

"Can't," he'd always say and wave goodbye with one freckled, muscled arm. Every morning Lawrence worked out with weights. He had the same muscles and build as all the other big jocks in the school, except that Lawrence wasn't a jock. He never went out for team sports; he liked the solitary kind—long-distance running, lifting weights, bicycling.

I knew, deep down, why Lawrence was staring at me. I knew it from the first moment that he began to look at me differently. But, as usual, I didn't want to hurt him, didn't want to make him angry at me. So what did I do? Nothing.

And it wasn't as if Lawrence was a loser or anything close to it. Lawrence was great. He had coppery red hair and sky-blue eyes, and he was cute and sweet, even though he was a little too serious, a little too formal, he was a good friend, a great pal. It's just that Lawrence was the kind of boy you could never call Larry.

"And that's just the trouble," as I told Candace the afternoon he asked me out. "He's a pal to me, not a boyfriend."

"Why can't a friend be a boyfriend?" she asked. We were sprawled on her big canopy bed, and I was twisting a corner of her ruffled, blue and white quilt around and around as I struggled for an answer.

"I guess, to me, a boyfriend has to be someone special. At least, that's the way I thought my first boyfriend would be," I said seriously.

"Then why'd you say you'd go out with him?" Candace asked, pulling her quilt away from me before I could ruin it.

"Because everybody's suddenly started dating this year, and I wanted to, also, and Lawrence came up to me today with that serious face of his—you know how he gets, Candace— and he asked me out to the movies!" I blurted out in one breath.

Candace crossed her long, pony-slim legs Indian style and waited for me to go on. Most of the time, I did the listening while Candace talked about her problems. But when I really needed her, Candace could be a great listener, too.

"Well," I continued, "I did say no at first. I swear I did!"

"Yeah, but I bet I know what happened," Candace said, nodding knowingly at me. "He got that hurt puppy-dog expression on his face, and you just fell apart. Right?"

"Right," I admitted. "I ran after him and said that I act really dumb sometimes and that this was one of those times. I said I really wasn't busy Saturday night, I was just sort of playing hard to get. And, I don't know, Candy, maybe I was, because I felt so relieved when he stopped looking sad and gave me a big smile."

"Boy, you've really got a problem," Candace said, shaking her head.

"I know. I just don't know what to do about it yet."

And that's how I began going out with Lawrence. Actually, our dates were kind of fun. One thing about Lawrence: I never ran out of things to talk with him about, mostly because we disagreed about a lot of things. If he liked the movie, I didn't, and vice versa. We'd spend the next hour talking and arguing out our opinions. Once we went to see a visiting ballet company that was performing in town. I loved it; Lawrence hated it. And for the next two hours, Lawrence told me *why* he hated it.

Sometimes Lawrence talked to me about me. "You're really something else, Lisa, do you know that? I mean, I think you're so different from all the other girls. Special."

Whenever he got started on me, I'd begin to

feel very, very uncomfortable and try to change the subject. I guess I felt uncomfortable because I couldn't return the compliment. Not in the same way. I mean, I felt Lawrence was special, too—but not extraspecial, not magical, the way he felt about me.

When I was getting ready for my second date with Lawrence, my sister Ellie, who was home from college for the weekend, came into my room to talk. In the month that she had been away, I had completely redone my room, and now she looked around admiringly.

"I like what you've done to your room, Lisa. It's really great."

I had painted the walls myself in lavender, my favorite color. There were splashes of white and purple all over, and on one wall I had hung a huge photograph of one of the prettiest cakes I'd ever decorated.

"And that cake!" Ellie exclaimed. "You really are a Michelangelo in the kitchen."

I met Ellie's eyes and saw that she really meant it. Always before, there had been a kind of invisible wall of coldness between us. Ellie would wind up making smart remarks about me, and I'd wind up getting angry without showing it. But since she'd gone off to college, something was different. Suddenly the wall was gone, and we were talking, really talking.

"You know, Ellie, you've changed. You're different, somehow," I said.

She smiled. "I was just about to say the same thing to you." Then we both smiled.

She noticed that I had on my favorite lavender blouse, the one that made my eyes look violet, and she asked, "Got a date?"

"Mm-hmm," I mumbled as I brushed my hair.

"Anyone I know?"

"Mm-hmm," I mumbled again. "Lawrence. Lawrence Kerr."

Suddenly she was the old Ellie again, the teasing, mocking sister who knew just how to make me squirm.

"Old Larry! Really? Oh, that's right, we never call him Larry."

"That's right." I smiled, but my flaming cheeks gave me away.

"No wonder you look so glum. You're going out with glum Lawrence!" But when she saw the look on my face, she softened. "Hey, don't get mad. I was only joking."

"Ha-ha," I said emptily as she blew me a kiss and left. But she was right. I *was* glum. Here I was, going out on my second date in my entire life—and where was the magic? Why, I hummed more contentedly when I was alone in the kitchen, baking my cakes.

Which brings me back to that Friday afternoon with a cake to deliver to the new Wiley family—and later, a date with Lawrence, which I wasn't looking forward to.

I strapped the big boxed cake onto the back of my bike. When my dad saw that this baking business of mine had to be taken seriously, he'd rigged up a special carrier for me on the back of my bike so I could deliver my cakes more efficiently.

"A successful business person can't afford to waste her time walking all over town carrying boxes of cakes," he said, then proudly unveiled the contraption he'd been working on secretly in the garage.

"Dad! It's super!" I cried. And for a short while, it really did make my life easier. But as more orders came in—and as I refused none of them—I was finding myself as rushed and harried as before.

One block from Mayview Lane, I heard someone calling my name. It was Lawrence.

"Hey, Lisa, where are you going in such a hurry?" he asked, helping to steady my bike when I stopped.

"I've got this cake to deliver, and I'm almost ten minutes late already."

He looked worried as he asked, "You're not going to cancel out on me tonight are you?"

I put my hand on his shoulder to reassure

him. "No, of course not. It's just that I'm a little frantic right now."

"Good." He sighed and smiled faintly. "That's really great because there's something, well, special that I want to give you tonight."

He was staring at me again, and I began to walk my bike to break the spell. Oh, Lawrence, Lawrence! I wanted to cry out. Don't give me anything. I'm not the girl for you. Why can't you see that?

"I know," I said. "I bet you want to give me your old sweaty T-shirt!"

Of course, Lawrence didn't laugh, and my joke fell flat.

"It's something I think—I hope—you'll like a little more than that," he said seriously. Then, determined not to give away his secret, he gave me a quick, awkward hug and said, "See you later." As he ran off, he called, "I'll pick you up at seven-thirty—sharp!"

"Okay!" I called back cheerfully and climbed back on my bike. But all the way down Mayview Lane I felt like turning around, catching up with Lawrence, and telling him, once and for all, that I couldn't see him anymore. But, of course, I didn't turn around, I didn't break up with Lawrence. I just continued to pedal down Mayview Lane, sinking deeper and deeper into a you-brought-it-on-yourself kind of misery.

I didn't check my order book for the house number, just as I hadn't checked my order book when I had begun baking the Wiley cake. I was fairly sure I remembered it, though.

The Wiley house was big and white with tall green hedges all around it. Our house was gray and white with big pots of red geraniums at the front door. The Wiley house had no flowers out front, perhaps because they'd just moved in, and yet, it still had a warm and friendly look.

I left my bike in the driveway, carefully carried the cake box to the front door, and rang the bell. As I waited, I held the cake box in one hand, and with the other I brushed my hair back from my face and tucked in my turquoise blouse. I've always been grateful that I inherited my mother's clear skin and slim figure. I've never had to worry much about makeup or wearing the "right" clothes. My cheeks are pink naturally, and since I wear jeans most of the time—and look all right in them—I generally don't worry about how I look. I know I look OK. Maybe not dynamite like Candace, but OK.

Now, however, as I stood before the big white door, I felt strangely self-conscious. Suddenly I wished I had time to check myself out in the small mirror I carried in my purse. Suddenly I wasn't sure I looked OK at all. My face and hands felt clammy, and I was sure my hair was frizzing up. I looked down at my turquoise blouse and noticed it was wrinkled and that there were two flecks of icing staining one sleeve. I was a mess!

Oh, why hadn't I changed my shirt? And why was I so worried? And why was it so quiet here? There was supposed to be a birthday party for a seven-year-old girl going on in there, and I didn't hear a sound, not one sound. I decided I'd better go home and check my order book. Just as I turned to go down the steps, the door swung open.

"Hi!" someone said. "May I help you?"

Slowly I turned around. There before me was the handsomest boy I'd ever seen in my life. He was tall, but not too tall, with dark wavy hair and sea-green eyes that were staring at me in obvious amusement.

Something about him was familiar, and before I could control the words, they were out of my mouth.

"I know you!" I cried. "I've seen you in the halls at school." Then I stood back in amazement that I had said such a dumb thing in such a ridiculous way. I had made it sound like it was the most important event in the world that I'd glimpsed him once or twice at school, that he wasn't entirely unknown to me.

So I tried to smooth it over by saying an even

dumber thing. "I mean, I know you, but I didn't *know* I knew you."

He laughed. He actually laughed at my dumb remark. He had the deepest, sweetest, most infectious laugh—the kind of laugh that makes me laugh, too. So there we were—me in my wrinkled, stained turquoise shirt and sweaty forehead, and he in his beautiful everything—laughing our heads off.

I leaned against one side of the door frame and caught my breath, and he leaned against the other. He folded his arms across his chest and said, "I'm Alex Wiley."

"I know," I said and burst out laughing again. Finally I managed to say, "And I'm Lisa Kentwood."

He held out his hand and said, "It's really great to meet you, Lisa."

I reached out to shake his hand and almost dropped the cake. Never before had I ever been so awkward and nervous. I'd always thought of myself as kind of graceful until this fateful Friday afternoon. Alex, thank goodness, didn't seem to notice.

"Here, let me take that from you. It looks like it weighs a ton," Alex said. "What's in it, anyway?"

"Don't you know?" I asked.

Again, Alex laughed. He thought I was making him play a guessing game, and he was all for it. He shook the box slightly, as if listening for a rattle of some kind.

"Hmm, smaller than a bread box but bigger than a loaf of bread." He smiled. "I give up. What's in it?"

"You really don't know, do you?" I said, panic seizing me. Something was definitely wrong, and I was beginning to suspect what had happened. A red flush of embarrassment began to creep right up from my toes to my cheeks. My nightmare had come true!

"Uh-oh," I said. "I think I've made a mistake. I think I've made a really terrible mistake."

"What's wrong?" Alex asked.

"Uh—do you have a little sister with a birthday coming up?" I asked cautiously.

Alex nodded. "Next Friday. Jennifer. She'll be seven years old. Why?"

"Oh, nothing." I shrugged. "Except that I just baked her a three-layer cake one whole week too early."

"Oh, you're the one my mother ordered the cake from. But I heard her call you. I'm almost positive she gave you the right date," Alex said earnestly.

"She did. It was me. I mixed it up," I said miserably, but his smiling eyes forced me to smile, too.

"What will you do now?" he asked.

"Freeze it, I guess," I answered.

Alex's eyes lit up again. "We have a big freezer. Won't you come in, Lisa Kentwood, and help me hide my sister's cake in the freezer?"

Suddenly my heart, my mind, everything simply stopped working for an instant with the sudden realization that *this was it!* Here it was, that magic that I'd always known was out there but never before had experienced. Here it was, and here I was, and at last it was happening to me.

Happily, in a wide-awake daze, I followed Alex into the house.

Chapter Two

The entire Wiley family must have been working night and day on the house because it looked as if it had been lived in for years, not for only two months. I followed Alex straight to the kitchen, but what a kitchen! The cakes I could bake in that kitchen!

Gleaming copper pots hung from a round rack over a big, round wooden work island. I know it's called a work island because sometimes I read home decorating magazines, and that's what they call a work surface like that in the center of a kitchen. While Candace pores over the latest fashion and beauty magazines every month, I look through decorating magazines, putting together in my mind my "dream" professional kitchen. The Wiley kitchen was about as close to my dream as I'd ever seen.

"This is—beautiful, unbelievable!" I gasped as I circled the kitchen, my fingers trailing over crocks filled with wooden spoons and wire whisks, my eyes taking it all in—every counter, every cabinet, every corner.

Alex shrugged, or at least I think he shrugged, but I wasn't really looking at him. "It's OK," he said.

Suddenly I realized that for five minutes I had actually forgotten all about Alex. From the first trance I had fallen into upon meeting him I'd immediately fallen into a second trance upon seeing his kitchen. Later, when I told my sister Ellie all about this strange and wonderful encounter, she had analyzed my second trance as a "flight" or escape from the intensity of the first one.

"You were so overwhelmed, you had to focus or concentrate on something else—the kitchen—to ease your self-consciousness."

Crazy as it may sound, I think she was right. I was overwhelmed. And I *was* self-conscious. And I did love that kitchen. But when I at last looked at Alex again, and our eyes met, I grew jumpy. I felt as if I had to keep moving, keep talking. If I stood still or sat down, I might blurt out my innermost thoughts and feelings, I might tell him that he was the boy I had been waiting for.

"Could I have the grand tour?" I asked. "I'd really like to see the rest of the house."

"Sure," Alex agreed. "Only I'm afraid it'll have to be a mini-tour. We've finished the downstairs, but the upstairs is still a wreck."

As I followed Alex, I wished we could walk for miles that way, me in back of him, looking at his black, wavy hair curling over his shirt collar and at his wide, wonderful shoulders.

His head turned in profile as he pointed out the living room to me, but I was more interested in looking at his fine, classic nose and thick, black lashes than in seeing the living room.

"Nice," I said, forcing myself to glance at the room. I think there were green velvet sofas and a green-and-gray-striped chair. Or, maybe the sofas were striped. The walls were gray— that I'm sure of because I leaned against one when Alex turned to me and said, "Life is crazy, isn't it? Ten minutes ago, I didn't even know you existed."

He stood before me, his arms folded across his chest, his head shaking in disbelief, his lips curled into an amused smile.

I couldn't speak. There wasn't a word in the entire English language I could think of at that moment, much less speak. All I could do was mimic him in agreement, shaking my own head in disbelief and smiling my own amused smile.

Just then the spell was broken by the ring of

the phone. Alex didn't run, but in what seemed like three huge glides with his long legs, he was in the kitchen, answering it.

"Yeah, this is Alex Wiley," I heard him say.

Immediately my heart began to race. Suppose it was a girl calling him up? What if he was going steady? Or what if it was my mother on the phone, demanding to know what was taking me so long?

"Really?" I heard him exclaim as I walked slowly and quietly back to the kitchen. "Well, great. That's really great. Sure, I can make it. Are you kidding?"

Then there was a pause as he listened to the person at the other end of the line.

But who *was* that person? Probably some girl inviting him to some party. Didn't he say he could make it? Probably girls were calling him every hour on the hour. Probably he had to schedule some dates in the morning before school just to fit them all in.

"No, you don't have to worry about a thing. If you say you're willing, then I'm committed. Absolutely."

He's asked someone to go steady, that's it!, I thought. And she's just called to say she's willing, and that's why he's smiling and looking so happy. Oh, I've got to get out of here!

"See you Monday at three o'clock, for sure. And, hey, thanks. Thanks a lot."

Alex replaced the receiver without looking at me. While he'd been talking on the phone, he'd absentmindedly been pulling on the string of the cake box. Now he sat at the big wooden table, winding the string around his finger. I hated to intrude upon his sweet thoughts, but I simply had to get out of there. It was just too painful watching him all dreamy-eyed over some dumb girl who probably could never appreciate him as much as I did. It was just too painful finding the magic at last—only to lose it so quickly.

"I've really got to go," I said sadly, about to head for the door.

"Go? You can't go!" Alex cried, startled. Then he got up, grabbed my hand, and pulled me down into the chair beside his.

He ripped open the lid of the cake box and gasped. "Wow! Perfect!"

He clapped his hands, then rubbed them together, then clapped them again. "Perfect," he said, peering into the box, a mischievous smile on his face.

Then Alex pointed one finger up in the air. "Watch this," he said, and the finger dive-bombed right down into the center of the cake!

Up it came, coated in white and chocolate. He licked his finger clean.

"Mmmm!" he exclaimed as I watched, my mouth open. "Know something? That is really great cake. I mean, really, really great!"

I was about to protest, but he shushed me.

"All my life I've wanted to do something like this," he explained as he dipped his finger down the center of the cake a second time. "And now I have the perfect excuse."

"But the cake! It's ruined," I finally managed to cry.

Alex stopped tasting, licking, and grinning. He looked at me and said solemnly, "It's worth it. Definitely worth it. This has been quite a day!"

I didn't know what he was talking about, and if it involved a girl, I didn't want to know. I got up, this time determined to go, and he smiled at me and said, "I got the part, Lisa. I tried out for the part of Romeo with the Roxbury Players in town—you know, the community theater—and I got it!"

Alex rushed to the refrigerator and pulled out a quart of milk and slammed it on the table. Then he took two glasses from a cupboard and placed them before us. Without even asking me if I wanted any milk, he started pouring. He was so excited he almost poured milk all over the table.

"Man! What a day this has been! First, I met you. And then I got a call telling me I got the part," Alex said, stabbing the cake a third time with his finger. Then, with his other hand, he scooped up a pink icing rose and held it out before me.

"To you, fair Lisa. A rose for a rose." Then, really getting carried away, he knelt on one knee before me, still holding out the rose.

I wanted to hug him. I wanted to stamp my feet and shout out my relief to the entire world. Alex wasn't going steady. Alex might not even have a girlfriend. What's more, he liked me. He liked me! And he had gotten the part.

"Oh, Alex, that's wonderful. I didn't know you could act," I said.

"Of course you didn't," Alex said, beginning to laugh. "You only met me a few minutes ago, you dummy."

"That's true," I said, beginning to chuckle. "Very, very true."

"Well," said Alex, still on his knee, "will you or won't you?"

"Will I or won't I what?" I asked.

"Accept my rose."

Giggling, I held out my hand, palm up. All the tension and fear were gone. I felt as light as whipped cream. "I do most graciously accept this rose from thee, Alex Wiley," I said with all my heart.

Then, I stabbed the rose with my index finger and transferred it to my outstretched palm. Now get ready for another admission about myself that you might find weird. I hardly ever taste my cakes because I hate overly sweet things. That is, I thought I did. But now, I brought the bright pink rose to my lips, intending only to pretend to lick it. Instead, I devoured it in two bites! It was creamy smooth, with a faint taste of vanilla. It was delicious.

"Atta girl, Lisa," said Alex.

I scooped up another rose from the top of the cake and offered it to him.

"Thou sweet," he said, continuing with the Shakespearean joke even though he was now back at the table.

"Nay, nay," I countered. "Thy rose is sweeter."

Alex again looked solemnly at me. "Thou art the sweetest rose of all, Lisa."

I couldn't tell if there was sincerity behind his kidding, but suddenly I didn't care. I wiped my finger all around the white whipped cream rim of the cake, licked some off, then leaned over and put the rest on the tip of his nose.

Trying to hold back my giggles, I said as seriously as I could, "It's not fair that boys can't wear flowers in their hair. I think you'd look really great with a flower in your hair, Alex." And with that, I scooped up one of the last roses, the biggest one, and crowned him with it before he could stop me.

I took one look at him and doubled over. While I laughed my head off, Alex rose silently, scooped up a handful of cake, and smeared it into my face.

I couldn't stand, I couldn't sit, I was laughing so hard. I rose, but my knees buckled, and screaming with laughter I half fell, half sat down on the floor. Alex used my defenselessness against me and sat down beside me with another handful of cake. Laughing as hard as I was, he tried to cover the few places on my cheeks and forehead that weren't already iced.

I tried to beat him off me, but he caught my two wrists in his one strong hand, and with the other he carefully completed the job while I lay wriggling and screaming on the floor.

"I've got to bring over a mirror so you can see what an excellent job I've done," Alex said.

"I'll get you, Alex Wiley!" I vowed, then took another look at him and dissolved again in laughter.

Now Alex held both my hands in both of his and leaned toward me. His smooth face with the silly, whipped cream nose was very close to mine. "So you're going to get me, huh? Can't you see it's I who have got you right in my—"

Suddenly Alex sat up pole-straight, his green, laughing eyes going dark, almost black. They were no longer on me but on something or someone in the doorway to the kitchen. Flat on my back I had to look over my head to see who it was. And there, upside down, was Mrs. Wiley, Alex's mother!

I knew who it was, though she wasn't saying a word and though I was looking at her upside down. But I caught a glimpse of black, lustrous hair and a very serious expression, and I knew.

Finally she spoke. "I can't believe this. I really can't believe this."

I sat up and looked around. There was icing and cake everywhere. I saw that we had knocked over a glass of milk. Milk was dripping off the table onto the floor and onto Alex's head.

That was the final straw. I didn't mean to be disrespectful, but I just couldn't help it. I had never seen anything so funny in my life. Drop after drop of milk plunked down on the rose on top of Alex's head and dripped down his cheeks to the collar of his shirt.

I couldn't help it. I fell back again, screaming with laughter. I gripped my sides because they always hurt when I laugh that hard, but it didn't help. I just kept laughing and hurting.

Maybe it was the best thing I could have done because Alex, who was momentarily jolted and embarrassed when his mother walked in, took one look at me and couldn't help cracking up again.

We laughed so hard that Mrs. Wiley actually began chuckling, too. "OK, OK," she finally said, waving her hand for us to stop. "Now Alex, suppose you help your friend off the floor and tell me what's going on in here."

Alex introduced me to his mother, but I couldn't shake her hand because I had globs of cake mashed into it. He explained what had happened, how I'd mixed up the date.

"But don't worry," he cautioned her before she could start fuming again. "This cake is on me. Let's say I bought it—and I'll pay for it out of my allowance. It was worth it, Mom. I got the part."

Mrs. Wiley's eyes warmed up at the news. She looked as if she wanted to throw her arms around her son, but maybe because I was there, or maybe just because he was such a mess, she gave him a quick kiss on the cheek instead. Nevertheless, I could see she was really thrilled for him.

I was led to a beautiful peach bathroom, where

I cleaned myself off, and then Mrs. Wiley and I went over the plans for next week's cake so that there would be no mistake this time.

"Stop worrying, Mom," Alex said, but he was looking at me. "Can't you see this could only happen once in a lifetime?"

I gave Alex a smile of gratitude. If he ever got to know me better, he'd see that only the part about meeting him was a once-in-a-lifetime moment. With me, fouling up could happen every day!

"Let me walk you to the door," Alex insisted when I'd said my goodbyes to his mother.

Suddenly I was nervous again. It had been so wonderful, but now it was over. Would I ever see Alex again? Would he just say goodbye and forget me?

"Thanks, Alex," I said casually, trying to hide my fear. "Thanks for everything." I opened the door and began to walk out without looking at him one last time.

"Wait a minute!" he said, chuckling, and grabbed my arm.

I turned and looked at him. He didn't look as if he was going to forget me as quickly as I had thought. In fact, he looked as if it was as difficult for him to let me leave as it was for me to go!

"Uh, I want to tell you something," he said,

and for the first time, he, too, seemed uncomfortable and at a loss for words.

"Yes?" I whispered.

"Uh, well, you know, when someone brings you luck—and you sure brought me luck today—you really should keep them with you. Uh, like a rabbit's foot or lucky charm or whatever."

I nodded in agreement, probably too eagerly. To stop nodding, I held my head very still, very rigid, until my neck actually cramped. I had to jerk my head to the side to release it.

"What's the matter?"

"Nothing," I said. "My neck cramps up sometimes."

"Well, anyway," he went on, smiling at me now, "I was wondering if you'd like to go out with me Saturday night. I know this is short notice, and I suppose you're probably not free but—"

"Oh, sure, I'm free. I'm always free on Saturday night!" I lied. "I never, ever do anything Saturday night." There it was. Yes, again. It was true I was free this Saturday, but only because Lawrence and I were going out tonight. But I couldn't say no. And I certainly couldn't tell him about Lawrence.

"Well, that's great," Alex said, sighing with obvious relief.

"I know," I said dreamily. "I mean, great. I think it's great, too."

I waved goodbye and began to back down the steps.

"Wait a minute!" he called again. "Where do you live? Where do you want to go? When should I pick you up?"

I stood there looking like a complete idiot. I *was* a complete idiot. I couldn't remember my address! My mind had gone completely blank.

"Oh, yeah," I said and stopped.

He took one look at me and cracked up again. That wonderful, catching laugh. My mind switched on again as I laughed, too.

As I got on my bike, I called out my address. "Maybe a movie, if that's all right with you?" I added.

"I'll call you tomorrow," he yelled as I rode away. "We'll set the time then."

I waved but didn't trust myself to speak another word. I just grinned and then sort of floated home. I drifted into the house without any memory of how I'd gotten there. One minute I was grinning at Alex, the next I was home. What happened in between, I had no idea.

There was the strong odor of meat grilling, hamburgers, probably, and onions frying. Without a word to anyone, as if I were more a silent, gentle breeze than Lisa Kentwood, I blew over

31

to the dining room table. The dishes were piled, waiting for me to lay them out. Setting the table was only one of my daily chores. I was also responsible for clearing the table and for putting the dishes in the dishwasher.

My dad, who was home from work now, and Ellie must have heard the clatter of the dishes, for they came to the table.

"Hi, Dad," I called, as if from far away.

He thought I was playing a game and cupped his hands over his mouth so that when he said hello it would also sound far away.

He was sweet. I smiled. Even Ellie was sweet. I smiled at her, too.

Dad looked at me quizzically as I placed a fork, knife, spoon, and napkin before him.

"You OK?" he asked.

I shrugged. "Sure. Why?"

"Get your hair cut today?" he persisted.

"Huh-uh," I said, shaking my head. "Same old style. It's just that it's—uh—a little wet. I—uh—wet it." Actually, I'd had to sort of wash my hair at Alex's house before leaving, and it still wasn't dry. "Why?"

"I don't know, exactly," my father said, still looking at me. "But there's something different about you." Then he turned to Ellie. "Ellie, doesn't she look different?"

Now Ellie stared at me. Mom walked in with a

big platter of hamburgers and fried onions.

"Dad thinks Lisa looks different," Ellie explained.

So now Mom, Ellie, and Dad all stared at me as I went into the kitchen and got the salad. They were still staring when I returned, but no one said anymore about it—for a while. They all kept sneaking glances at me throughout the meal, however.

Nevertheless, we managed to get into one of our usual dinnertime conversations. Essentially it was a wrap-up of what everyone had done that day.

Mom went first and told us about another house she was on the verge of selling. In the midst of her slightly boring tale, she managed to interrupt herself twice to prod me to eat fast so I wouldn't be late for my date. Mom really liked Lawrence. She called him "a nice boy." Plus, Mom had this big thing about being late. "It's rude, rude, rude, I don't care what you say, to be late," she always said. Naturally, I was always late, and she was always trying to get me to hurry.

Then Dad told us about his day. At least he had the honesty to admit it was kind of uneventful, and he was considerate enough to cut it short.

Ellie said, "Well, as for me, I've definitely,

positively decided to become a psychologist."

Last month, she'd definitely, positively decided to become a psychiatrist. Frankly, I didn't understand the difference. They both seemed like the same thing to me.

"There's a world of difference," she insisted and went into a long explanation of just how, but I couldn't follow it.

Suddenly it was my turn. I found out it was my turn because Mom poked me and repeated over and over, "Lisa? Lisa? Lisa?"

I guess I don't have to tell you what I was daydreaming about.

I bolted upright, about to speak, and suddenly was reduced to giggles. I sat there with all of them staring at me, and I just gave into wave after wave of giggles.

"Lisa, you sure you're all right?" Dad asked, concerned. At times like these, he often turned to his oldest daughter for confirmation. Sometimes I suspected he did that very consciously, to make her feel included and important. Anyway, it was a special thing between them, and she always rose to the occasion, giving him her opinion. "Ellie, do you think she's all right?"

Ellie looked at me. My giggling finally died down, and I met her eyes.

Suddenly I knew Ellie knew. She looked into my eyes and could see the circus there, a circus in which white ponies carried ladies wearing pink tutus, and everyone wore sparkles in their hair, and the music and the drum-rolls and the proud lions and the trumpets signaled an exciting, magical event. I didn't hide it from Ellie, and Ellie saw it.

"Oh, I see," she said softly, kindly. "I see." She turned to Dad and said, "Lisa's fine, just fine."

Her terse answer to Dad stopped him short, and we all went back to eating. But I knew that the moment dinner was over Ellie would follow me up to my room. And I was glad. I needed her, more than ever before. For the first time, I was thankful I had an older sister. Very thankful.

Chapter Three

When dinner finally was over, Ellie rose from the table, crossed over to my chair, and whispered in my ear, "It's all right. I'll clear the table. You go up and dress. I know you want to look your best for your date tonight. I saw it in your eyes before, and I wanted you to know how happy I am for you—and that I understand."

Suddenly, the doorbell rang.

"Oh, no!" I cried. I stared at the door. I stared at my sister. How could everything be so right and so wrong at the same moment? Ellie thought what she saw in my eyes had to do with my feelings about Lawrence! She thought it was Lawrence who had made my eyes look so bright, who was making me act this way. And why shouldn't she? She knew I was dating him and that I was seeing him tonight. She knew that he was standing in front of the house, leaning on the bell so eagerly that the chimes were bouncing off the ceiling like church bells inside a church on Sunday morning.

What she didn't know was how I felt about Alex. How could she? I myself had only met him, so how could she assume it could be anyone but Lawrence? And yet, I was furious with her.

As Dad rushed to the door, I turned to Ellie and sputtered, "You think—I mean, you thought—!"

"It's all right," she said soothingly, patting me on the back. "Don't be embarrassed. I'm your sister, and I've been thinking that we haven't been close enough lately. But all that's going to change from now on. So you don't have to feel embarrassed with me anymore."

"Embarrassed? Embarrassed!" was all I could manage to hiss between my teeth.

Then, hearing my father lead Lawrence into the living room, I pushed past my sister and ran up to my room. I was too angry, too exasperated, too rushed, even too happy to help her out of her confusion. Her eyes were on me as I stormed up the stairs, two at a time. Even after I slammed the door behind me I could feel her still staring after me, but I didn't have the time to do anything about it.

I heard Mom return from the kitchen and discover that I hadn't cleared a thing off the table. I could hear her sniffing and complaining about me to Ellie, and then I could hear Ellie—

not the words exactly, but her oh-so-mature and consoling tone. She was probably saying something like, "Lisa's in love, Mom."

"Lisa? You mean, my Lisa?" Mom probably responded with her eyes as wide as two fried eggs.

And then, in that same even, soft tone again, Ellie was probably saying, "Of course, *your* Lisa. What other Lisa would I be referring to? Mom, you're just resisting. You have to face it. Lisa's in love. And, since falling in love is like a state of madness, we will have to excuse Lisa's behavior for the time being. I'll clear the table."

Half of me wished Ellie would forget the table and come up and talk to me the way I'd thought she was going to earlier. I wanted to set her straight, and, even more, I just wanted to say Alex's name out loud. But the other half of me was grateful that she was taking charge downstairs. At least she was keeping Lawrence busy.

As I tore off my clothes, I could hear Ellie joking with Lawrence, and then I heard plates clattering, which meant she was clearing the dishes as well. Meanwhile, I was rapidly becoming guilty of the rude, rude, *rude* offense of lateness, to quote my mother.

In twelve minutes I emerged showered, shiny,

and miserable. I clomped down the stairs in my clogs, and Lawrence jumped up when he saw me.

"I'm really sorry I'm so late," I apologized. "But dinner just went on and on tonight."

Lawrence didn't seem to hear me. "You look—you look sparkling new," he sort of whispered in a rush, as if he couldn't help himself.

"I do?" I said, melting. I'm not the kind of person who's so secure that when a compliment comes along, I can just take it or leave it. I mean, I'm confident that I look good. All right, that I'm even pretty. But not *that* confident! Which is why I can't treat a compliment casually. I have to hear it, and I have to blush, and I have to hear it again, and I have to ask, "Do you really mean it?" and then, maybe, I can leave it.

So I said to Lawrence, "I do? I mean, do you really mean it?"

And Lawrence nodded and stared at me and said seriously, "Yes, I really mean it. You look—uh—"

"Sparkling?" I helped him.

"Yeah," Lawrence agreed and continued to stare at me. Dad, who was sitting on the sofa kind of forgotten, began to grow restless. He looked at his watch, cleared his throat, then looked at his watch again.

Then Mom came into the room, and Dad nodded to her, and she nodded to Lawrence, and Lawrence just continued to nod and stare at me.

Thank goodness for Ellie. She, too, came into the room, but she didn't stand there and stare and nod like the rest of us idiots. Obviously Mom had already told Dad the "news" about the state of madness I was going to be in for a while, and they were both in a state of shock. Ellie, however, was still calm. She walked right over to Lawrence and placed her arm lightly around his shoulders and began leading him toward the door.

"So where are you two off to? The movies?"

Lawrence nodded.

"We're meeting Candace and Mike at Candy's house, and they're driving us to the movies," I said, trying to be helpful.

Ellie opened the door and smiled at Lawrence. "I'm going to tell my psych professor your psychiatrist joke. And next month when I'm home again, you must bring me another joke. Between the two of us, maybe I can pull an A in this course after all!"

Lawrence nodded. Of all of us, only Ellie retained her cool. Mom and Dad just stood gaping at the two supposed lovebirds, Lawrence and guess who!

"Have a good time!" Ellie called after us as we marched out of the house like two zombies. "And, Lawrence, don't forget. I'm counting on you!"

Finally the door closed behind us, and Lawrence and I were alone. We looked at each other, and Lawrence smiled, so I did, too. But I couldn't help the sudden thought that if he were Alex, we'd be screaming with laughter right now.

As we walked hand in hand to Candace's house, I got the feeling that Lawrence was trying to summon up his energy or his courage to tell me or ask me something. Probably the same something he'd hinted at earlier.

Suddenly I felt exhausted. It was all just too much! Baking the cake and rushing to finish it, then bumping into Lawrence, then meeting Alex, then seeing Ellie get everything all mixed up, and now going to the movies with Lawrence, who, I was sure, was going to ask me— or tell me—something terribly important any minute. I knew I should stop it, should try to prevent it, but I just didn't have the energy.

I loved walking with Lawrence and making the dry leaves crackle like frying bacon under our feet, but I didn't want him to say anything. I was afraid of what he might ask me; I didn't want to deal with it. If he asked me

what I suspected he was going to ask me—
that is, to go steady—I knew I might say yes,
I really might, because I just didn't have the
will to say no. I was afraid, yes, *afraid* to
say no.

We were under a large elm, and Lawrence
slowed and turned to me.

"Lisa," he began, fumbling in his pockets for
something. That was as far as he got because
two big, bright yellow-white car headlights
flashed on and half blinded us for the moment.

"What took you so long?" Candace called from
the passenger window. "You were so late, we
came to get you. Get in, get in!" So Lawrence
and I piled into the backseat, and Mike zoomed
off to the movie theater.

"If we miss that opening horror scene, I'm
going to kill you, Lisa," Candace said. "I hear
it's really scary, and I'm just in the mood to be
scared." She said all this as she stared straight
ahead, so I concentrated on the blond curls at
the back of her head.

"I hate scary movies," I said miserably.

Suddenly Mike pulled to a stop at a red light
and quickly turned around to face us. He was
wearing a Frankenstein mask, and nearly scared
me half to death. I screamed out loud, I couldn't
help it. Mike laughed a little too long and a little
too loudly to hide his own surprise and embar-

rassment at having really scared me. This made Candace glower at Mike.

"She just said she hates scary movies. How could you?" said Candace, attacking Mike and defending me.

Meanwhile, Lawrence used this as an excuse to put his arm around me and pull me close to him. As he hugged me, he reassured the two of them. "She'll be OK. It's just that Lisa's a little more sensitive than most people realize."

I liked the way Lawrence said that. I even liked the way his solid, protective arm felt around my shoulder. Even Candace seemed to like it. She turned around to say something to me but wound up eyeing Lawrence kind of dreamily.

By the time we were all seated in the dark movie theater, I was sure that if Lawrence asked me to go steady I wouldn't be able to say no. Not tonight. Not after I had let him put his arm around me in the dark car. Not after I hadn't pulled away and had actually smiled up at him gratefully. It would be just too cruel.

All I could hope for was to try to put it off. But, of course, Lawrence couldn't be put off all night. After the scary movie and after the ice cream and Cokes and after the crazy, giggly ride home, Lawrence and I found ourselves standing alone outside my front door.

"Just drop us off," Lawrence directed Mike. "I'll see Lisa into her house, and then I think I want to walk home."

"Oh, but—" I began to protest, but the words died on my lips when I looked into Lawrence's eyes. This time he was determined, and I knew that there was nothing I could do any longer to prevent it.

"Bye, Mike. Bye, Candace. Talk to you tomorrow," I called as I climbed out of the car. I wished I could go home with Candace and tell her all about the extraordinary day I'd had and the extra-extraordinary boy I'd met, but I knew I'd have to wait until tomorrow for all that. In fact, the night was still not over. There was much yet to happen, and I braced myself for it.

It came as soon as Lawrence sat down beside me on my front steps. This time, Lawrence didn't have to search and fumble in his pockets. Swiftly and smoothly he pulled out a shining gold chain and held it out before me.

"Lisa," he said very formally, "I'd like you to go steady with me, and if you agree, I'd like you to wear this gold chain."

I stared at the chain swinging silently between Lawrence's two hands. I knew he was looking at me, waiting to meet my eyes, waiting to hear my answer, but I continued to look at the chain. How pretty it looked in the moonlight! For months I had been begging my parents to buy me a gold chain.

"Please!" I had begged my father only last month. "It'll be my first piece of really good jewelry. I don't own anything real. Please!"

So, now, at last, I could have my chain. It was long and brilliant, and the weave was tight and close. It was beautiful, and Lawrence must have been saving up for this for a long time.

"Please, Lisa, say you'll go steady with me. Lisa, I care about you so much. I don't think there's another girl like you in the whole world!" He went on in a deep, intense voice that kind of hypnotized me. While he talked, he kept staring straight ahead.

"I guess we've known each other so long, and been friends for so long, that you may have gotten into the habit of thinking of me more as a brother than as a boyfriend." Then he looked me in the eyes as he said, "But, Lisa, I don't feel brotherly toward you."

Now it was my turn to stare straight ahead. His words made me feel warm all over. It felt so safe and good to be cared about like that. It made me want to be held and kissed softly. And that's what made me stare straight ahead.

"If you don't like me, I guess I'd better know it now. Lisa, what do you say? Don't you like me even a little?"

"Oh, of course I do!" I cried instantly, touching his cheek. "I like you a lot. Lawrence, I like you a great deal."

Lawrence smiled shyly and leaned over to clasp the chain around my neck.

"No, don't!" I said. I couldn't believe my own words. Part of me wanted to wear that chain more than anything.

Immediately Lawrence backed off, and I could see the happiness in his eyes instantly change to hurt and confusion.

"Lawrence, wait. Don't get the wrong idea. It's just that—well, I've never gone steady before. Not ever, not with anyone—and, well, this is all so sudden."

Lawrence looked at me seriously. I could see that he heard me and that he was struggling to understand, just as I was struggling to make him understand.

"I mean, I'm just so surprised, I just don't know what to say," I told him, finding that it was more true than I had imagined. Even though I'd guessed what he was going to ask me, I didn't know it would shake me up so much when he did. I was less prepared for it than I had realized. In fact, one small tear began rolling down my cheek as I turned to Lawrence and took his hand in mine.

"Please, oh, please don't be mad at me. It's just that I need time—just a little bit of time—to think about it," I said desperately.

Lawrence patted my hand and nodded in agreement. "Sure. Of course. I understand," he said bravely.

We had both been very brave and very admirable, and if we'd left it right there and said good night, it would have been great. But naturally, or should I say unnaturally, I got scared that Lawrence was secretly hurt and angry. I couldn't leave it alone.

"Probably—almost definitely—I'll wear your chain. You hold on to it until then." It broke my heart to close his hand around the shining chain, but I did.

"You really think you will?" Lawrence asked, searching for a bit of reassurance.

Naturally, I gave it to him.

"I'm more than ninety-nine percent sure. I can almost promise you for a fact that I will feel pleased and proud to go steady with you," I said, and part of me absolutely believed it.

Lawrence smiled. "Ninety-nine percent is better than nothing, I guess."

Then we finally said good night. Lawrence

leaned over and kissed me lightly on the cheek. He might have kissed me on the lips, but I turned my head ever so slightly away.

Lawrence shrugged. "I guess I'll have to wait for you to be one hundred percent sure to earn a real kiss." I nodded, too embarrassed and scared and, yes, complimented, to speak. I opened the door and quickly ran inside. When I got up to my room, I found a note from Ellie on my pillow.

Dear Lisa,
— If you look under my door, you'll notice the light's still on. If you enter, you'll find me wide awake. And if you begin to talk, I'll listen.

Love,
Ellie

I smiled at the note. Once again I felt grateful to have an older sister, to have Ellie. I undressed quickly, creamed the mascara off my eyes, then knocked softly at Ellie's door.

"Come on in, Lisa," she called, and I did.

Ellie was sitting up in bed and was blanketed by books. Some books had notepaper stuck between certain pages, and some books were open, and I could see notes written on the margins. Sliding down off her nose were the roundest pair of tortoise-shell glasses I'd ever seen. She was wearing a white Victorian nightgown with a ruffle at the neck.

"What are you staring at?" Ellie asked.

"You."

Ellie's hands flew to her hair. "I'm a mess, right?"

I shook my head. "No. You look so pretty I can't believe it," I said honestly. Never before had I thought of Ellie as pretty—or as ugly, for that matter. Always before, Ellie was simply, well, Ellie. "That nightgown. It's so romantic. I love it. And those glasses. I never knew you wore glasses."

Ellie pulled off her glasses and squinted. "I just got them. Seems I've needed them for some time but didn't know it. They make me look ridiculous, right?"

I sat down beside Ellie on the bed. Suddenly she seemed very small and not very sure of herself at all. Suddenly I felt that my older sister needed me and that I could actually help her!

"Ellie, don't you know how pretty you are? You really don't know? Why, I'll never have your sense of style, never!" With that, I pulled her glasses away from her and tried them on in front of her mirror.

"See?" I insisted, turning to her. "Who else but you could look great in these glasses?"

Ellie held out her arms, and I rushed into them. We hugged a long, deep sisterly hug, full of closeness and caring.

"Thanks." She sighed. "I needed that. I haven't been feeling too great about myself lately. But you really helped."

"Something wrong?" I asked, concerned.

Ellie put her glasses on again. "Oh, it's just that college is a little harder than I thought it would be. I'm finding I really have to *work* for good grades. I guess I'm used to being the smartest girl in the class, and I'm finding, for the first time, that I'm not."

"Yeah, I guess that can be tough, especially when you're used to everything coming so easily," I agreed.

"Exactly!" said Ellie. Then she took a hard look at me. "But enough about me. I said in my note that if you wanted to talk, I'd listen. The offer still holds, you know." She cleared a place for me on the bed where I could curl up.

The tears came out then, in a flood. There was no single little tear rolling down my cheek this time. This time my eyes filled up and overflowed. All the hurt and fear and confusion and turmoil I had been feeling turned to salty liquid and gushed from my eyes.

Ellie stroked my back, but she didn't say anything. She just let me cry.

Suddenly Mom knocked on the door and without waiting for an answer, entered.

"I heard you crying in here, and I wanted to see what was going on," she said softly but with concern.

I couldn't lift my head to look at her. The sound of her voice just made me cry harder. Ellie must have sensed this, and just as Dad was about to join the "party," Ellie got out of bed and whisked them both out of the room, saying, "She'll be just fine. Remember what I told you. We just have to understand she's going to be like this, off and on, for a while."

"Lisa, are you sure you don't need me?" Mom called.

My sobs were my answer.

"Love," Dad said. "The silliest thing I ever heard of at her age."

Ellie closed the door behind them, then picked up a glass of water from the stand beside her bed. "Here, drink this," she said. "Then tell me all about it."

I looked up at her through blurry eyes and knew there was nothing in the world I wanted more.

Chapter Four

I told Ellie everything. I told her about my mixed-up feelings for Lawrence and about his clear and transparent feelings for me.

"I just knew he was going to ask me to go steady tonight. I just knew it!" I moaned.

Ellie frowned. "There's something I don't understand. A little while ago, you described yourself as a girl who just can't say no. But I get the feeling there's more bothering you than just not being able to tell Lawrence you can't go steady with him."

I nodded in agreement, and then I smiled. Now came the part that I was dying to tell her—the part about Alex. I told her every detail of the crazy and wonderful way we met. Part of the time I had her laughing out loud as I relived our hilarious cake orgy.

"Oh, that's a riot! I can just see him sitting there with that pink rose on the top of his head!" Ellie exclaimed and giggled. Then I described Alex to her, from the sound of his voice to the color of his eyes.

"He sounds really special, Lisa," she said.

And then I told her everything else. I told her about how he'd asked me out for Saturday night and how I'd accepted. And the dilemma that that raised.

"You see, Ellie," I said seriously, "I've almost promised Lawrence I'd go steady with him, yet I'm going out with Alex tomorrow night. I'm crazy about Alex, but I can't seem to refuse Lawrence. I'd die if I ever hurt Lawrence or got him mad at me. Oh, Ellie, what should I do, what should I do?"

"The first thing you have to do is take it easy," Ellie advised in a nurselike tone. "You're all wound up like a tension wire. And that's not going to help you think clearly. You must feel as if you're being torn in two right now," she said.

I stared at her in amazement. "That's exactly it. You couldn't have described it better. I feel completely torn."

To emphasize the point, Ellie drew a picture for me with words. "You're like the guy standing on one side of a chalk line, wringing his hands in anxiety because he doesn't think he wants to stay on that side and doesn't know if he should cross over to the other side. If he stays, he'll never know what it was like on the other side, and if he crosses over, he'll lose whatever he had on this side."

"That's me, all right," I admitted.

"Then you've done enough for one night. You've revealed what has been bothering you, and you've identified some of the problems. Now it's time to take a few deep breaths, relax, and go to sleep."

I looked at her in astonishment. "But you haven't told me what I should do. We haven't solved the problem yet. How can I go to sleep?"

Ellie smiled at me patiently. "Breathe deeply. Relax. And remember, the problem took months, maybe years to develop. It can't be solved in an hour."

"But what am I going to do?" I wailed.

"You're already doing it. You're facing the problem, talking about it, and in time you'll unravel the answer."

Suddenly I was furious. "Oh, stop playing the noble, patient doctor with me, Ellie. Tell me what to do!"

"I can't," she said calmly.

"You can't?" I echoed, exasperated.

She shook her head. "No, I can't. Even if I had an answer and could tell you what to do, you wouldn't like it."

"Why not?"

"Because it would be my answer, not yours. And you've got to find your own way, your own answer. So it'll feel right to you."

I looked at my hands in my lap. Somewhere, deep down, Ellie's words had quieted me. My heart wasn't racing quite as fast. But on the surface I was still worried. And I was still annoyed with Ellie for not giving me a quick tip to make it all come out right.

As if reading my thoughts, Ellie leaned over and took my hand in hers. "I wish I could give you a quick solution to all your worries. All I can tell you is trust your deep down, basic instincts about what is right and what is good."

We looked at each other, and I was the first to smile. Ellie believed that, deep down, I really was a good person and would find a way to do the right thing. It made me kind of believe it, too.

"I feel so much better," I told her and yawned.

"I'm glad," she said and gave me a push. "Now, get to bed. You're absolutely exhausted." Then she yawned, too, smiled guiltily, and said, "I guess I'm tired, too."

Deep under the covers that night, I vowed I'd tell Lawrence on Sunday that I couldn't go steady with him. I pictured us having a nice, quiet talk and agreeing to remain good friends forever. There'd be no angry words, and at the end Lawrence would say, "I wish you the best with Alex. He's a lucky guy." Feeling calm and confident, I fell asleep immediately.

The next morning I skipped downstairs singing old Beatles songs. Mom was in the kitchen making homemade corn muffins for breakfast.

"Don't beat the batter too much," I told her, peeking over her shoulder. "In fact, I'd say it's ready to be poured into the tins and baked."

Mom raised an eyebrow and put one hand on her hip as if she were about to say something like, "Oh, is that so, Miss Smartypants?" But I flashed her a great big smile, and she just shrugged.

"Want me to take over?" I offered. I just couldn't help it. The minute I saw a bowl of batter and a mixing spoon, I couldn't stand to watch anyone else botch it up.

But Mom was used to it and took it the way she often did these days, merely as help. "Sure, honey. I could use your help. While you're doing the muffins, I can make the coffee and slice the grapefruits."

I gave the mixture a final stir, poured it into the tins, and put the tins in the oven, checking the temperature dial to be sure my mom had set it right. Baking was the one thing in the world I felt totally confident about. Some people have a green thumb in the garden; some people have a head for numbers. I, on the other hand, have a talent—yes, a remarkable talent—for baking, and I know it. I just wished Mom would recognize it. Most of the time she behaved as if my baking business was just one big nuisance that created mess and clutter in her kitchen. Or else she acted as she did now, as if my expertise was ordinary and my mastery was merely a helping hand.

Well, the National Olympic Bake-Off would change all that. I'd entered the national recipe and baking contest secretly. Then, when I'd been notified that I was being considered as one of the semifinalists and was asked if I could come to Madison, Wisconsin, for the bake-off, I couldn't contain my pride and excitement.

"I did it! I did it!" I cried when I got the letter. But when I told Mom and Dad about the contest and showed them the letter, Mom sniffed and said, "It seems to me that the least they could do is pay your airfare."

"Maybe they will," I said, feeling just the tiniest bit deflated. "They didn't say they wouldn't. They just want to know if I'll come."

Dad gave Mom a look as if to say, "Come on, Joan, give the kid a little encouragement," but she ignored it. The funny thing was, Dad was all for my baking business. I could never figure out what about it bothered Mom so much, what really bothered her, I mean. I'd made a mental note to speak to Ellie about it, but I hadn't gotten around to it yet.

And this morning the last thing I wanted to do was analyze my mother. I had better things on my mind than that. Actually, I had only one thing on my mind—Alex and our date that night. The very thought of him made me all shivery and trembly.

Suddenly the phone rang, and Mom and I both jumped up to answer it. She was eager to hear whether or not some clients had decided to buy the house she'd shown them yesterday, and I was eager to hear from Alex. I was closer to the phone and picked it up, but not before bumping heads with Mom. She and I both rubbed our heads as I said hello into the phone.

It was Alex.

Mom must have seen the expression on my face change or heard the tone in my voice go from pained to syrupy. At any rate, she sat down and watched me, instead of walking out and giving me privacy the way she usually does.

"So, whaddaya wanna do tonight?" Alex asked, trying to sound like a gangster.

I giggled—and then I played right along with him. "Well, well, if it isn't Romeo, Romeo!" I said in my best gun-moll accent. "How ya doin'?"

"Swell, doll. Peachy. So, uh, how 'bout it?

Wanna take in a few of the sights tonight? Whaddaya say, doll?"

When I glanced at Mom, I saw she had a quizzical look on her face, and I quickly looked away. Otherwise, I'd have cracked up and spoiled all the fun.

I put a pencil in my mouth and let it dangle like a cigarette. "That sounds swell to me, Romeo. Whaddaya have in mind exactly?"

I could almost see the smile on his face as he said, "I thought maybe we'd catch that horror flick. And then maybe I'd take you dancing. So put on your best duds."

My heart flip-flopped. I'd seen the horror film last night with Lawrence. But dancing! It sounded great.

"Now you're talkin'!" I said. "Why dontcha pick me up here around seven-thirty. I'll introduce ya to the folks."

I gave Alex my address again, and without ever coming out of character, he said goodbye.

"Yeah, see ya later, good-lookin'," I said and hung up. Mom's eyes were wide with disbelief.

"*Who* was *that*?"

"Alex."

"Alex Romeo?"

I laughed. "Of course not, Mom. Alex Wiley."

"Wiley?" Mom looked confused. "But you called him Romeo."

I couldn't straighten her out because the phone was ringing again and the coffee was perking and Ellie and Dad were hungry for breakfast. Now that Alex had called I wasn't that eager to get the phone, so I let Mom reach for it.

"It's for you, Lisa," she called. "It's Candace."

"Lisa, I've got to talk to you," Candace said desperately. "I couldn't sleep all night."

My eyes were on Mom as she pulled the muffins from the oven. I winced when she slammed the hot tin down on the counter. Naturally, a rap like that is death to a just-risen cake. Gloomily I watched as the muffins sank, sank, sank.

"We're just about to sit down to breakfast, but if you really need to talk—"

"Oh, Lisa, you're wonderful. I really do," Candace said.

"Okay. Do you want to come here, or should I come there?"

Candace probably hadn't had breakfast yet because she said, "Um, hold a place for me at the table. I'll be right there."

But when Candace arrived, she said she was too miserable to eat, so I grabbed a muffin, excused myself from the table, and led Candace up to my room.

Candace said she was too nervous to sit, so while I stretched out on my bed, Candace paced up and down, nibbling on my muffin. I could have kicked myself for not bringing another one up for her, no matter what she'd said about not being hungry, but I could see that she was upset, so I didn't interrupt her until she'd finished every last crumb.

Finally, fortified with food, Candace looked ready to tell me what was on her mind. She had an odd, sort of guilty look on her face.

"Come on, Candace," I encouraged her, "out with it. Take a deep breath and say it, whatever it is."

If I'd known what she was about to say, I doubt if I'd have encouraged her so much. But Candace, taking my advice, got right to the point.

"I like Lawrence. I like him a lot. I guess you could say I'm really crazy about him." She looked up at me for a second, then covered her face with her hands as if she were about to cry. "I never would have told you except that you told me you don't like Lawrence. If you like Mike at all, you can have him, Lisa. I broke up with him last night."

I stared at Candace in amazement.

"I can't help it," Candace persisted. "I can't help how I feel. And, Lisa, I've been feeling this way a long time now. But last night when we double-dated, I couldn't stop staring at him. I knew I had to tell you today, or I'd burst."

Candace was waiting for me to respond, but all I could think of was how easy it had been for Candace to break up with Mike. All my good feelings flew out the window. Late last night I'd been determined to break up with Lawrence. Now something told me it wasn't going to be that easy. That, in fact, it would be even harder.

"Well, why don't you say something?" Candace prodded.

"What do you want me to say?" I retorted.

Candace shrugged her shoulders. "I don't know. How you're feeling about what I told you, I guess."

I felt my face growing hot with anger and jealousy. Everything came so easily to Candace. Even breaking up with a boy. She never seemed afraid of anything. Now she wanted Lawrence, my Lawrence. Oh, I was so mixed up again. How could I call him my Lawrence when I was supposed to be breaking up with him?

"I never said I didn't like Lawrence. I like him a lot," I said. There was an edge to my voice.

"Oh," said Candace.

"As a matter of fact, he asked me to go steady last night."

Candace looked both disappointed for herself

and happy for me at the same time. "Oh, you lucky thing. Did you accept?"

"I'm thinking about it, but—" Suddenly I remembered that I hadn't told Candace about Alex. Just as suddenly, I realized I didn't want to. Not yet, anyway. I wanted to keep Alex my secret for the time being.

"You mean you might not?" Candace asked excitedly.

When I nodded, she said, "Oh, Lisa, promise me you'll tell me as soon as you know. You know I would never do anything about Lawrence—like flirt with him or anything—unless you said it was OK."

"You'll be the first to know," I promised her.

Then Candace wanted to know what I was doing that evening. I didn't want to lie to her, but I just didn't want to tell her about Alex yet. So I said, "I'm not sure. I'll give you a call later."

The next minute Candace was out the door, calling loud goodbyes to my whole family. Then it was quiet, and I was left alone with my thoughts and dreams about Alex. I wondered what I could possibly wear on my date and became frantic when a search through my closet revealed nothing even halfway suitable. Then I remembered that Ellie had a beautiful Victorian ruffled blouse that would look great with my black velvet pants.

"If it fits, it's yours for the night," Ellie agreed readily, when I begged her to borrow the blouse. Then she stood there waiting, perhaps waiting for me to say something more about what I was going to do about Lawrence. But I didn't have time to talk. I had to bake two pecan pies for a customer that afternoon, and then I wanted to take a long, luxurious bubble bath before my date with Alex.

By the time Alex called for me, Mom had asked me six times how I happened to be going out with him when I was supposed to be so in love with Lawrence. I kind of enjoyed the idea of everyone walking around wondering about Miss Mystery Woman and decided to keep up the suspense for a while. Not that I knew the answers yet myself. I still hadn't spoken to Lawrence, but I vowed I'd do that on Sunday.

The blouse looked terrific with my black velvet pants, just as I knew it would. I wrapped a glittery belt around my waist and slid into my medium-heeled black sandals. My cheeks were so hot with anticipation that I didn't need any blusher, but I coated my lips with my favorite bright pink gloss, and then I took a final look in my floor-length mirror.

"Wow!" I cried out loud. I was surprised at my own reflection. I couldn't remember ever feeling so grown-up—or pretty.

I took my time going downstairs to greet Alex. First of all, I didn't want to trip on my shoes. I really wasn't used to wearing heels. Most of the time I wore sneakers or clogs. Second, I wanted to enjoy every moment of anticipation. And third, I knew Alex could hear me from the living room, where he was waiting for me, and I wanted the anticipation to build for him, too.

I entered the living room very quietly, but Alex looked up instantly from his conversation with my mother. It had worked! I could see that Alex had been counting the steps— and the moments—until I arrived. It was just a little thing, but it made me feel good to know he might be looking forward to this date as much as I was.

Alex didn't say anything, and neither did I. He just stood up and smiled at me, and I smiled at him.

Neither Dad nor Ellie were home, so Mom walked us to the door. For a moment I was afraid Alex would start his mobster routine, which I didn't think my mother would particularly appreciate, but he seemed to understand this and said a simple good night.

Alex's father's car was big and black, and as soon as I sat down on the plush seats and caught Alex smiling next to me, I knew this was going to be the most wonderful night of my life. And it was.

"OK, first some serious movie-watching and then some serious boogeying," Alex announced as he started the car. I didn't think it was really a lie not to have told him I had already seen the movie. The truth was that I didn't care if I'd seen the movie fifty times. It was being with Alex that was the important thing.

"You're a good driver," I told him as I settled in.

Alex reached inside a pocket for his wallet and showed me his license.

"I just got it," he said proudly. "But I've been driving since I was twelve years old."

"How could you be allowed to drive at twelve?"

Alex explained that for two years, when he was twelve and thirteen, his family had lived in what he called "the sticks" of Wyoming.

"Our closest neighbor was thirty-two miles away. My father wanted me to know how to drive in case there was an emergency."

"Do you miss it? Wyoming, I mean." I really wanted to get to know Alex. His every thought, every feeling interested me. Unlike Lawrence, whom I'd known for so many years, Alex was new and fascinating.

"I miss the long, empty stretches of land where

you can be completely alone with the wind and the mountains. Ever climb a mountain?"

I shook my head. "Just the thought of it panics me. I guess I'm a little afraid of heights."

We'd stopped at a red light. Alex turned to me and touched my hair softly. "If we were on a mountain together, I'd never let you fall."

Then the car behind us blew its horn, and Alex had to attend to his driving again.

I almost hated going into the dark, quiet movie theater because there was so much more I wanted to talk with Alex about. But in another way, sitting beside him in the dark house had its compensations, too. Alex put his arm around my shoulder as soon as the lights went down, and he kept it there throughout the entire movie. Every once in a while, he'd stroke my hair, and it would make me feel like purring.

I had to pretend to be shocked at the scariest parts of the movie, but even that was kind of fun because every time I did, Alex's arm would tighten around my shoulder.

In any case, I knew that the best part of the evening was yet to come, so I leaned back and enjoyed every minute of being with Alex. As the words The End appeared on the screen, my heart began to pound a little faster. I pictured the two of us dancing together in a strobe-lit room to the driving beat of some great rock group, and I just couldn't wait.

"That movie really got you all tensed up," Alex said as we filed out of the theater.

"Yeah, it was really scary," I agreed. "Once we start dancing, I'll loosen up, though."

But when we climbed into Alex's car, he said he had a better idea. And he did. It was just about the best idea in the entire world.

Chapter Five

"Come on, Alex. Tell me. Where are we going?" I begged, giggling and almost quivering with curiosity and excitement.

"Huh-uh," Alex grunted, shaking his head.

"Pul-eeeze!" I begged. It was crazy. Part of me felt that I'd die right that second unless he told me, and the other part of me felt as if it couldn't have mattered less where we were going, as long as we were going there together.

"Welcome to the Alex Wiley Magical Mystery Tour," Alex said, then laughed. We were driving through the center of town, which, even on a Saturday night, is not one of your liveliest places. The radio was turned up loud, and we were making up our own words to the songs, almost screaming them out to be heard over the radio. Alex was singing this teasing song about his Magical Mystery Tour and how he could promise it wouldn't be a bore and how I'd beg for more.

"I wanna dance; he won't let me; I wanna

dance; he won't let me," I sang back at him.

Suddenly Alex pulled into one of the many parking spots along Main Street.

"Wait here!" he commanded, winking and leaping out of the car. "And look that way!" he said sternly, pointing in the opposite direction of which he was heading.

I shook my head no. "I warn you, I'm going to follow you."

Alex put his elbows on the ledge of my rolled-down window. He leaned in so that his face was close to mine.

"Don't you like surprises?" he asked.

I melted. "Yes, but—"

"Well, then," he interrupted cheerfully, "look that way and don't turn around! I'll be gone a few minutes."

I obediently turned my head and stared in the opposite direction. I wanted to see where he was going, but I didn't peek. This was the fun of being with Alex. He was always making things magical. Who was I to spoil it?

In a few minutes I heard the trunk of the car unlatch. I knew Alex was shoving something into it, but I couldn't see what because even when I gave in and peeked in the rearview mirror, all I could see was the open trunk hood.

"All set?" he asked as he climbed back into his seat.

"Alex Wiley, I'm going to strangle you!" I growled.

"No, you're not," Alex said, smiling confidently. "Know why?"

"Why?"

"Because you wouldn't strangle me *before* you found out what the secret was. You're not that dumb," Alex said and started the car.

After a few minutes, I noticed that we were driving away from town, away from where the rock club was. I didn't want to give him the satisfaction of seeing my curiosity aroused again, so I bit my lip and kept silent.

Creston may be a city, but it's a very small city, and I've lived here all my life. I pride myself on knowing its streets fairly well; I have to, or I'd be lost every other week when I'm delivering a cake to someone in an unfamiliar area. But the route Alex was taking was totally unfamiliar to me. I stared at the houses and the streets as we passed them, and I had absolutely no idea where we were.

Suddenly there were no more houses, only trees and darkness. On Alex drove while I remained silent.

This was ridiculous, I began saying to myself. Enough was enough. I decided I'd ask him to tell me—and this time, I'd tell him I meant it. I was getting just a tinge annoyed.

And that's when Alex pulled to a screeching halt. I looked up, and there before us was a small but shimmering lake. Tiny pink and blue and white lights were strung from the trees around the lake, giving it the look of a fairy-tale land. I could hear a rock band playing somewhere across the lake, and automatically my foot began to thump to the muted beat.

"Like it?" Alex turned to me and asked softly.

"Alex, I just can't believe you. You're too much. I mean, I've been living in Creston practically my whole life, and you moved here just two months ago—and—Alex—where did you ever—how did you find this place?" I sputtered.

"Some actors from the Theater took me here after my audition," Alex said casually, climbing out of the car.

I just sat there, staring at the lake, at the lights, at the night. Whoever that band was across the lake, one thing was sure—it was no amateur band. They were good. And Alex, oh, Alex, wasn't he just the best? Every moment with him was fun and special. Sometimes he reminded me of a little kid, always involved in planning the next mischievous scheme. He had an impulsive, spontaneous quality that I just loved.

I heard the trunk hood slam and realized Alex

72

had been fiddling around at the back of the car, so I got out to investigate.

"Here, hold this," he said, grinning, handing me a brown paper bag with what felt like a jug or bottle inside. He himself was carrying another brown paper bag and what looked like a blanket.

Then Alex led the way, guiding me to a velvety patch of grass where he dumped everything, including my package. Then he spread out the blanket, unpacked potato chips, crackers, cheese, and what looked like a jug of wine.

As he was laying out napkins and cutting up the cheese, I said, "I hate to sound like a kid, Alex, but I've never had wine before."

"Oh, this isn't wine. It's cider. My father works for a chain of newspapers, and before we moved here, we lived in Paris for two years. The French drink a lot of cider, usually what we call hard cider. This is just the regular stuff, but it's good."

Then he handed me a cracker smeared with the smelly cheese, and I wrinkled up my nose and shook my head.

"In Paris, they eat a lot of cheeses with strong smells. I didn't like them at first, either. Now bland cheeses bore me. The stronger a cheese smells, the more I know I'm going to like it."

I bit into the cracker. The way Alex talked about Paris, I could tell he loved it there. I didn't even have to ask him. And he sort of made me love it, too. Alex made me almost *see* Paris and the way the French did things there. I began to want to do things that way, too.

After a few sips of cider and two crackers with cheese, I was about to stretch out on the blanket when the band across the lake began playing a really wild number—and playing it really loud. I looked at Alex, and he looked at me. Then, as we both burst out laughing, he got up and held out his arms.

"Shall we?" he asked.

I nodded. "We shall." And I stood up and went to him. To my surprise, Alex was not a great dancer. Until that moment, I guess I thought there was nothing that Alex couldn't do superbly. But dancing? Why, he was so awkward, he was funny. He sort of jumped up and down, getting red in the face almost immediately, and dancing too fast for the music.

I couldn't help it. I began to laugh.

"I know, I know." Alex groaned, throwing up his hands. "I'm the worst, right?"

I grabbed his arm. "Oh, Alex, no. Not the worst!" I felt panic at the thought that I might have hurt him. "Not the worst. Just—different."

Alex patted my head and smiled. "It's all right. I'm not supersensitive about it. I just wish I could dance better, that's all."

"Want me to teach you?" I asked, the words popping out of my mouth before I could think about them. I guess they were just about the best words I could have said, for Alex's eyes grew wide and bright, and he said, "Hey, would you? That'd be great, really great." And by saying that, he made me feel so special that I almost burst. Suddenly I had something to give to Alex. Something I could do for him.

"OK," I said, kicking off my shoes and getting serious. "Let's begin with your shoulders." And I showed him how he was moving them too much and twisting his arms too quickly.

"Watch me and then you do it," I said, and did a few steps before him. Now I'd always considered myself an all-right dancer. I mean, I never felt embarrassed on a dance floor—at least I didn't if there were twenty other people dancing, too. But suddenly, dancing before Alex, I felt like one of those pink and blue lights sparkling out over the lake, shimmering in the blackness of the night. I felt dazzling.

At first, Alex danced with me. Then he backed away to give me more room and leaned against a tree. I felt him watching me. I couldn't believe it. I wasn't embarrassed. I wasn't dropping to my knees, giggling with self-consciousness. And, I wasn't avoiding his eyes!

I was enjoying it, all of it. The dancing on the

grass with my shoes kicked off, the feeling of Alex's eyes upon me, liking me, liking to look at me. I'd never felt like that before. I danced until I was gasping for breath. And when, finally, I gave up and threw myself down on the blanket, Alex clapped.

"You're really something, do you know that?" he said, lying down on the blanket and putting his head in my lap. "That's the way I'd like to be able to act. As well as you dance."

"Oh, but I've never danced this well in my life," I insisted. "I never felt this free."

Alex turned his head so that he was looking up at me now. His hands reached up to my face and pulled it down to his.

The kiss was the softest, sweetest, tenderest thing I'd ever known. After it was over, we stared at each other for a while.

"I like looking at you," he said gently.

"And I like looking at you," I whispered.

So that's the way we stayed for a long time, just staring at each other, the stars, and the trees.

But after a while, my stomach began sending me signals it was hungry. Alex got my signals, too, because his head was in my lap, and when I get hungry, my stomach begins to gurgle and growl.

Alex had been staring at the moon for a while,

but now he turned to me and gave me a quizzical look as if to say, "What's going on with your stomach?"

Suddenly I was too embarrassed to look at him. I covered my face with my hands, and in the littlest voice I could manage (so, hopefully, he wouldn't even hear my ridiculous explanation), I told him, "It's hungry."

"What's hungry?" He'd heard, all right.

"My stomach."

"Well, then," said Alex, jumping up, "let's feed it!"

In a split second, Alex had the potato chip bag torn open and a pile of them poured out right on the blanket beside me.

To cover my shame, I teased him. "I never knew the French ate potato chips. Very elegant."

Now it was Alex's turn to be embarrassed. Mimicking me, he covered his face with his hands and in the littlest voice said, "I couldn't help it."

"Why couldn't you?" I asked sternly, fighting back the giggles that were bubbling up inside me.

"You won't tell anybody if I tell you something, will you?"

"Cross my heart," I vowed, still fighting to keep a straight face.

"Well," he said, dropping his hands from his

face so he could see me, "I'm a potato chip freak. I'm like a junkie. Gotta have my chip fix or I go bananas. And today, I hadn't had one potato chip all day. So you can understand that by now, I'm going slightly out of my mind."

I tried to make myself frown so that I wouldn't laugh. "So, then, you admit that you have this potato chip addiction and that even though the French would never bring potato chips on their picnics—especially their nighttime picnics—you risked getting caught and bought a bag."

Since Alex was in the middle of biting into a big potato chip, he couldn't really talk. But he smiled and put up his arm as if he were taking an oath or as if he were saying, "Believe me, I confess. It's all true. Every word of it."

I started laughing and grabbed a handful of potato chips from the pile. We ate until the grumbling in my stomach stopped and Alex's potato chip compulsion was eased for a while.

The chips made us thirsty, so Alex poured a tiny bit more cider, and we sat back and talked and laughed some more. After I'd asked him a million questions about his acting career, he asked me a million questions about my baking business.

"My dream is to become the owner of a great line of bakery shops, all across America," I told him, although I'd told no one else in the world.

"I used to want to become a dessert chef at a great restaurant," I continued, really spilling out my dreams. "But just a few days ago, I was thinking that it would be even nicer to work for myself. I think it would be wonderful to fly to some big city somewhere in the United States and see my name above a clean, white bakery with luscious cakes in the window."

"Yeah, I know what you mean," said Alex. "I feel the same way about my name. It would be the same kind of thrill, I think, to fly to some city and see my name on a big, bright theater marquee."

That's when we made the vow. Looking back on it now, it seems a little silly and a little dramatic. But at that moment, that night, on our first beautiful date together, it was so moving I almost cried.

We put our hands together in one enormous, four-handed fist and looked into each other's eyes. "Let's vow," said Alex, "that ten years from now, both our names will be in lights. Yours lit up over your bakeries and mine lit up over the title of my movie."

"I promise to do everything in my power to make it happen," I swore solemnly.

The moment was so intense that when it was over, we burst out laughing just for sheer relief.

"Come on, I'd better get you home, or your

parents will never allow my name to be mentioned, much less put up in lights." And, still laughing, we gathered up our things and began to head back to the car.

I didn't want to leave. I wanted to remain there at that lake, lit up by those lights, forever. The best I could do, however, was to turn back and take one last look.

"So long, lake," I called out sadly. Alex came to stand beside me. Suddenly, strangely, a wind came up from—well, out of nowhere. It shook the branches of the trees and made the lights tinkle lightly. In the water, all was dizzying, darting light.

"Look!" said Alex. "The lake is waving goodbye."

We loaded our stuff back into the trunk and pulled away. We turned on the radio, and as Alex drove, I rested my head on his shoulder. There didn't seem to be any need to say anything more that night; already we'd said so much.

Pulling to a quiet stop in front of my house, Alex got out of the car but left the motor running. I liked that. Even though I wished the night would never end, I liked that he wasn't planning on pressuring me into making it even longer. He knew it was late and was obviously planning only to walk me to my door and say a quick good night.

As we walked up the steps to my front door, Alex plucked a small branch of leaves from a hedge. "Maybe it's not exactly a rose, or even a daisy," Alex joked as he handed it to me, "but the sentiment is the same."

"Very sentimental," I agreed.

Suddenly Alex was in the role of the tough guy again. "So—uh—babe, how 'bout it? Next Saturday night? And remember, you still owe me."

"Oh, yeah?" I said with exaggerated toughness. "What do I owe you?"

"Dance lessons," Alex said, then kissed me quickly on the cheek and left.

I wanted to watch him leave. I wanted to stand out there all night and all week, until it was time to go out with him again next Saturday night. But I couldn't. So I let myself into the house and walked into the kitchen to pour myself some milk. My grandmother used to heat hot milk for my mom whenever she was up late at night.

"It settles you," Grandma would say, and now, I often drank a glass of milk before going to bed. Not heated, but still milk.

"Shh," Mom said as I walked into the kitchen. I was about to turn on the light, but Mom said, "Leave it dark, please. Or you'll scare him away."

"Who?" I asked, peering out the window where Mom was looking.

"The deer. See him?"

I was just about to say that I couldn't see anything, when something brownish with white spots ran right past our window. Its eyes glinted in the dark, and it turned its head to face us for one brief second before darting away. When she was sure the deer was gone, Mom turned to me and said, "You're home kind of late."

"Yeah," I agreed. "But it was so wonderful, it was hard to leave."

"Want to talk?" she asked, placing her hand on mine.

I shook my head. "I don't think so, Mom. I'm kind of tired now. But, thanks."

"Well, all I can say is that this time last night you were sobbing hysterically. Now you're purring like a kitten."

I smiled with sudden understanding. "I guess being a teenager isn't only hard on me. I guess it gets to you sometimes, too."

"Sometimes," Mom admitted. "Although this moment isn't one of those times." Suddenly I was in her arms, and we were hugging the way we used to when I was little.

"Good night, Mom," I said finally. "I love you."

"Good night, Lisa," she echoed. "And—I'm

happy you're so happy, even if I haven't the faintest idea of what's going on."

"You will," I said, smiling, then climbed the stairs to bed.

Now I know that you'd expect me, after a first date with Alex like the first date I had with him, to climb into bed and do nothing but dream about him. To relive the evening from beginning to end, from the moment I saw him glance up at me in the living room, to his arm around my shoulder all through the movie, to our Magical Mystery Tour car ride, to our picnic on the lake, to the very moment when we said good night. I know you expect that, but I didn't do it.

I thought about cakes, instead.

I was inspired, and as I was getting ready for bed, all I could think of was this lavender-and-white cake that I'd make for Alex's sister. I'd make lavender irises out of frosting, and, if I could get one, I'd put one real, fresh iris right in the center.

Maybe I couldn't think about the evening because it was so special, so perfect. Or maybe, too, to think about it was also to think about what I was going to do about Lawrence and how, exactly, I was going to break up with him. Those were not the thoughts I wanted to have right now. So I decided not to have any. Thoughts, that is, about Lawrence and breaking up and my fears and doubts and everything.

So, instead, I thought about cakes in general and the cake I'd design for Alex's sister. It brought the smile back to my face, and I did not shut my eyes until I had the whole thing planned in my head. Then I turned off the small light beside my bed and sank into the pillows.

I went to sleep smiling, but deep down inside I was quaking because I knew that the next day I'd have to face what I couldn't and hadn't been able to face for some time—Lawrence.

Chapter Six

Maybe I successfully avoided thinking about Lawrence before I fell asleep that night, but I certainly couldn't on Sunday morning because he called at nine and woke me up. I have a phone right near my bed, and when I heard it ring, I thought it was the alarm clock going off. I reached out my arm and tried to press in the alarm button. The alarm button was already pressed in, but the ringing continued. Finally I had to force my eyes open and answer the phone.

"Huggmllgh," I said, or something like that.

Lawrence, however, understood me perfectly. "Hi, Lisa. Did I wake you up?"

"Mmmmm," I mumbled, closing my eyes again.

Lawrence sounded as if he'd been up for hours. His voice was crisp and cheerful. Never one for small talk, he got right to the point.

"So, have you made a decision yet?"

I winced, and then my eyes flashed wide open. My mouth felt dry and sandy, and my heart began racing wildly. I had thought I would call him later in the day and ask to see him. When we got together I would tell him what I had decided. I hadn't expected him to call me the first thing in the morning.

Help me! I thought wildly. Somebody tell me what to say! Somebody put some words in my mouth, please, oh, please!

"Lawrence?"

"Yeah?"

"Um, I haven't exactly made a decision yet, but I tell you what."

"What?" he asked, but he sounded a little discouraged already.

I sat up straight in bed, propping the pillows in back of me. If I'd felt terror before, the sound of Lawrence's voice dropping down a note or two made m feel almost sick with panic. Instead of breaking up with Lawrence, I wanted to *make up* with him. Everything must come out all right, I vowed. I can handle it. I must.

"Um, I've almost made up my mind—I mean, I am ninety-nine and forty-four-one-hundredths-percent sure that we can really just go along almost as if I'd told you yes."

Lawrence breathed a little impatiently. I always seem to be able to hear every little change in a person's voice, every sigh or mutter or grinding of teeth.

"Listen," he said shortly. "What kind of an

answer is that, Lisa? I mean, really. You're starting to get on my nerves. Just say yes or no. I'm not made of paper, you know. If it's no, I'm not going to fall apart. I can take it."

"No, you don't understand," I pleaded. "It's just that going steady is a big deal for me. I mean, I never even went out on a date until I started going out with you. It's really important to me to be mature about this. I want to think it through and not feel pressured so that I don't wind up saying one thing and wishing I'd said another. You know what I mean."

Lawrence hesitated. "Yeah, I guess I sort of know what you mean. Independent decisions, and all that."

It was amazing. Lawrence did know what I meant. I didn't even know what I was saying, but Lawrence heard me. Lawrence understood.

"Yeah," I said softly.

"So does that mean you'll go out with me next weekend, or what?" Lawrence persisted.

"Oh, certainly!" I said enthusiastically. "Uh, that is, certainly Friday night."

"Why not Saturday night, too, being that we're practically going steady?" Lawrence persisted.

I shrugged my shoulders and tried to get a casual, sincere tone in my voice, even though I didn't feel either casual or sincere.

Oh, why was Lawrence pressuring me? Why

was he persisting? But I knew the answer: because he liked me so much. Because I was that important to him. And if I broke up with him, I'd disappoint him that deeply, that's why.

"My parents. They get on my case if I go out twice in one weekend. So let's definitely go out Friday night, OK?" *And that will give me Saturday night with Alex.*

"OK," said Lawrence. Then we didn't seem to have anything else to say. It was unusual for us, but the conversation we'd just had was unusual, too.

"Bye, Lawrence," I said, trying to sound cheerful.

"Bye," said Lawrence, not even trying.

I felt really lousy after that. I wanted to call Lawrence right back and tell him everything. But I couldn't tell him about Alex. I just couldn't. Not yet.

Oh, Alex! A strange, melting sensation shot through me as I thought of Alex. Then came a familiar stab of guilt as I thought of Lawrence again. The situation seemed more hopeless than ever.

From out beyond my window, I heard a familiar tinkling. Bells. And bells could mean only one thing—Candace. A few months ago she'd attached tiny silver bells to the front and back of her bike. It made her sound like she was riding around in a Christmas sleigh.

"That's such a cheerful sound," I heard my mother tell her at the front door one day.

"Yes, isn't it?" Candace had agreed enthusiastically. "I feel as though I'm sprinkling cheer over each street and house as I pass it."

I rolled my eyes but said nothing. Frankly, between you and me, Candace didn't put those bells on her bike to "sprinkle cheer" around. Candace likes attention. And she'll do the wildest things to get it.

Actually, the bells really did pay off with Mike. Everyone in school knew Candace had a thing for Mike, but although he seemed to like her, too, he was going with a girl named Roberta. Come to think of it, Candace always seemed to go for the guys who were already attached. The fact that Mike was already taken didn't seem to bother her at all. Maybe it even made him more interesting. She just got on her bike and jingled past his house every Saturday and Sunday morning, wearing her tightest jeans and T-shirt. Finally, Mike couldn't resist, and one morning he came running out of his house shaking this huge cow bell. Two days later, Candace called to tell me she and Mike were going steady. Now she'd broken up with Mike and had her eye on Lawrence.

I peered out the window, about to call out to Candace that I'd be right down. A bike ride would be just the thing to do on a bright, sunny fall morning like this. But what I saw below made my heart screech to a sudden stop. There, side by side, were two bikes. Sitting on the first, the one with the bells, was Candace. But sitting on the second, the ten-speed number, was Alex.

"Leeee-sa! Wake up, Lisa!" Candace called, cupping her hands around her mouth.

I stepped back from my window so she couldn't see me. I needed a few minutes to stop shaking. What was Candace doing with Alex, *my* Alex? Then I remembered she didn't even know he was *my* Alex; I'd told her nothing about him so far. But as I pulled on my clothes, I thought *she must know now*. Alex must have told her. But how did they meet? And what right had she to bring him here?

I slipped into my clogs and hurried down the stairs. Before I opened the door, I took one second to breathe in deeply, the way Ellie had taught me. I can't say it did much good, but I figured I needed all the help I could get at that moment.

"Hi!" I cried, grinning madly. "Why, what in the world—?" I hoped my fake surprise was fooling them.

As I walked out onto the front lawn, Candace said, "Lisa, this is a new friend of mine, Alex Wiley. Alex, say hello to Lisa."

Grinning in that impish way of his, Alex held out his hand to me and said, "Hi, it's good to meet you, Lisa."

Alex was always playing games, but this was one time when I just couldn't go along. I was too confused, too worried.

I shook Alex's hand, but I turned to Candace. She didn't even wait for me to ask. She could hardly wait to tell me about Alex.

"I know. You're wondering how Alex and I met—and when—and you're right to wonder because it only happened an hour ago. At his garage sale."

I looked at Alex.

"My mother held a garage sale this morning to get rid of some things from our other houses so we'd have room to buy more things for this house. We'll put them exactly where the old things were, and eventually we'll put them up for sale, too." Ordinarily this would have gotten a laugh out of me, or at least a chuckle and a smile. But now I just glared at Alex, and then I glared back at Candace.

"Yeah, so anyway," Candace continued, looking puzzled at the way Alex was looking at me, "I went along with my mom to Alex's mother's garage sale because I was feeling lonely and blue—and, Lisa, you didn't even call me last night to tell me what you were doing—and so, since I broke up with Mike, I had nothing to do today—"

"So you came to our garage sale, and there you met me and brought me over here to show me off to your best friend," Alex said a little impatiently. Alex had only known Candace an hour. He didn't know what it was like to be Candace's best friend and have to listen to some of her rambling stories that went on for two hours! Well, *I* had to listen to them—at least I felt that I had to if I didn't want to risk her getting annoyed at me. Normal people like Alex just cut her short.

"Yes, so I met Alex there—and here we are!" said Candace. Thanks to Alex's influence, that was the shortest sentence Candace had ever uttered.

It suddenly dawned on me that Alex hadn't told Candace about us. I wasn't sure if he was waiting for me to make the big announcement or if he planned to do it, but just as I was beginning to shift from one foot to the other uneasily, he broke the news in his own way. He started laughing hysterically, obviously pleased at this ridiculous state of affairs.

Candace stared at him as if he were losing his marbles. I just continued to glare.

"Candace, I'm sorry to laugh, but when I tell you, you're going to crack up, too." As Alex said this to her, Candace looked at him as if she didn't plan to laugh again for fifty-nine years. I could tell she was suspecting something, and, although she didn't know what it was, clearly she didn't expect to like it.

"You see," Alex said, walking over to where I was just hanging on by a thread, "Lisa and I"—he put his arm around me—"are already friends, very good friends."

I was amazed at how soft his voice got when he said this. All the laughter was gone now, and he looked down into my eyes with nothing but sincerity and seriousness. I melted. I was through glaring. I'd forgotten, in that instant, what the word glare even meant.

"Really?" said Candace. "Why didn't you tell me, Lisa?" She seemed hurt. I didn't blame her; after all, she was my best friend.

"I—wanted to. I was going to, today, as a matter of fact. On our bicycle ride."

Candace stared at me as if I had gone crazy. "What bicycle ride?"

"Well, when I heard your bike tinkling up the street, I thought—oh, forget it. But, Candace, I mean it, I was going to tell you."

"Well, it was no big secret, and now you know—Lisa and I are, well—" said Alex, and embarrassment stopped him.

"Going steady?" volunteered Candace.

Both Alex and I turned tomato red. "Well, no. Not steady." Then Alex looked down into my eyes again. "At least, not yet."

I thought I was all melted, but I managed to melt some more, somehow.

Trying to soften the blow to Candace, I said, "Candace, I'm so glad you and Alex met. I myself only met him Friday night."

"Friday night? But you couldn't have. Friday night you went out with—"

"Um, I met Alex when I delivered a cake to his house around six o'clock," I interrupted before Candace could speak Lawrence's name. Alex wasn't dumb, however. He heard. He just was too polite to say anything—then.

"So, um, now that we all know each other, how about if we do go for a bike ride?" I suggested.

They must have wanted to escape from that sticky situation as much as I did because they agreed instantly. I ran to the garage to get my bike, and Candace followed after me to get a few quick details. Alex politely waited outside.

As I unlocked the garage door, Candace whispered softly enough so only my entire house—but no one down the block—could hear.

"Did you go out with Alex last night? Is that where you were? Is that why you didn't call me? Now I can understand why you've kept him a secret. You're going out on Lawrence!"

"Don't say that!" I shouted and fell apart. Enormous tears filled my eyes and rolled down my face, and each tear seemed to represent one of the many feelings tearing me apart. There were tears of frustration, tears of confusion, tears of misery, and tears of joy. With each tear, I seemed to experience the feeling that went along with it, and the tears kept rolling down my face. I sobbed and sobbed.

"Oh, Lisa," Candace said softly, "I'm so sorry I said that. Please don't cry. I know you could never do that to Lawrence."

But that just made me cry harder. Candace hugged me and patted me and told me everything would be all right.

"Will it?" I sobbed and looked up at her, my eyes brimming over again.

"Oh, Lisa, if you don't stop, I'm going to cry, too," said Candace, and sure enough, her eyes began to fill up.

"I can't stop. I feel as if I'll never stop crying," I wailed. The tears dropped from Candace's eyes, but when we each caught a blurry glimpse of the other, we burst out laughing amid the sobs. And that's how Alex found us, laughing and crying hysterically.

"Have you girls flipped out?" Alex asked. And that remark was enough to set us off again. Finally we stopped laughing and jumped onto our bikes. And the three of us rode together until it was time for Alex to help his mother clean up after the garage sale.

As we waved goodbye to Alex, Candace turned to me. I caught the look; I knew it well.

"Oh, no, Candace! Don't tell me!" I cried.

She gave me an embarrassed smile and nodded. "Just remember," she said. "I'm first in line. They're both great—Alex and Lawrence. So, whoever you drop, I want."

I had to laugh. "I know what you mean. I think they're both kind of great myself. But I'll remember you're the first in line."

Somehow, that broke the ice, and Candace and I were back to being best friends again. We went to her house and talked for hours. Candace's mom brought up a tray of milk and doughnuts, and as we ate and talked and laughed, I realized a great weight had lifted. I didn't feel worried. I didn't feel guilty. I didn't feel anxious. Just as Ellie had said, I'd begun to deal with the problem. It couldn't be solved in a day, but at least I was talking about it.

"I'm so glad you know," I told Candace. "I mean, it's such a relief to have you here to talk to."

"That's what best friends are for," Candace said. And I knew she meant it and that she was right. Candace and I are very different in some ways, but she's a good and loyal friend. I didn't have to worry that she'd steal my boyfriend away. She'd never do anything like that.

The rest of that Sunday was sweet and peaceful. Ellie, Dad, Mom, and I sat down to a rousing game of Scrabble after dinner, and Ellie won, as usual. She won when she made the word *vertigo*, which made me jump up and gasp because it was one of the words on my vocabulary test the first thing Monday morning—and I hadn't studied at all!

I raced up to my room, looked at my vocabulary list, then dialed Lawrence's number.

"Hello?" Lawrence said sleepily.

"Hi, it's me. And I guess it's my turn to wake you up. Uh, Lawrence, what does *vertigo* mean?"

"Remind me to get you a dictionary for your birthday," said Lawrence dryly.

"No, really. Of course we have a dictionary. But it's downstairs, and I don't want my parents to know I haven't started studying yet."

"*Vertigo*," said Lawrence, "is the feeling of dizziness and imbalance you're giving me, Lisa.

Oh, Lisa, won't you at least wear my gold chain? I got it for you. The least you could do is wear it. If you promise to wear the chain, I'll promise not to mention going steady with you for a while. What do you say?"

"OK," I said instantly. It suddenly seemed such a little thing, and it would make him so happy. Not that I minded wearing the gold chain. I think by now you know my feelings on that subject. But it wouldn't be much fun since I knew that when I wore it, I'd have to hide it from view or risk a million questions from everyone.

"You will?" Lawrence said in amazement.

"Uh-huh," I answered dumbly.

Lawrence asked me to meet him in front of school in the morning so he could place the chain around my neck. I agreed. I would've agreed to just about anything that night because I just knew it would all work out. It had to.

"Need the definitions of any other vocabulary words?" Lawrence offered. He was like a grateful puppy, ready to do anything for me now.

"No, the rest are kind of easy. Only *vertigo* stumped me," I told him.

We said a sweet good night, and then I lay down on my bed and thought about that word *vertigo* for a while. Soon my eyes closed, and I dreamed about the word. I was standing on top of the highest wedding cake in the world and suffering vertigo. Suddenly millions of gold chains were lowered from the ceiling, and I hung onto one for dear life. Then I saw Alex down below saying he'd catch me, so I let go of the chain. Then Lawrence appeared and asked me why I'd let go of his chain. I didn't know what to do, whether to reach out for the chain again or jump into Alex's waiting arms. I woke up sweating. I looked at the clock and saw it was one in the morning. I was still dressed, but I was too tired to get ready for bed, so I just crawled under the covers and was instantly asleep.

As Candace and I walked to school that morning, I kept trying to think of a way to leave her before I had to meet Lawrence. I told Candace all about my telephone call with Lawrence—we were that close again—but I needed to be alone with Lawrence. But Candace can be a little dense sometimes. And on this particular morning, instead of running off to say hello to this friend or that one, Candace clung to me as if we were stapled together.

Lawrence was waiting for me, but when he saw that Candace was right beside me, he stuffed his hands in his pockets and hunched his shoulders. I was terrified that Lawrence might take out the gold chain right in front of Candace—and everyone else—but he didn't. He just said hello to both of us. When neither Candace nor I seemed capable of saying anything, Lawrence surprised all of us.

Smoothly taking my hand in his, he said to Candace, "You wouldn't mind excusing us for a few minutes, would you? I've got something really important to speak to Lisa about."

Candace just shook her head and stared silently after us as Lawrence pulled me away. We walked around the corner of the school, out of sight of the kids walking in the front door.

"Well, here it is," he said, pulling the chain out of some crinkly tissue paper.

After he placed it around my neck and locked the clasp, he came around to face me. He put his two hands in my hair and pulled my face up to his. Then he kissed me sweetly. I didn't break away. I really didn't want to. It was too caring, too sweet to stop. We didn't even touch, except for our lips, but we were very close.

And when the kiss was over, we just floated apart like two clouds in the sky that lightly blow away. We walked toward the front door.

"See you!" I called softly as we walked into the school.

"See you," Lawrence called back. Then we each turned down opposite directions of the corridor.

I wasn't entirely in dreamland, however, because I remembered to tuck the chain under the neckline of my sweater as soon as I turned a corner. Then I entered my English class and sat down at my desk. Mrs. Stewart, my English teacher, passed out the exams. I looked down at mine, and there it was—the very first vocabulary word on the test—*vertigo*.

Chapter Seven

That whole week was filled with so many Big Moments that it felt more like a month of events. First, of course, was Monday morning's Big Moment—when Lawrence gave me his chain to wear.

Later that day all kinds of tests were announced. I had exams scheduled for every single class. I planned to work out a study program for myself during my free period, but as I was walking into the library, Alex Wiley came up behind me and swung me around. I'd noticed him a few times in the halls before we met, but now that I knew him, now that I was dating him, now that he was *my* Alex, it was exciting to know that at any moment of the school day, I might see him.

"I just realized that I don't even know your schedule," he began immediately. "I mean, maybe we have the same free period and can spend it together sometimes."

"I know," I said eagerly. "I was thinking the

same thing." Actually, in a way, I was thinking just the opposite. It had occurred to me that spending time with Alex in school—or Lawrence for that matter—could get very sticky. The thought of one of them discovering me laughing or holding hands with the other made me want to ask for a sick pass and leave school immediately.

"So, what's your schedule?" Alex insisted.

I looked around to see if Lawrence might be turning the corner or something.

"What's the matter? Is this classified information or something?" Alex asked, amused at my behavior.

What I wanted to tell him was that Mondays, Wednesdays, and Fridays I always had this hour free and that I'd always be here, waiting for him. But the thought of what it might do to Lawrence to discover us together made me tongue-tied. I simply had to risk checking out the halls one more time for any signs of Lawrence.

"You know, you're acting kind of strange, Lisa. I mean, I haven't exactly asked you for your family's financial statement. What's the big secret?" Alex said.

I grabbed Alex's hand and pulled him inside the library.

"I didn't want Mr. Blomberg to see me. I told

him I was going to be finishing up my report this period—I'm two days late already."

Alex looked at me, and a few very big seconds elapsed before he said, "Are you sure it's Mr. Blomberg you don't want to see right now, Lisa?"

If ever there was a prime opportunity for me to tell Alex about Lawrence, it was right then and there.

"Alex," I began, and that's as far as I got. I didn't have the whole speech planned out, but I did know what I was going to say first. I was going to say that, yes, there was someone I didn't want to hurt. I wanted to explain that if this someone saw us together, it might be difficult to explain at the moment, but that I was working on it and it would be cleared up in a day or two.

Well, I really meant to say all that. I'd had it. I was tired of the panic; I didn't want to sneak or hide. Out with it. I was ready. I was willing. But Mrs. Greeley, the librarian, wasn't at all willing. She slammed a book shut and rushed over to us.

"Look, you two," she said in a voice that was a cross between a whisper and a screech, "this, as you may or may not know, is a library. What we do in libraries, for your information, is read. Silently. That is *all* we do here. Do I make myself clear?"

I nodded. Alex nodded.

"You staying?" Alex asked.

"I've really got to do this report. I'll see you later," I whispered.

Mrs. Greeley was standing there, glowering at us. Alex looked at her and pantomimed the word *sorry*. Then, in exaggerated steps, like the great actor he is, Alex began tiptoeing out of the library. But when he got to the door, he turned back to me and said, "Want to come with me to rehearsal this afternoon?"

Mrs. Greeley gave an exasperated sigh, so I just smiled and nodded yes. Then Alex said in a loud, deep voice, "Bye, Mrs. Greeley. Nice place you've got here," and quickly, quietly closed the door behind him.

A few of the kids sitting at tables near me were chuckling. If Mrs. Greeley hadn't been staring me down, I would have joined them. But, instead, I kept my eyes down and found an empty seat at the table farthest from Mrs. Greeley's desk. Then I spent the rest of the hour dreaming of Alex.

He'd asked me to his first rehearsal! I couldn't get over it. To me, it seemed such a brave and trusting thing to do. I mean, I would be proud to show Alex one of my finished cakes or pies, but I don't think I'd want Alex to see me testing out a new recipe.

Alex must really like me a lot, I realized. It gave me a warm and satisfied feeling. It made me just want to sit there and doodle sketches of Alex's beautiful face and write his name over and over. The last thing it made me want to do was study or plan to study—or least of all, write up my report.

When the bell rang, signaling the end of the hour, I was positive all the school clocks had broken down at the same moment. I checked my own watch and found that it, too, must have broken. Surely I hadn't spent an entire hour dreaming of Alex! But I had.

Candace was waiting for me in front of school at the end of the day. She was standing with two other girls in our class, Amy and Karen.

"You just missed your mother," Candace said, running up to me.

"My mother? She came here? To school?" I asked, suddenly envisioning a major catastrophe. "What's wrong?"

"Nothing," said Candace. "She just drove by and when she saw me, she asked me to give you this letter."

The letter had been opened. All last year Mom and I had had a major difference of opinion over the issue of my mail. She had felt she had a right to open my mail, and I had disagreed.

"Mail is personal, private property," I would argue.

"I get the mail in the morning, after you leave for school. What if there's a letter for you that's important, that can't wait?" she had argued.

We argued and argued until one day, when she opened a letter addressed to me from Ellie. Ellie had written: *What shall we get Mom for her birthday? I was thinking of a purple velvet robe. I saw one in a shop here. Shall I buy it?*

With the opened letter in her hand, Mom finally admitted she was wrong. "You were right, Lisa. Mail is personal, private property. I'll never open another letter of yours again. I'm sorry, Lisa, really I am."

That's what I like about Mom. She's very strong, very opinionated. When she's wrong, though, she admits it.

But now as I looked at the envelope ripped open along one side, I wondered if Mom had really changed at all. Candace saw me eyeing the ripped envelope, not even reading the name or address on the top left corner. "Your mom said for me to tell you she's sorry she opened the envelope, but when you see who sent it, you'll understand. That is, she said she hoped you'll understand."

"National Olympic Bake-Off, Madison, Wisconsin," I read. Then I pulled out the letter, and an airline ticket fell to the ground. I picked it up as I read, "Thank you for entering the Olympic Bake-Off. Congratulations! You have been chosen as one of the four official semi-finalists."

The letter went on to give details of the final bake-off. The date was set for Saturday at noon in two weeks. A limousine would be waiting to pick me up at the Wisconsin airport. I looked at the envelope and began to laugh.

"Look," I said, handing the letter to Candace. "Mrs. Lisa Kentwood. Boy, are they in for a surprise when they see a fifteen-year-old kid climb off that plane!"

"Then you're going?" she asked, barely looking at the letter.

"You bet I'm going," I told Candace with pride. "This is my career we're talking about. I need all the honors I can rack up, starting now."

"Do you think you'll win?"

I really didn't know the answer to that question. I knew I'd be up against adults, maybe even professionals, with years more experience than I had. I hadn't even decided on which one of my personally developed recipes I'd use at the bake-off. I just knew that I was going and that I'd bake the best cake I'd ever baked in my life.

Just then, Amy and Karen called, "Congratulations, Lisa. Good luck!"

I looked at Candace, and she shrugged. "I

couldn't help it. I was excited for you. Your mother left in such a hurry, and I was dying to talk to someone about you. You don't really mind that I told them, do you? I'm really proud of you, Lisa."

Actually, I had much more important things on my mind, such as: what was I going to do about Lawrence, who had just come out of the school and was standing at the top of the stairs?

"I don't mind, Candace. But now," I said urgently, "I have to ask you a very big favor." She's crazy about secrets, as long as she's in on them. "I have to go somewhere with Alex, but I don't want Lawrence to be hurt. So, could you—"

I didn't need to say more. Candace interrupted me, her mind whizzing a mile a minute. She came up with a scheme that sounded all right to me, except for the fact that she seemed a little too enthusiastic about it.

"I know!" she gushed. "I'll tell Lawrence I want to start jogging. It's true. I've got to get into shape. And I'll ask him to go with me now."

I wasn't exactly crazy about the idea of the two of them running along together on some romantic, secluded path, but I was in a hurry, so I just said, "You're a friend, a really best friend. I just knew I could count on you."

The next minute Lawrence had walked over, and she was tugging at him, pulling him away from the school, away from me. "Oh, come on, Lawrence. You know how it is. Until I get into a routine, I need someone pulling me, pushing me to get out there and run. If you weren't here, I'd never even think of jogging this afternoon. Oh, you're such a pal!" she cried.

It was really kind of funny. There was Candace, pulling and pushing Lawrence, while he kept turning back to look at me. Meanwhile, all she was talking about was how good it was to have someone pulling and pushing *her*! Well, Candace can be very convincing when she wants to be, and pretty soon Lawrence was shouting to me, "I'll call you tonight!" and jogging home beside Candace.

Turning back toward the school, I saw Alex, who was talking to two other guys. When he saw me, he broke away and took my arm.

"Ready for a little Shakespeare?"

"Shakespeare, Shakespeare, where art thou, Shakespeare?" I said.

"At the moment, he's at the community theater on Main Street. But he won't be there all day, so we'd better get going."

Laughing, talking, joking, we hurried downtown. But when we entered the darkened theater, we immediately stopped talking. The director and four of the actors were standing on the bare stage, holding scripts in their hands. A bright spot lighted the stage.

When the director heard us enter the theater, he shaded his eyes with his hands and peered into the audience. Alex rushed up the aisle and jumped up on the stage.

"Ah, Romeo! Good," said the director, patting him on the back. "Now all we need is our Juliet, and the rehearsal can commence."

I quietly slipped into a seat, suddenly aware that I'd never been to a theater rehearsal. I felt kind of important, the only person sitting in the dark and empty audience. I relaxed and sat back, really starting to enjoy it until Juliet emerged from the sidelines. I don't even know her real name because everyone was referring to everyone by their characters' names. All I do know is that I was sitting there, watching Alex get his script, watching the light twinkle in Alex's beautiful eyes when a fluff of exquisite long red hair kind of slithered onto the stage.

"Alex, darling!" she cried, and ran up to him and kissed him right on the mouth. Now I have read that theater people tend to be superaffectionate and dramatic, but this was going entirely too far! Especially since anyone could see that she was at least a million years older than he was. It was a clear case of an old lady taking advantage of a young boy.

But Alex didn't seem to notice anything wrong. "Ah, Juliet, I've been waiting under your window, wondering when you'd appear."

She was about to respond, but the director clapped his hands and said, "All right, all right everyone. Let's get started."

Everything was all seriousness after that. Even though it was all very interesting—even exciting—watching the play unfold as everyone read their lines unbelievably well for the first time, I couldn't really enjoy it. I sat up straight in my chair, never taking my eyes off Juliet. If she so much as touched Alex's arm, I vowed I'd go up there on that stage and quote some choice lines of my own to her. But I didn't have to because she was obviously a very good actress, and once the rehearsal began, she was all business.

At six the rehearsal ended, and Alex jumped down off the stage and came up the aisle to be with me. He said goodbye to everyone, and we were gone. He didn't say one special, individual word to red-hair, for which I was everlastingly grateful.

"What'd you think?" Alex asked me as soon as we were outside.

"It was wonderful," I said.

"You'll come opening night, won't you?"

My heart seemed to take a leap. "Opening

night? I've never been to one. Don't you have to dress up in gowns and tuxedos?"

Alex laughed. "I don't think you'll see any tuxedos in this audience. It's only a community theater."

"I'd be happy and proud to attend," I told Alex, and he squeezed my hand.

Spending the afternoon with Alex made me even more behind in my schoolwork. I ate a quick dinner and ran right up to my room, planning to spend the night catching up. But then I remembered I hadn't looked in my order book, and sure enough, I'd forgotten that, in addition to the birthday cake I had to bake for Alex's sister, I'd also promised to bake two pecan pies for a Mrs. Greene. Oh, no! I was feeling swamped again. That old familiar, but horrible, feeling of panic was returning. How can I handle it all? I wondered.

At dinner Mom apologized again for opening my letter. But, in addition, she suddenly seemed superinterested in the whole bake-off business. Wanted to know every detail. We even had a small argument about it when I said, "How come, suddenly, you're so interested?"

"It's not a sudden interest. I've always been interested," she said.

"Well, it seems to me your interest has perked up only now, when it's suddenly the big time.

Before, you always seemed annoyed at my baking business," I said, remembering the hurt I'd felt at times because of her attitude.

Mom saw how red my face was, and she heard the anger in my voice. I saw her stiffen the way she sometimes does when she thinks I'm getting what she calls "impudent." But then, to my surprise, I saw her take a deep breath, relax, and reach out for my hand across the table.

"Maybe I haven't been as supportive as I should have been, but I want you to know right now that I've always been very proud of your baking talents, Lisa."

Dad sat quietly at the table; Ellie was back at school. I couldn't figure out if Mom was finished or not, so I kept still, which was a good thing because then she said, "Sometimes, as a mother, I get caught up in trying to correct the things that aren't going right. I think about helping you with your problems so much that sometimes I forget to give you credit for the good things you've done."

Again Dad and I were silent. Mom had never spoken this way at the table before. And only once or twice in private. It was so special, so intimate that I didn't want to say anything that might ruin it.

"So I think I should correct that right now," Mom continued, "by telling you I think you're terrific. I'm so proud of your accomplishments. Why, at the age of fifteen—"

"Fifteen-and-a-half," I said.

"Right. Fifteen-and-a-half. But for someone so young to have such a thriving, successful business is really quite special. I just wanted you to know how I feel about it."

I guess that was about one of the most rewarding days I have ever had. The rest of the week was like that, too. I somehow managed to bake the two pecan pies for Mrs. Greene on Wednesday, as well as buy the ingredients for Alex's sister's cake. Thursday and Friday I worked on the cake and also managed to get in a lot of studying. Then I phoned Ellie long distance at school and told her the remarkable thing Mom had said at dinner.

"It's true, Lisa," Ellie said. "Mom thinks the world of you. She's always telling people about her daughter Lisa, the entrepreneur."

"What's an entrepreneur?" I asked.

"Someone like you who starts up her own enterprise. But, as Mom says, you're something more because you're also an artist."

Sometimes—usually for very brief moments—life can be so sweet, so special that everything gets colored in that warm and rosy hue. At times like these, when you look in the mirror, your skin looks clear, without one zit, your hair falls right, your belly looks flat, and your favorite shirt is washed and starched just the way you like it. When you speak, the right words come out, and when you're spoken to, only beautiful thoughts are expressed.

I thoroughly enjoyed those few, special, perfect days. They gave me strength and confidence, but, as I found out, you can never have enough strength or confidence. I certainly could have used a few barrels more.

The first dark cloud appeared when I was supposed to go out with Lawrence on Friday night. We'd set the date for seven-thirty, but at six when I arrived at the Wiley house to deliver the cake, Alex pulled me inside.

"Stay for a little while," he coaxed, helping me off with my sweater.

Mr. and Mrs. Wiley waved hello and called me into a room decorated with balloons and silver streamers. Alex's little sister was wearing a white party dress. She had the same dark good looks her brother had.

The little kids were so cute, eating their hot dogs and potato chips and playing their fun little games, that I sat with Alex and laughed and watched for quite a while. Then, when Mrs. Wiley brought out the birthday cake, she insisted that I stay and have a piece.

By the time I got home, Lawrence had already

arrived and was sitting in the living room, talking to Mom and Dad. Since we were planning to go bowling, time wasn't crucial, but I could see that Lawrence was a bit annoyed.

At least Mom didn't embarrass me by asking where I'd been. In fact, she kind of came to my rescue by joking, "You know, Lisa, if your business gets any busier, you're going to need a secretary—and an accountant!"

"Well, if I win the bake-off, maybe I will need to hire a secretary," I said, sliding into a chair next to Lawrence. I wisely gave up the idea of changing my clothes for our date. Instead, I thought that if I sat right down near him, I might be able to smooth out the frown line on Lawrence's forehead.

"What bake-off?" asked Lawrence.

So I told Lawrence all about the contest and how I'd be flying out there in two weeks and how proud and excited I was.

"My father began reading medical books when he was fourteen," Lawrence said to my parents as well as to me. "So I think it's never too early to begin preparing for your career in life."

I had to look away, or Lawrence would have seen me roll my eyes. This was Lawrence at his most formal, and when he got like that, he was dull, dull, dull. I thought of the fun I'd just had with Alex, the life and excitement going on at his house, and I longed to run back there. Was the party still going on? Was Alex out with some other girl? Did red-hair phone him and say they simply had to have a private rehearsal together?

Suddenly I realized Lawrence was talking to me and waiting for me to answer.

"Lisa. Lisa? Are you ready? Want to go?"

I nodded and rose. I gave my parents elaborate goodbyes and kisses—anything to put off being alone with Lawrence. But then, as we left the house, I tripped over Lawrence's foot and fell onto the grass. I burst out laughing, and Lawrence, to my amazement, burst out laughing, too. I looked at the hill in front of my house, then looked up at Lawrence. "Let's roll down. I haven't rolled down this hill since I was a kid. Remember when we used to roll down together?"

In a flash Lawrence was beside me. "Ready, set, go!" he said, and we folded our arms close in to our chests and rolled. The night, the sky, and the grass went spinning, and I thought to myself: maybe this won't be so bad after all.

Chapter Eight

Mom and Dad heard the commotion out on the front lawn and came out to look. What they saw there were two teenagers making complete idiots of themselves. Just as Mom and Dad came out, Lawrence and I were racing up the hill again for another roll. We were laughing and shouting.

"Remember the time you rolled right into the tree!" Lawrence called to me as I huffed up the hill.

"Yeah, and remember the time you just conked out? You rolled over once, and then your body just stopped. I pushed you, we tried everything, but you just couldn't get yourself rolling."

Lawrence laughed at the memory. Boy, if only he'd laugh more, I thought. He has a great laugh.

We waved to my parents, and Lawrence actually said, "Come on! Try it. It's fun!"

They shook their heads and smiled at us as if they felt sorry for two people who'd really gone off the deep end. Then they went back inside. But we didn't leave.

Instead, we began doing all the old things we used to do when we were kids. We ran down the hill, and even though it was dark, we climbed up into the branches of the tree I'd once rolled right into. Lawrence rocked back and forth to make the branches shake, and I cried out just as I used to when I was young and a little afraid.

We sang all our old camp songs. I tried to harmonize, and Lawrence simply tried to stay on tune.

"You are, without a doubt, the worst singer I have ever heard in my life," I told him, laughing.

"You should hear my father sing. He's so bad he's good," said Lawrence.

Then we got down on all fours in the grass, and staying within the light of a streetlamp, we searched for four-leaf clovers. We kept bumping into each other as we crawled madly around until finally Lawrence said, "I give up!" He stretched out on the grass and turned his head to see if I was going to give up. Then he decided to play his old four-leaf-clover trick. Once again, although I was years older now, I fell for it.

"Oh, wow!" Lawrence cried, sticking his nose down into the grass. "Yes. It is! It is!" He plucked something up from the grass. Then he stood up, turned his back to me for a moment, and then held out the four-leaf clover to me.

"How did you—I don't believe—ooh, can I have it?" I cried.

"Well, I don't know about that," Lawrence said hesitantly. "I mean, a four-leaf clover is pretty rare. I don't know, maybe I could sell it for a couple hundred dollars." He looked at me, scratched his head, then looked at me again.

"Well, all right," he said. "Here."

I reached for the four-leaf clover, and Lawrence opened his palm to reveal two clovers held together to look like one.

"All you need is a little bit of tape or glue," Lawrence said, making me laugh even harder. I couldn't believe he'd fooled me with that old trick after all these years.

What's more, I realized, I couldn't believe Lawrence was playing tricks at all! Serious, formal Lawrence had rolled down the hill with me, climbed a tree, laughed a belly laugh, and played a trick!

When I finally stopped laughing, Lawrence asked, "Are you wearing it?" I knew what he meant—the gold chain. I reached down inside my sweater and pulled up the necklace so he could see.

Lawrence gave me a smile of such sweetness that I just couldn't help it—I reached over and kissed him on the cheek. He put his arms around me and held me silently for a long time. When we broke apart, he was still smiling.

"Let's bowl," he said. So hand in hand we went off to town.

Lawrence never plays sports he's not good at. I, on the other hand, will try anything. I can have a great time playing basketball in the school gym without ever getting the ball in the basket. But Lawrence can't stand to lose at anything. I guess losing is a big blow to his ego, so he only plays to win.

"Hey, Lawrence, you're taking this game too seriously!" I complained, after we'd been bowling for about ten minutes. "I mean, it's only a game."

Suddenly Lawrence was the other Lawrence again, the formal, stiff, humorless one. "I think if you're going to play a game, you should try to play it the best you can—and nothing less."

I rolled my eyes. "Oh, come on, Lawrence. Sure, it's good to try to play it well. But it's just as important to have fun doing it." I couldn't stand it. Lawrence could be so wonderful one minute and such an idiot the next. Right now, he was being a total idiot.

I decided to lighten things up a bit. As Lawrence began to bowl, I shouted out, just like a cheerleader, "Go, Lawrence, go! Go, Lawrence, go!" It threw his aim off slightly, and he hit only one pin. He turned to me, and his face was red with anger.

"You deliberately ruined my shot. That was really dumb!"

I was getting angry myself. We had been having such a great time. Lawrence had been so much fun, so sweet. But now he was back to being a real grouch, and I couldn't stand it.

"Lawrence, what's bothering you? I mean, I can't believe you're really that upset because you didn't get a strike. So what's making you act this way?" I demanded.

"What way?" Lawrence asked, looking as innocent as a child.

Now I was really angry. I was about to really let Lawrence have it, but something stopped me. My old fear, I guess. Even at that moment, when I was boiling mad, I couldn't just express my feelings. I got afraid that maybe I was too angry and that my words might come out too harshly and that then I'd hurt Lawrence.

So there I was, all red and choked up with anger, when Lawrence surprised me.

"Let's sit down," he said. Then he jumped up and bought us sodas. Then he sat down again. I didn't sit very close to him because I was so angry, but he didn't seem to notice.

He picked up a pencil and began doodling all

over the scorecard. Neither of us said anything, but I could tell that Lawrence was closer to speaking than I was.

Finally, without looking at me, Lawrence said, "I guess you know me better than anyone, Lisa. Tonight, when we were remembering how we used to play together as kids, I realized how well you really know me. But, Lisa, I'm not sure I know you very well anymore."

"What do you mean?" I asked, my heart sinking suddenly.

Lawrence shrugged and continued to doodle on the scorecard as he talked. "I just get the feeling you're not being entirely straight with me."

My heart was somewhere down around my toes by the time Lawrence finished. "What—what specifically are you talking about?" I stammered.

"About the chain! The chain, Lisa. Is that specific enough?"

My spirits rose slightly. Wasn't I wearing the chain? Hadn't I shown it to him? How could he complain about that?

"But I'm wearing the chain. I showed you," I protested.

"Yeah, you're wearing it, but under a million layers of clothing. Lisa, you're not wearing it—you're hiding it!" Lawrence said angrily.

"I'm not hiding it!" I insisted. "I'm just not showing it off."

"Well, why aren't you?" he asked. "I thought you'd be proud to wear it. At first, when you showed me the chain around your neck, I felt proud, too. But since then, I've been thinking. And something about it has been bothering me. I keep asking myself why you wear it under your sweater."

"Because," I said, almost yelling, "we're not officially going steady. It's just like the bake-off. Until they announced I was an official finalist and sent me my plane ticket, I didn't go around talking about it."

"Well, why aren't we officially going steady?" Lawrence persisted. "I've tried to understand. Sometimes I tell myself that I do. But the truth is, Lisa, I don't understand. I don't understand at all."

Now I was really furious, and I couldn't hold it in any longer.

"Maybe it's not important for you to understand. Maybe it's only important that you respect my feelings. If I say I'm not ready to commit myself, why can't you just respect that?"

Without a word, Lawrence stood up and took a bowling ball in his hand. He walked over to the alley, aimed, and bowled. The ball rolled straight down the center of the alley and knocked every single pin down. He waited, his back to me, while the pins were set up again. Then, again he played, and again and again.

I began to worry. Wasn't he ever going to talk to me again? Was this it? What I'd been fearing? I should have known that what I was fearing would cause a much bigger blowout than this. I should have known, but I didn't.

Suddenly, just as I was about to go up to him, Lawrence put down the ball and returned to where I was sitting.

"I promised not to pressure you anymore if you wore my chain, and tonight I broke my promise. I'm sorry. I still feel that you're not being completely honest with me, but I'm willing to let it drop. I really don't know why I keep hammering away at you. I mean, I know you like me, and I know I like you, but somehow your promise to go steady has become a really big thing in my mind. I think I've got it under control now, though. OK?"

I smiled. "Sure."

We never really got back to the way we were at the beginning of the evening, but at least we weren't fighting anymore, and at least that dread feeling of panic at the pit of my stomach had gone away. We said a quick good night at my door and made a date for the following Friday.

Mom and Dad were playing cards in the living room with some friends of theirs. I didn't feel at all sleepy, so I joined them for a while, nibbling on some nuts that my mother had put on the table and peeking at their hands. Mom and Dad played a really interesting game of cards. They didn't play for money; they played for services.

"So, if I lose, I'll pay you by helping you organize your closets," I heard Mom saying to one of her friends one night. "And if you lose, maybe you'll do a small drawing for me, since you're an artist."

It seemed to me a really nice way to win and lose. Everyone seemed to like it. Mom and Dad always had lots of friends over who were eager to trade services as well as play cards.

After a while I said good night and went to my room. Mom knocked on my door a few minutes later. "Feel like talking?" she asked.

As a matter of fact, I did, but I didn't want to take her away from her friends.

"That's all right. I was losing anyway," she said. "Sally or Joe will fill in for me." She sat down in my wicker chair. "Lisa, I just want you to know that I'm here for you. If you have problems, I want to know about them—if you want to tell me. I love you, Lisa, just remember that."

I stared at her, aware for the first time that I'd shut her out of my life almost totally lately.

She was being really kind about it, but I could see I'd hurt her a little.

"Oh, Mom, I don't even know where to begin!" I cried.

To my surprise, she said, "Begin at the end." Most people will tell you to begin at the beginning, but not Mom. She said, "Tell me what's bothering you right now, and from there we can go back to what caused it at the beginning, if you want to."

So I told her about Lawrence and how he'd asked me to go steady and how I'd agreed to wear his gold chain. "I'm so confused. Sometimes I want to say I'd be happy and proud to go steady with him, and other times I want to break up with him. Whenever I try to break up with him, I wind up more deeply committed to him. Isn't that crazy?"

Mom shook her head. "It's not so crazy. But why do you want to break up with Lawrence?"

"Well," I said slowly, "if I tell you that, I guess I'll have to tell you about Alex."

"Ah," Mom sighed. "Alex Wiley. The boy you went out with last Saturday?"

"Yes," I admitted and told her all about Alex. Just then, the phone rang. It was Candace.

"Did I call too late? Did I wake anyone up?" she asked, although she wouldn't have waited until the morning even if the wires had been cut. Nevertheless, she made her voice sound just as sorry and worried as it could be.

"It's all right," I told Candace. "No one's sleeping yet."

She breathed a sigh of relief. "What are you doing right this moment?"

"I'm talking to my mom," I told her.

"Oh, Lisa, you have the greatest mom in the whole world. She'll understand," Candace said desperately.

"Understand what?" I asked.

"When you tell her that you're coming over here to sleep over."

"I am?" I asked.

I glanced at Mom. She was waiting patiently for me to get off the phone. I hated the thought of running out on her, especially since I'd have to ask Dad to drive me over. Nevertheless, deep down, I knew I was going to accept Candace's late invitation. It was a great idea. And it was what I really needed—to sit up all night talking to a best friend the way only best friends can talk.

When I got off the phone, I broke it gently to Mom, and she took it real well. There was no "But we were talking!" or "I'll remember this, Lisa!" Instead, she simply said, "We'll finish our talk another time. I'm glad we were able to make a start. Now you go to your friend, and I'll go back to mine."

I hugged her and squeezed her and thanked her for understanding. Candace was right. Mom was the greatest mother in the whole world. At least, tonight she was.

Dad mumbled and grumbled, but he drove me over to Candace's house rather than let me walk there alone in the dark. And as he drove, he said that he gathered I was going through a really rough time. "If you need to talk, I want you to know that I'm here."

I couldn't believe it. First Mom and now him. I felt encircled by this warm and caring family. Instead of feeling all alone, it was as if I suddenly had almost too many people to talk to!

"Dad, thanks," I said, "but I really don't feel like talking just now."

I thought I noticed a hurt look in his eyes for an instant, but then he said, "Oh, I didn't mean just now. I have to get back to our guests. I just meant whenever you felt like it. Sometimes it's just good to know someone's there."

"Yes, it is," I agreed, and gave him a big hug, too.

I suddenly realized, as I walked into Candace's house, that I'd never seen Candace's mother or father ever hug her. Her mom often did thoughtful things, such as serving us milk and doughnuts. But they didn't touch each other very much in Candace's family. So the first thing I did when I walked in was to give Candace a big hug.

She stared at me a moment afterward as if she were really surprised. Then she just smiled, took my hand, and pulled me up to her room.

"I forgot to pack anything," I told her.

"No problem," said Candace, going to her bureau. "Come here. Pick out your nightgown for yourself." I walked over and peeked into the drawer Candace held open for me. I had realized Candace had lovely clothes, but I had never really noticed how many she had. Now I looked at and touched all the nightgowns. There must have been at least twenty different gowns and pajamas in that drawer. Blues, pinks, lavenders, yellows.

"You're so lucky. You have so much," I told her.

"Things, yes," she admitted sadly. "Lots of things. But I hardly have a father, he's away on business so much. And Mom is so mad about it that most of the time she's walking around in a rage, and everyone has to keep out of her way."

Candace was my best friend, but until that moment I'd always thought she had everything. I remembered guiltily how supportive, how *there* both my parents had been. I couldn't even imagine what it would be like to have parents like Candace's. No wonder she was always coming over to our house for breakfast!

I pulled on a pair of satiny yellow pajamas, but the legs were too long. Candace looked at me, then ran to the closet and pulled out a pair of high boots.

"Here, tuck the legs in these," she commanded.

I pulled on the boots and looked in the mirror. It was a sensational outfit. It looked more like something to go dancing in instead of something to sleep in.

"You should become a fashion designer. You have great style, do you know that?" I asked Candace.

Candace's big blue eyes rolled up toward the ceiling. "Oh, wow! You're absolutely right!"

"I am?"

"Yes," she insisted. "That's exactly what I think I want to be—a fashion designer. I spoke to Ms. Kramer, my art teacher, about it, and she thinks I've got the talent."

As Candace talked, I pulled off the boots and climbed into bed. Candace put on a silky pink gown with pink bows at the wrists and joined me.

"Lisa," she said slowly, plumping up her pillow, "have you made up your mind about Lawrence yet?"

"Do you still like him?" I asked.

Candace nodded.

"Oh, Candace, I feel like such a rat. Here I am, holding on to Lawrence, when you like him so much. But you see, I like him, too!" I cried.

"I know," she said miserably. "But at least you have Alex."

"I know," I admitted.

"Lawrence and I went jogging three times this week," Candace confessed. Maybe she was trying to make me jealous. Maybe she was trying to make me give him up. Or maybe she just had to relieve her conscience. But whatever she was doing, she had no idea that what she was confessing didn't disturb me at all. If she'd only known how Lawrence was pressuring me to go steady with him, she would have realized she had no reason to feel guilty. She'd have seen that she was getting nowhere with Lawrence. But I couldn't tell her. To tell her that would be to hurt her too cruelly. So I just said, "Well, good luck."

We spent the next few hours talking about everything under the sun—clothes, school, our futures, our parents. It was very late when we finally turned out the lights and went to sleep. We'd had such a close night together there was almost nothing left to say. But, of course, there was plenty more to talk about in the morning.

The one thing we didn't talk anymore about was my dilemma—until I was about to leave.

"You know, you're not being fair to Alex, and you're not being fair to Lawrence—"

"I know," I interrupted.

"But you're also not being fair to me," Candace continued.

So I made Candace a promise: "As soon as I get back from the bake-off, I'm going to break up with Lawrence."

"Promise?" Candace said, her eyes sparkling with hope.

"Promise," I vowed. Little did I know how true that promise would turn out to be—except that it wouldn't happen the way I had planned it all. It would happen in the worst possible way, the very way I had most dreaded.

But for the meantime, things were fine. I baked my cakes, made plans to go to the bake-off, went out with Lawrence and Alex, and finished my talk with Mom.

"You know what you've got to do," Mom said when I talked to her some more about Lawrence and Alex. "Now it's just a question of doing it."

"I'm going to," I told her. "I promised Candace—and I promised myself—that I'm going to break up with Lawrence as soon as I return from the bake-off."

"If you really want to break up with Lawrence, why wait?" she asked.

"I—I just can't face doing it now, not before the pressure of the bake-off is over," I told her. It was true that I was feeling nervous about the bake-off and didn't want any more problems on my mind until it was over. But it was also true that I was just stalling for a little more time, a little more fun before the difficult moment came.

So I took the extra time, and I had the extra bit of fun with Alex and Lawrence, but eventually, the difficult moment came. And when it did, it was worse than I'd ever imagined.

Chapter Nine

The night before the bake-off, I was a nervous wreck. One of the contest requirements was that you had to bake your cake from memory; you couldn't use a written recipe at the event. But I just couldn't seem to remember the list of ingredients!

"What'll I do?" I wailed.

"Lisa, you're just nervous," Dad said soothingly. "It'll all come back to you tomorrow when you get that mixing bowl and wooden spoon in your hand."

"But I can't even remember the name I gave my cake! Oh, why did I give it such a long name!"

"Now, Lisa, you've baked your Black-As-Night Chocolate Cake with Moonbeam Frosting at least fifteen times," Mom said firmly. "We went over the procedures until you were blue in the face. You know everything backwards and forwards."

It was true. Mom had been an angel, testing me and helping me until even I had to admit that "if I don't know it now, I never will." Yet, I had this uneasy feeling that I was going to make a fool of myself the next day.

"What if the other three semifinalists are all at least thirty-five, with years and years of experience?" I whined.

"Well, what if that's so?" Dad asked. "All the more reason why it's not so crucial for you to win. To have gotten this far at your age is an achievement in itself."

"But I don't want to be laughed at," I said.

"You won't be laughed at, silly; you'll be applauded."

Ellie phoned from school to wish me luck, and she said the same thing: "Prepare yourself for applause, not laughter."

Then Candace called to wish me luck. "Break a leg," she said cheerfully.

"What kind of nasty thing is that to wish on me?" I said testily.

"Haven't you ever heard that expression? It's a theater expression that means good luck."

"Oh," I said flatly. "Sorry." But I made a mental note to remember it and use it on Alex at opening night when I got back.

"What are you going to wear?" Candace asked.

My mind went blank again. "I don't know. I can't remember what I decided on." I called out to my mother, "Mom, what did I say I was wearing tomorrow?"

"The last thing you told me was that you were going to wear either the blue skirt and blue striped blouse or jeans and your gray sweater," she called back to me from the other room.

"Oh, no! That was ages ago! I rejected those ideas and a million after them!" I cried.

Candace asked, "Want to come over and borrow something of mine?" It was sweet of her to offer, but the offer annoyed me. Everything annoyed me at that moment. "No! I decided on a great outfit, and that's what I'm going to wear—if only I could remember what it was."

"Why don't you just get some sleep?" Candace advised. "In the morning you'll remember everything."

Everyone was being so sweet, and I hated myself for being so grumpy, but they just didn't understand how important this contest was. Winning could mean a lot for my future. Maybe I'd even be accepted at one of the great culinary schools in the country. Oh, so much depended on this!

"I know what," Candace was saying. "Why don't you wear my yellow pajamas and the boots you tried on the other night? I didn't tell you because I was a little bit jealous, but you looked really great in that outfit."

"Candace, are you crazy?" I almost screamed into the phone. "That's a disco outfit. I can't go into that contest looking like I'm ready to boogey. This is serious."

"Sorry," Candace said.

"I'm sorry, too. I guess I'm just very nervous," I explained.

No sooner had I hung up the phone than the doorbell rang. To my amazement, a messenger handed me a big white box filled with long-stemmed roses.

I tore open the envelope and read the card: *You take the cake, kid. Love, Guess who.*

My eyes filled with tears. Here were these beautiful flowers and this thoughtful, adorable card. But the crazy thing was, I couldn't guess who had sent them at all! One moment, I decided that only Alex, my Alex, could have sent flowers like these. And the next moment, I was sure that only Lawrence, my oldest, dearest friend, could think of such a caring thing to do. Back and forth I went, first Alex, then Lawrence.

Who did I thank? I wondered. What a ridiculous mess! If I thanked Lawrence and it turned out to be Alex who'd sent the roses, I'd be in deep trouble. And vice versa.

How, I wondered, could something so beautiful cause so much grief? The only answer, I decided, was to thank neither of them and try to forget about it until the bake-off was over. But I went to sleep that night with the roses sitting in a vase beside my bed, their aroma a constant reminder of the unresolved conflict waiting, waiting, waiting for me when I returned.

Mom and Dad drove me to the airport in the morning. I had been too nervous to eat any breakfast and had told my father that I thought he was lingering over his coffee just to taunt me.

Maybe I was just grumpy because I had to give up my date with Alex in order to go to the bake-off.

"No sweat," he had said. "The play is opening next Friday, so I'll be busy with rehearsals this weekend anyway."

"Next Friday?" I asked, unable to contain the shock in my voice. "So soon? It's really opening next Friday

I'd promised Lawrence I'd go out with him on Friday night. Of course, I couldn't miss Alex's opening night, but it meant another lie to Lawrence.

"It sure is. We work fast. Do you want to sit in the audience or stand in the wings?" he asked.

"The audience. I don't want to miss one word, one gesture, and if I stand in the wings, I might miss something."

Alex told me he'd leave my ticket at the box office. "I can't pick you up because I'll have to be at the theater early. But afterward, we'll go out and celebrate."

As the plane lifted into the sky, I curled up in my seat and pictured Alex in costume, Alex in the spotlight, Alex backstage after the performance. I imagine myself throwing my arms around him, congratulating him. And this thought, of course, made me think of Lawrence. How would he take it when I told him I couldn't see him on Friday night? I had decided to tell him I could go out with him on Saturday night instead, that my sister was coming in from school on Friday and I wanted to be with her.

Then I remembered that I'd vowed to break up with Lawrence when I got back from the bake-off.

All right, Lisa, I told myself. You promised, and you're going to do it. You'll do it face to face Saturday night on your date—your last date—with Lawrence.

That decided, I felt extremely relieved. I closed my eyes and realized that my nervousness had vanished. Poof! It had gone like a puff of smoke. And in its place I felt excitement and a growing sense of confidence about the coming event.

I was sure no one in Wisconsin had ever tasted anything like my Black-As-Night Chocolate Cake with Moonbeam Frosting. Maybe I wouldn't win the grand prize, which was a check for five thousand dollars and a silver loving cup, but at least I'd wow them, of that I was sure.

A limousine was waiting for me at the airport, just as they had promised, and a bunch of contest officials were there to greet me. Sure enough, when they saw me, they all exchanged glances as if to say, "Why, she's only a kid!"

Then this public relations person who was standing next to the photographer said, "Listen, I think this is a great bit. We can stress the angle that you're never too young—or too old—to be a winner."

A woman in a black, serious suit said, "Not bad. I like it." Then she said to the photographer, "Can we get a shot of Lisa waving and smiling in front of the plane?"

Everyone was talking about me as if I hadn't arrived yet. I felt like going back up into the plane and making my entrance once more so I could be sure they knew I was really there.

But once we got to the test kitchens and the contest began, everyone forgot my age. We four semifinalists were given kitchen areas, and we each were observed by the judges as we worked.

I measured, poured, mixed, and whipped. I was glad I hadn't worn my gray sweater because I would have been too warm. My green shirt with button-down collar and green slacks were just right. Not too casual and not too dressy and cool enough to work in. (Those ovens get hot!)

When I had placed my last "moonbeam" on top of the cake, I glanced up at one of the judges. She was smiling at me. I felt as if her eyes were saying to me, "It's all right, Lisa. You did well, really well. You can relax now."

I smiled back and breathed a deep sigh of relief. While the judges went about their tasting, I went to the ladies' room and washed my face.

The president of the flour company that was sponsoring the bake-off read out the winner a few minutes later. I was back at my kitchen area, standing before my half-eaten cake, about to begin getting nervous again. Suddenly I heard my name being called out. "Lisa Kentwood." I gasped. Again the company president said my name. I caught the eyes of the kind judge, and once again they seemed to be reassuring me: "It's all right, Lisa. You did it. You did it!"

Everyone had been right; there was no laughter, only applause. I stumbled up to the small microphone. The silver loving cup was placed in one hand, and the check was placed in my other hand. I clutched both prizes to me and said tearfully, "I'll never forget this moment as long as I live. Thank you."

At the airport I called home and told them the unbelievable news. Dad, to my amazement, actually sounded teary as he said, "I'm very proud of you, Lisa. My little Lisa."

The thrill of triumph stayed with me until Wednesday. Mom and Dad met me at the airport with another bunch of roses. For a moment it reminded me of the other roses and the Problem with a capital P. But when Mom asked me to tell her everything that had happened, I lost myself in reliving it all. It was almost as much fun reliving it as actually living it!

A local newspaper reporter came to my house to interview me, and at school kids kept running up to me for days afterward to ask me all about my "big win." Even Mr. Bromberg wrote a little note of congratulations on my report when he handed it back in social studies: *Congratulations, both on this fine report and a certain culinary achievement I happened to hear about.*

Meanwhile, Alex was so busy racing to rehearsals after school that we didn't get to say more than hi to each other all week. Lawrence, however, was waiting for me at school on Monday morning. I didn't have the heart to tell him I had to change my date with him from Friday to Saturday night. Instead, I concentrated on telling him all about the contest, from beginning to end.

That was the wonderful thing about Lawrence; he really cared. I mean, he stood there listening to me, really listening, and didn't even interrupt when he saw we were about to be late for our first class.

"That's great, Lisa," he said, squeezing my shoulder. "You really did it."

I told Lawrence about the roses my parents had given me, hoping that if he was the one responsible for the other bunch, he'd give some sign, but he didn't. Suddenly, though, I knew it was Lawrence just because he gave no sign. He was waiting for me to say something.

"And Lawrence, thanks. The roses were really thoughtful. I loved them," I said quickly.

Lawrence squeezed my shoulder again and said, "I'm glad I thought of them first—before your parents."

"So am I," I agreed.

But when Lawrence waited to walk home with me from school on Wednesday, I told him about the change in my plans.

"Ellie's coming in from school Friday, and I really want to spend the evening with her. You don't mind, do you?" I said, hating myself for lying. It's only this one last time, I told myself.

On Saturday night, when you break up with Lawrence, you'll end the reason for all this hiding and deception.

"No, that's fine," Lawrence said easily. "I prefer Saturday night. There's a basketball game at school on Friday that I really wanted to go to anyway."

I hope you'll still feel that way when Saturday night is over, I prayed. Oh, Lawrence, I don't want to hurt you, but this time I mean it. I'm going to break up with you.

I knew at last I'd solved my Problem. I even felt that Lawrence and I might be able to remain friends. Finally I stopped feeling afraid.

Everything I wore for Alex's opening night was borrowed.

"I just don't own anything dressy enough!" I wailed to Candace. It was true, too. I just never wore dressy things, even for dates.

Candace, on the other hand, owned an outfit for every possible situation—even a gown—"in case I get invited to a wedding," she explained.

So Candace wound up lending me a silk two-piece outfit, Mom let me borrow her black silk evening bag, and Ellie said I could wear her gold pantyhose and her gold eye shadow.

Dad was waiting for me at the bottom of the

stairs. When I saw the expression on his face, I didn't even have to ask how I looked. I just looked at him, and we both smiled at the same instant. Then he bent down and planted a small kiss on my forehead. Mom waved to me from the window as Dad drove me to the theater.

"Would you like me to wait with you until it's time to go in?" Dad asked.

I told myself, Lisa, this is good training. If you can tell your father that, no, you don't want him to wait with you, that you'd kind of like to stand in the lobby and experience this all by yourself, then you can tell Lawrence on Saturday that you want to break up with him.

Then I heard the words come out of my mouth, and I told myself that that proved it. Everything would work out Saturday night.

I kissed Dad goodbye and stood in the center of the lobby, watching the people in their dressy clothes hurrying into the theater. When the lights flashed, signaling that it was time for people to take their seats, I crossed my fingers and sent Alex a silent wish: *Break a leg, Alex.*

Then the lights dimmed and went all the way down. Instantly the hum of people laughing and talking quieted to absolute silence. As a small group of musicians began to play a lively madrigal, the curtain rose to reveal a beautiful set representing a street in Verona.

When Alex came on stage, I didn't recognize him at first. In his costume and stage makeup, he looked older and taller. But when he spoke his first lines, my heart stood still, and I realized, *It's Alex! My Alex!*

After that, I didn't even mind that old red-hair was playing Juliet. I was completely entranced. Alex was as good as I knew he'd be, even better. He seemed very professional to me, not at all like the kids who act in our school productions. I even had to admit that red-hair was a good actress. I loved every minute of it—except for intermission.

The ten-minute intermission was a lonely time because I longed to be with someone with whom I could share my feelings about the show. It was just too exciting to keep inside until the show was over. As soon as the lights flashed, I rushed back to my seat. By the time the play was over, and Romeo and Juliet were dead, and the tears were streaming down my cheeks, and the prince had sadly recited his last two lines: "For never was a story of more woe/Than this of Juliet and her Romeo," I knew I had witnessed something really special and that Alex was a major part of it.

I clapped and clapped until my hands were red, and my cheeks hurt from grinning with pride as the cast took bow after bow. Then I rushed outside to pace back and forth while I waited for Alex. Even now, I sometimes wonder why I had to stand outside the theater. Because if I'd waited in the lobby, maybe I would have looked through the glass doors of the theater and seen Lawrence coming up the street after the basketball game. Then I could have moved away from view, and he never would have seen me. Everything could have happened the way I'd planned it to happen. Instead, I blew it. I really blew it, and everything I'd dreaded most became real, like a nightmare, only worse because it wasn't a dream about imaginary people. It was real, and it was about real people, people I loved.

Chapter Ten

It happened so quickly. One minute I was all alone in front of the theater, waiting for Alex. The next minute, I was surrounded—by Alex and Lawrence!

From one side, Alex emerged. The audience and most of the actors had already left. Alex was alone when he threw open the side door of the theater. The first thing I noticed was how his face was shining. I guess he had to scrub his face to get all the makeup off, but I also like to think he was shining with a golden glow of happiness.

"I'm sorry I'm late," he said. "I had to say goodbye to the cast and everyone, and then I had to spend a few minutes with my parents."

I nodded that I understood and that it was all right, that now everything was all right.

"Well, what did you think?" he asked. We were standing about two feet apart from each other. I'd planned this moment so many times in so many different ways in my mind. In one version, I had planned to clap and shout "Bravo!" when Alex came out. In another, I would rush up to him and throw my arms around him and hold him tight. But the truth is that when I saw him, I became really shy and couldn't move or speak at all.

"Was it all right? Did you enjoy it?" Alex asked again, moving closer. He reached out to brush a strand of hair from my face, and I caught his hand and squeezed it. We stood there for a second, holding hands, and then I found the words.

"It was wonderful. You were wonderful. It was great. You were great. I loved it, I loved it, I loved it!"

That was all Alex had to hear. He grabbed my arms and whirled me around. *And that's when I saw Lawrence.* Alex spun me around, laughing, and I was laughing, too. Then suddenly I stopped laughing and stopped spinning. Standing before us was Lawrence, and his face looked stung with pain and anger.

I broke out of Alex's grasp and tried to catch my breath as I faced Lawrence. Alex sensed something was going on and quietly stood beside me and put his arm protectively around my shoulder. Lawrence winced when Alex held me, and my heart went out to him.

"Hello, Lisa," he said weakly, as if he were

fighting a losing battle for control of his emotions and control of his voice.

"Hello, Lawrence," I whispered.

In the awkward silence that followed, Alex, who was in a really jubilant mood, tried to be pleasant and charming.

"Hi, I'm Alex Wiley," he said, holding out his other hand to Lawrence.

But Lawrence wasn't having anything to do with pleasantness. He ignored Alex's hand and stared straight at me.

"How's your sister?" Lawrence asked cuttingly.

"Oh, Lawrence," I cried. "Please don't be angry." My heart was pounding so loudly I was sure both of them could hear it.

"Don't be angry?" Lawrence parroted. "Just what do you take me for, anyway, Lisa?" His face was getting really red now, and I realized, miserably, that there would be no stopping him.

Alex, beginning to catch on now, dropped his arm from my shoulder and asked, "What's the problem, Lisa?"

But it was Lawrence who responded. "What's the problem? What's the problem? Take a look at her neck and you'll find the problem."

Then, without waiting, Lawrence reached over and pulled the gold chain out from under my neckline.

Lawrence's face, filled with hurt and anger, was very close to mine as he said, "I think this is really rotten of you, Lisa."

I guess seeing the gold chain around my neck was the final straw. His eyes were beginning to fill up, but he kept fighting for control.

"All these weeks I've asked you to tell me the truth," Lawrence continued. Then, turning to Alex, he said, "She told me, 'I'm ninety-nine and forty-four one-hundredths-percent sure.' Did she tell you that, too? Did she agree to wear your gold chain, too, and say she'd go steady with you? Did she ask you to respect her feelings when she couldn't make up her mind, making you feel like an idiot when you complained? And did she ever make a date to go out with you and then cancel it with the excuse that her sister was coming in from school and she just had to be with her?"

A sob escaped from his throat, and turning even redder, Lawrence—humiliated, furious, and beaten—ran away before anyone could say another word.

He left Alex and me standing in the street in the cool, dark night.

"Is it true?" Alex asked after a while.

"Most of it," I had to admit.

"Ninety-nine and forty-four one-hundredths?" he asked coldly.

I looked at Alex, and there was no sympathy, no warmth in his eyes. Only a cool, distant look of disappointment.

"Please try to understand," I pleaded. "I've been so torn. It's been so difficult. I've been so afraid."

"I *am* trying to understand," said Alex. "In fact, I understand a lot more than you think I do. You think I'm angry because there was another guy in the world that you also liked. But I'm not mad about that."

"Then what is it?"

"I feel really bad for that poor guy. How could you do this to him, Lisa?"

I looked at Alex with surprise.

"You know, boys have feelings, too. And it's pretty tough on a guy to fall apart in front of the girl he likes and in front of another guy. He must have cared about you a lot. And you must have really hurt him. You must have given him the impression he could be pretty sure about you. Then he saw you with me, with my arm around you. Man, that really must have cut him up. I mean, I'm sure he was trying to act cool. So what does he end up doing? Crying. Did you know that boys cry, too? That they can feel hurt and pain and embarrassment?"

In my whole life, I had never felt smaller, meaner, or more awful. I just stood there and let Alex tell me off. He was right; they were both right. But I couldn't even tell them they were right because—well, how could they believe anything I said now?

Then Alex reached for the chain around my neck and fingered it for a moment. "You really wore his chain while you went out with me?"

"Oh, Alex, stop!" I cried, trembling. My cheeks were hot with shame, but my body was strangely cold, and I couldn't stop shivering.

"I'll stop under one condition," said Alex.

"What condition?" I asked.

"That you promise not to break down in tears. I really couldn't stand it if you started crying now. I don't want you to try to make me feel sorry for you. My sympathies are with Lawrence."

He was silent a few seconds, then added, "Look, I'm not in the mood for celebrating now. I think I'd better just take you home."

Just hearing his harsh words made me want to cry my eyes out right there and then. But I promised not to cry, and we got in his father's car in silence. We rode all the way to my house without saying one more word. It wasn't until we were at my front door that Alex spoke again.

I was still shivering, so Alex took off his jacket and put it around my shoulders without looking at me. Then he said, "Lawrence came first, didn't he? I mean, you knew him first?"

I nodded sadly.

"Then I don't think we should see each other again until you clear up your relationship with him."

The only bright spot was when Alex said, "Lisa, I really do want to see you again. This may be a crazy time to tell you, but I actually was thinking about asking you to go steady with me when this whole thing with Lawrence blew up."

"Alex, I don't want you to feel sorry for me or anything like that, but I do want you to understand something," I finally said. "And it's something that I've never told another boy—not Lawrence, not anyone."

Alex didn't say anything, but at least he did look at me, so I continued.

"All my life—well, certainly since I've been a teenager—I've been afraid of anyone, but especially a boy, being mad at me. I've been so afraid that I've often hidden or denied my feelings. I always thought that if I said how I really felt about something, no one would ever want to speak to me again."

Alex still didn't say anything, but he didn't look away, either. He really seemed to be listening.

"That's what happened between Lawrence and me. I couldn't tell him how I really felt. I was afraid of hurting him. Afraid he'd get angry."

"So you wound up really hurting him and really getting him angry," Alex added.

"I see that now," I admitted. "But I didn't see that then. And if it helps at all, I was planning to break up with him tomorrow night. Truly."

"And what about me?" Alex demanded. "Did you plan to tell me about Lawrence? You were afraid of bumping into him that day in the library, weren't you? That's why you were so nervous, wasn't it?"

"Oh, Alex, I didn't want to hurt you, either!" I cried.

"Well, you did," Alex said angrily. Then he just couldn't seem to stand it anymore. He took back his jacket, looked at me, and said, "Call me when it's all straightened out and you're free again, OK? I just can't talk about it anymore tonight."

He just turned around and began walking away. I watched his back, remembering the first time I'd met him. I remembered how, as he walked in front of me, guiding me through his house, I was happy to look at the back of his head, his hair curling around his neck, the width of his shoulders, and the shape of his back. Now he was walking away, and I wondered if I'd ever see him again.

Alex had made me promise not to cry. Now that promise seemed so easy because I felt beyond tears. I'd done all the crying I was going to do. My eyes were dry, but I felt a sadness so deep that for a moment I couldn't think, couldn't move, couldn't do anything.

Mom and Dad were waiting up for me and asked brightly, "How was the play? You're home kind of early, aren't you?"

"I'm really tired," I managed to choke out. "Could we talk in the morning?"

My voice and my expression told them enough; they didn't need the actual words. They let me alone, and I stumbled up to bed, where I immediately fell into a deep and exhausted sleep.

Sunday drifted by. I felt as if I never really woke up from that sleep. Candace met me at school first thing Monday morning and wanted to know, "Did you do it?" Of course, she wanted to know if I'd broken up with Lawrence.

"Oh, I did it all right. I really did it," I said and walked away sadly as she stared after me.

For the next two days, I dragged myself to classes and back home again. I felt tired and limp. Candace called several times, but I just didn't feel like talking. Mom came up to my room many times. She even tried fixing me my favorite dinners, but nothing seemed to get me out of the miserable slump I felt caught in.

Then, on Thursday, I passed Lawrence in the hall at school. We both looked at each other and then looked away. But after that, I knew I had to do something. I couldn't just let it go on this way. It was up to me. I had to take responsibility.

Suddenly I was aware of my heart and my brain humming again like motors in good working condition. It was as if the Sleeping Beauty had awakened—although not with a kiss. Probably, more like a slap, but at least she'd awakened.

That night I sat down at my desk and wrote Lawrence the longest, most honest letter of my life. It went on for seven pages, most of it recalling the good times we'd had together in the past. Then, at the end I wrote this:

Oh, Lawrence, I've learned so much at your expense. I've hurt you, and all because I was trying to spare myself— yes, myself—the thing that is most difficult for me—to say no. If only I'd said no weeks ago! But I didn't because I was afraid you'd think I didn't like you. But I do, Lawrence, you must believe that. It's true that I didn't want to go steady, that I also liked Alex. But I liked you, too, and that's partly what made it so difficult.

It breaks my heart when I think that we might not be friends anymore. I can't imagine going through high school without having you there. But I'm prepared to, if that's what you want. I can even understand that you might not want to talk to me again. Or look at me when we pass in the halls.

But at least, please believe this: that I've always liked you and I always will. You've always been one of the best friends I've ever had. I know I disappointed you; I know I hurt you. Maybe you can't forgive me, but at least you should know that I've changed after all that has happened; I've learned something. I think now I know how to say how I feel—to a boy as well as a girl. Maybe I'll never stop feeling afraid, but at least I'm willing to take more risks than I was before.

So, Lawrence, if our friendship is over, I'll just have to accept that. But if you ever want to say hello, I want you to know that you'll make your dear old friend Lisa deeply happy.

I carried the letter around with me for days until I found the right opportunity to pass it to Lawrence. The right opportunity came on Wednesday, when I knew he had social studies the last period of the day. I just went to his classroom, walked to his desk, put the letter down before him, and walked out. After school I waited in front of the building. But he didn't come out. He must have left by a side entrance.

The same thing happened the next day. But when I came home on Friday, a white envelope was waiting for me in front of my door.

I tore it open and read: *Dear Lisa, Thanks for your letter. Lawrence.*

Nothing more. But it was enough. Enough to make me feel I could start to live again.

I raced upstairs and without thinking, began dialing Alex's number.

As soon as he said hello, I said, "Alex? I've cleared up that—uh—other relationship."

When there was silence at the other end, I grew nervous.

"Alex? It's Lisa. And I was just telling you that I'm, well, free."

Then I closed my eyes and prayed very hard for a second or two before Alex finally said, "Well, then, in that case, how about going to a party with me Saturday night?"

I was so relieved I began to laugh. Alex still liked me! And Lawrence had thanked me for the letter! Maybe, just maybe, everything was going to be all right.

"Well, you look like your old self again, Lisa," Mom said when she came home from work.

"I am my old self again. I'm going to a party with Alex tomorrow night."

In bits and pieces over the days, I'd told Mom what had happened. Now she smiled and patted my head. "I'm glad for you, Lisa. Will Lawrence be at this party, too?"

Suddenly my heart lurched. Lawrence! Of course! It was a school party, and a lot of the school crowd would be there—maybe even Lawrence.

"Maybe," I admitted.

"Well, maybe that's a good thing. Maybe it's time you two met each other eye to eye again."

I wasn't as sure as Mom and spent the next twenty-four hours thinking about what I was going to wear and how to do my hair to keep my mind off worrying about what Lawrence might say or do if he saw me there with Alex.

I called Candace. "Hi. Can I borrow your yellow outfit and the boots? Remember?" I said desperately.

"Well, hello, stranger," said Candace. "Of course you can borrow the yellow outfit and the boots, and of course I remember, even though you haven't called me or spoken to me in a year."

"Candace, I'm sorry, but I just couldn't help

it. I was going through a really bad time. Lawrence saw Alex and me together. It was the worst moment in my whole life, and I just didn't want to talk to anyone about it, not even you."

"I know what happened," Candace said softly. "Lawrence told me. That's why I haven't been bothering you."

"Lawrence told you?"

"Well, he's been pretty miserable. He needed to talk to someone," she said defensively. "We go jogging together, you know."

"Oh, sure, right."

"He's even taking me to Tim's party tonight. I hope you don't mind."

"Candace, how could I mind? I guess I'll see you there. Alex and I are going, too." I had to admit to myself, though, that it would be strange to see my best friend and my ex-boyfriend together so soon.

My first few minutes with Alex that night were shy and awkward. Neither of us knew what to say to each other. But as soon as we were alone in Alex's father's car, he relaxed. In fact, I almost wished he had stayed shy because the first thing he said was, "Lisa, when you called and said you were free, I was really happy. I've missed you. A lot. So, I want to know if you will go steady with me."

I knew my mouth was hanging open, but I

163

was so surprised that I couldn't control my reaction.

"What's the matter? You're free now, aren't you?" Alex asked.

"Oh, yes," I said quickly. "That's not the problem now."

"Well, what *is* the problem?"

So I took a deep breath and thought to myself: Well, Lisa, this is it. Here's your first test since your disaster with Lawrence. Remember to think about how you're feeling and tell him honestly.

"I—I—I'm really, well, honored that you asked me to go steady with you, Alex. Really. But I'm ninety-nine-and-forty-four-one-hundredths-percent sure that I'm just not ready to go steady right now."

"You mean, you might want to date other guys?"

"Well, I might. I like you more than I've ever liked any other boy, Alex. But I want to get to know you better before I start thinking of going steady."

To my surprise, he didn't get angry or upset. "All right," he said calmly, "as long as we have plenty of chances to get to know each other. How about next Friday and Saturday nights?"

"It's a deal," I said with relief.

But I felt myself begin to tense up again when

we walked into the party and the first person I saw was Lawrence. I walked over to a corner of the room and turned my back to the party while Alex got me some cola. I prayed Lawrence hadn't seen me, but, sure enough, a moment later he tapped on my shoulder.

"Want to dance?" Lawrence asked, smiling.

I smiled back. "Sure."

Compared to Alex, Lawrence was a great dancer. At least he kept to the beat, and we could move in time together. I was really beginning to enjoy myself when Lawrence said, "Lisa, do you have my gold chain? Are you wearing it by any chance?"

A moment of fear stopped me. What should I tell him? If I told him I wasn't wearing it, would he be angry? Once again, I took a breath and passed my second test.

"No, I'm not wearing it, but I do have it with me in my purse," I said honestly.

"Oh, good," Lawrence said easily. "Well, now that you don't wear it anymore, you wouldn't mind returning it, would you?"

Actually, I'd thought of giving the chain back to Lawrence at the party if the chance came up. That's why I'd brought it along. But I hadn't quite expected it to be this easy.

"You see," Lawrence said mischievously, "there

may be someone else I might want to ask to wear it soon."

I began to smile. I realized that I was so glad for Lawrence. He looked happy—and he didn't seem angry at me anymore.

Suddenly he became serious. "You know, Lisa, I could never remain angry at you for long. Everything you said in the letter was true. You're still one of my best friends, and you will always be."

"Oh, Lawrence!" I cried and gave him a quick hug.

Suddenly someone was tapping me on the shoulder again, only this time it was Candace.

"Sorry, Lisa." She smiled and took Lawrence's arm. "You had your turn."

We all burst out laughing. Alex, who was waiting for me, saw the whole thing, and came up to us. Before he took me in his arms, I grabbed Candace's hand and whispered, "You're right. It's your turn now. And good luck." Then I winked and let her go as Alex's arms encircled me. For the first time, I felt completely free of fear. Breaking up had been hard to do, maybe harder than it ever should be. But making up was the most wonderful experience of my life.

Chapter Eleven

Making up began at the party with Lawrence. How good it felt to have Lawrence a part of my life again. And it continued with Candace. Dear, beautiful Candace. At last she had someone to care about her. She was radiant; when she looked at Lawrence, she positively glowed. I felt even closer to her now.

But it was with Alex that I did the best making up. We danced and joked and laughed and talked. And when the party was over, we both knew, without even saying it, that we just couldn't go home yet. We just couldn't let the evening end. So Alex took my hand and waved goodbye to everyone and led me to his car.

When he started up the engine and began driving away, I worried that he was taking me straight home. "You're not taking me home, are you?" I had to ask.

"Nope," he said.

Satisfied for a moment, I sighed happily

and rested my head on his shoulder. Then I said, "Well, where *are* we going?"

Alex looked at me with his dark, beautiful eyes and said, "Don't you know? Can't you guess?"

"I was hoping you'd take me there, but I was afraid you'd forgotten about it."

Alex shook his head. "I'll never forget. It's our place."

So, once again we sped down the unfamiliar streets with the unfamiliar houses until we came to the place where the houses ended and the trees began.

As soon as Alex stopped the car and turned off the engine, I could hear the faint music coming from the band across the lake. I turned to Alex, and he turned to me.

"This will always be our place," he whispered as his lips touched mine.

"Always," I echoed as I held him close. Then his lips touched mine again. Soon he was kissing not only my lips, but my cheeks, my nose, my forehead, my eyes.

"I really like you so much, Lisa," he said huskily. "But there's a confession I've got to make to you."

We pulled apart and left the car so we could walk down to the lake's edge. There we stood, our arms around each other in the cool, clear night, watching the lights reflected in the water.

It was only later, when I was back home and

snuggled up in my bed, that I realized I hadn't panicked when Alex said he had a confession to make to me. In fact, I'd felt calm and patient and hadn't said a thing. I just waited until he was ready to tell me. I knew he would, and I was in no rush. It was so nice just to stand there, holding him, feeling him close.

And when he finally did tell me what was on his mind, tiny little tears began to trickle down my cheeks. As they slid down my cheeks, Alex smiled and kissed each one. For they were not tears of misery. They were tears of sadness, maybe, but they were also tears of relief, of wonder, and of freedom.

"I'm glad you don't want to go steady with me. I mean, I like you more than any other girl I know or have known. And yet, I'm relieved you don't want to go steady with me," he told me quietly.

"Why?" I asked.

"Because I kind of feel the same way about it that you do. I'm just not ready. Only, I guess I felt you expected it. I felt I had to ask you, or you'd be upset," Alex admitted.

"Oh, Alex!" I cried. "Don't you see? You sound just like me! We're exactly the same!"

"Yeah, I guess we are," Alex slowly admitted. "Maybe, deep down, everyone is. We're all afraid of people being mad at us."

Then we didn't say anything again for a long

while. We just stared at each other, and every so often I'd brush a hair from his face or caress his cheek, and every so often he'd kiss the tip of my nose or hug me tighter.

Even when Alex finally drove me home, we just couldn't say goodbye. We sat in his car with the motor running and kept finding new things to say. But finally we were yawning more than talking and feeling so exhausted that our minds were beginning to stand still. And yet we still couldn't part.

So we sat together in silence, happy just to look at each other and hold hands.

It was late, and it got even later. Then, when my mind was standing almost completely still and I didn't even have the energy to hold Alex's hand anymore, I found the way to say goodbye.

I looked deeply into Alex's dark eyes and took his face in my hands. "This was the best night of my whole life," I said softly. "The best."

Alex nodded. "The best for me, too."

"Good night," I whispered. "But not good-bye."

Alex smiled. "I'll call you," he said, and led me to my door.

I'd found the way to say goodbye—by not saying goodbye at all. Instead, I'd said hello. Hello, night. Hello, day. Hello, Alex. Hello, Lawrence. Hello, the whole rest of my life.

Athena was stunned. She dropped her fork down onto the counter. It clattered loudly.

"What?"

"I need you to become my wife. And when ur marriage is over, I will set you up with enoug money to live whatever life you choose."

"But..."

"Freedom, Athena. I offer you freedom after a time. Real freedom. The kind that comes with having the financial assets that you require."

"Marriage..."

"Is likely the only thing that will keep you safe from Hamilton. If you are married to another man, particularly one of my status, then you will exist. And you will exist out of his reach."

"Are you a man of status?"

"Yes. Or at least I was, once upon a time, and with you on my arm, I will return to that place."

Millie Adams has always loved books. She considers herself a mix of Anne Shirley (loquacious but charming and willing to break a slate over a boy's head if need be) and Charlotte Doyle (a lady at heart but with the spirit to become a mutineer should the occasion arise). Millie lives in a small house on the edge of the woods, which she finds allows her to escape in the way she loves best—in the pages of a book. She loves intense alpha heroes and the women who dare to go toe-to-toe with them (or break a slate over their heads).

Books by Millie Adams

Harlequin Presents

His Secretly Pregnant Cinderella
The Billionaire's Baby Negotiation

The Kings of California

The Scandal Behind the Italian's Wedding
Stealing the Promised Princess
Crowning His Innocent Assistant
The Only King to Claim Her

Visit the Author Profile page
at Harlequin.com for more titles.

Millie Adams

A VOW TO SET THE VIRGIN FREE

ISBN-13: 978-1-335-58414-4

A Vow to Set the Virgin Free

Copyright © 2023 by Millie Adams

Harlequin Enterprises ULC
22 Adelaide St. West, 41st Floor
Toronto, Ontario M5H 4E3, Canada
www.Harlequin.com

Printed in U.S.A.

A VOW TO SET THE
VIRGIN FREE

To Jackie Ashenden, who is such a legend that her book inspired me and is why this book happened at all.

CHAPTER ONE

ATHENA COULDN'T REMEMBER life before the compound.

On the Black Sea, in Russia, with high walls and heavy security, it was nearly a fortress. It dominated her memories.

She knew she must have had a life before the compound, she just didn't remember. She had been eight years old and she had been brought there. That's what she remembered. Being eight and standing before a sad, beautiful woman. She'd had tears on her cheeks and she had smiled when she had looked down at Athena. "My daughter," she'd said.

And that was who she had become that day. Their daughter.

A doll for her mother to play with, and never let out. The outlet for so many of her fears...

Her disappointments.

Athena knew enough to know her life was not terribly normal. She was never allowed out of the compound for a start.

And her only friend was a girl named Rose, who served as a maid.

Athena often wondered why Rose was a maid, and Athena was treated as their daughter. She couldn't fathom it.

She had far too much time to wonder about things. Especially after her friend Rose left. After that, she was alone. Lonely.

And then her father—the man who had always acted as her father. The man she *remembered* as her father, had told her that she would be leaving too. That it was high time she got married.

Athena was twenty-eight, though in many ways, younger. She had no practical life experience, so she knew enough to know that she couldn't compare herself to a twenty-eight-year-old woman who hadn't just taken her first plane ride.

She had been surprised when her father had told her of the marriage bargain, because she hadn't truly thought that her mother would ever let her go. For as long as she could remember, she'd known the name Naya. Naya had been her mother's first daughter. Her perfect, treasured daughter. Athena had been adopted to replace her.

She could only assume that she had been an orphan. That her being taken in was an act of charity. She was grateful. She had never truly thought that she would have a life outside the compound. Marriage. She had wondered at first if that might be exciting. No, she did not know the man that her father was giving her to, but… She did not know anyone. So what did it matter. Perhaps it would be wonderful. Perhaps it would be exciting. A chance to live a different life.

To see something. To be someone new.

Romance had always been a distant fantasy for her. She had not ever truly thought that she could have it.

And so, she had decided to see what might happen. And then she had met him. An older man, with a deadly energy. Her mother had wept. *"Don't give her to him."*

But he was intent.

"You indulge her," her father said, as though Athena wasn't in the room. "You have indulged yourself most of all. She has been your doll to dress up and play pretend with, but now she will be of use to me. She will marry Mattias, there is no other option. We had debts and they must be paid."

"Surely when Ares bought Rose, we were able to settle those debts."

"I will not go to Ares again. And it was not enough."

A doll.

The words had jarred her, and yet she'd known they were true. She had been a stand-in for her mother's beautiful only child who had died as a young woman after she'd left the compound and gotten married. Athena had been her replacement and her mother had both depended on her, and resented her.

Athena understood. She'd always been aware of Naya's place in her mother's heart. And the ways in which she'd been different.

But she'd been loved, she'd thought, even if it wasn't always easy, it was the only love she'd known. She'd been a daughter, or she'd thought she had been.

Rose had been the maid, Athena the daughter.

In the end, both would be sold to pay her father's debts.

She must not have been a good enough daughter in the end. For what good daughter would be sent to such a fate?

Mattias scared her. He looked at her as though he had plans for her. She did not wish to know what those plans were. She could see it in his eyes. He was a man who enjoyed hurting others.

Even Athena, for all that she had never left the compound before, understood that.

She was now being delivered to him, to be married. Mattias made his home in the Northern Highlands of Scotland, which is where they were driving now, after a long flight from Russia. The scenery couldn't have been more different here.

She was in the back of a shiny black SUV. A convoy of them.

For safety.

Her father had said.

No one could know which of them was in which vehicle.

The spread would be advantageous to her.

She would've loved to have been excited by the view.

The mountains were craggy and awe-inspiring, the sky gray, the clouds heavy with rain. It was so very different than the stern view of the Black Sea she was accustomed to.

She had spent her life in a beautifully gilded cage. The compound was styled as a luxury villa. It was the heavy security, the isolation from the outside world that gave it its name. Her rooms were soft and safe.

She was under surveillance at all times.

Never alone, yet somehow lonely. It had been part of her life from the time she could remember, and it had only been as she grew older that it had become notable.

It had begun to feel oppressive just a few years ago. It was like something in her had clicked.

Naya, her predecessor, had gone off to have a life. Athena had no life at all. She'd asked her mother once, when she could be free to go live her life.

"Naya died living outside these walls. I will not lose you, Athena."

It was not a proclamation of tenderness, but of desperation, and Athena could see she had no choice.

The compound was too secure. Too isolated.

Perhaps that was when she had become aware that she was a prisoner.

Such a prisoner that for a moment, marriage to a stranger had seemed an adventure.

She was wide awake now, and she could never go back to before she'd realized how astonishingly wrong that was. She knew now. She was not their daughter, she was a prisoner. She was being used as a bargaining chip.

She would not go quietly.

She had no choice now. She had to do this. Or she would spend the rest of her life as this. This creature who had been fashioned to be pliable and dependent. To exist for others only, and never herself.

A doll, the man who had called himself her father, had said.

He was not wrong. A thing to be dressed up, looked at, played with.

She was nervous. But she was resolved. Her decision was made, she would not waiver from it now.

She had pretended to be excited for the wedding. She had peppered the man she'd come to think of as her father with questions, and because he underestimated her, he had answered them all. He'd told her how they would travel, when, where. She'd told him she was just so excited to travel. She'd pretended to be starry-eyed about the marriage.

She had not known she was duplicitous, but it had turned out she was when need be.

He had given her every detail she needed. Then

she'd used the limited access to maps and the internet that she had to study the area.

There was a forest they would drive by in two miles, she could see it in her mind's eye. It would be her chance. Her one and only chance. And she would take it. She would get caught, very likely. She could not imagine a scenario wherein she was not captured and restored immediately by one of her father's men. She was fast, but they would overtake her. They had guns.

She had to.

She had to try.

Athena had spent her life shut away, and every decision in her life had been made by others. It had been the only reality she remembered, so she accepted it. That reality had broken when she had seen the true nature of her father. First when she had discovered that he had sold Rose to Ares, as though she were an *object*, and then with his willingness to marry Athena off, completely disregarding her feelings.

And more than her feelings, her safety.

She no longer accepted what she was given.

She would escape, she would find out the truth of who she had been the first eight years of her life. Perhaps the truth was not a good truth. But what did it matter? Her present truth was not especially good either. So she would run. In futility, but with bravery.

She only had to wait for the moment.

And then it happened. They rounded the corner just next to the woods, right at the very edge. If she could make her way through them, then she could run out the other side and there she would find a village. She would be able to get refuge. Help.

Eventually, to find herself.

She needed that to be true.

She was wearing a cloak, which was very dramatic but her parents—she hesitated now to call them her parents but didn't know what else to call them—hadn't commented, it wasn't unusual for her to be dramatic. She'd hidden a small bag in the folds of it and had been quite warm on the plane, but it was worth it. And she had a small amount of food and water to carry her through, plus something to offer protection from the elements.

She needed to try, she quickly unbuckled her seatbelt, opened the door and held her cloak tightly around her and flung herself out of the moving vehicle.

She guided herself toward the forest, tucking and rolling as she did, landing sprawled out on the grass before scrambling, not bothering to look at what was behind her, and if the limo had managed to stop. She ran. She ran as if the hounds of hell were on her, because they were. She ran with all her might. She ran for all she was worth. The forest was dark, the trees dense. She knew that. Because she had done her research.

She hopped a short left, just as she had planned, because she knew that was the direction that would take her to the village. She wove under trees, and around them. Taking the thickest and most impassable way, one that they would never guess she had taken, because it would be so difficult to traverse.

Everybody simply thought her a cosseted girl. Nobody knew the fire that was inside of her. The fire that had been ignited by all of this betrayal. The determination that she carried with her.

They underestimated her, and they would lose her for it. She ran until trees started to thin out, and she felt nothing but confusion. She could not recall this on any map. But then, this was an extremely remote forest, and it was possible that there were pieces of it that remained unknown.

She walked until her legs ached. Until she was freezing. It had started to rain, and as the foliage grew wet, it became a liability. Everything she touched left water droplets on her, which bled into the fabric of her billowing cloak—protective, she had hoped—rendering it a sodden mess.

She was lost, and she could hear twigs snapping in the distance. She didn't know what sort of creatures were in these woods. She had missed a very important piece of research.

Exhaustion and hypothermia were becoming a fear for her.

And then, there in the dimness, she saw it.

A small heap of stones with a straw roof. It was in disrepair, but she imagined the inside would be dry.

She scrambled forward and pushed the wooden door open.

It was silent inside. All thick stone walls and a stone floor. It was dry. Surprisingly warm, and she imagined the lack of moisture and the efficiency of blocking any wind contributed to that.

If they were to find this place, surely they would look inside for her.

But what other option did she have?

Curling up outside under a fern wasn't going to work, and she was about to collapse.

She sat down on the floor. It was hard, but she felt safer in here. She would actually be able to rest for a while. She curled up into a ball of soggy misery and tried to stop herself from shaking.

Eventually she fell into a fitful sleep, consciousness hovering about the edges, tinged by fear. Dreams mixed in with a strange sense of wakefulness, and she could feel herself suddenly floating above the earth. Warm. Held tightly. She clung to that, tried to savor the feeling. She felt secure then when she'd otherwise felt alone.

But then everything went to blackness, and she lost her hold on the brilliant dream that had made her feel so safe.

She awoke with a start.

She was sitting in a plush chair, her feet up on

an ottoman. To her right was a table, and on it was a steaming mug of some sort of hot liquid, and beside that was a pastry.

She was starving, and still so cold.

She looked around the space, her eyes still bleary. It was all gray stone and gothic details. It looked like an old castle. She wasn't in the little hovel she'd fallen asleep in earlier.

She thought back to the dream...

Of being lifted. Of being held.

That hadn't been a dream. Someone had found her there and brought her...here.

She looked around the room, and then suddenly, the large fireplace against the back wall ignited.

It was a rush of flame and sound, and she recoiled in shock.

"Who's there?" she asked, her voice trembling.

She did not believe in magic.

She had never seen it. Not living as she had in the compound.

This... This did seem like an enchantment. The entire thing. Or a dream. That this place could be here, in the forest. That someone had found her, sleeping, hidden away in that shack and brought her here...

She reached her hands out, and realized that they were still quite cold.

Then, shaking all over she reached out and picked up the mug. She knew she perhaps shouldn't trust the substance in it, but she also knew she was thirsty and hungry and freezing. She had to let her more immediate needs take precedence.

And once she was warm, and full, she found herself drifting off to sleep again.

Something woke her. She could not pinpoint it. A strange sensation that filled her and made her chest feel like it was expanding until she was jolted from her sleep.

"What do we have here?"

The voice was rough, with a heavy Scottish accent, deep and frightening, and she found herself gripping the arms of the chair hard.

She was trying to shake off her sleep.

"Speak, lass."

She tried to find the source of the voice, looking to her left and right, but she couldn't find it. She felt the voice, as much as she heard it. A rumble through her body.

"I... My name is Athena."

"Athena. Goddess of war. Tell me, Athena." The voice became lower, rougher, close to a growl. "Have you come to make war with me?"

She looked all around, and she could not see where the voice was coming from.

"No. I've run away. From my...from my captors. And someone brought me...here."

"Captors?" He said the word hard and harsh.

"Yes. Well... My father. My adoptive father. I

came to live with him when I was eight years old. He's selling me into marriage now."

"I see. And you are running away from your arranged marriage?"

"Yes. Wouldn't you?"

He laughed. Hard and harsh. "No. I've no need to run from anyone."

It was nearly a growl, that voice, and she tried to imagine what sort of man would accompany such a voice, and failed.

"Who are you?"

"An interesting question. And not one that I am obligated to answer. You are the intruder in my house. Keep talking."

She had nothing to say except…except…

"Will you protect me? If my father's men come for me, will you protect me?"

"That all depends, wee Athena. In what manner will they be armed?"

"They have guns."

"Guns. Barbaric, don't you think? There were days when men engaged in hand-to-hand combat. Broad swords. And they were called barbarians. At least then you could look your foe in the eye. At least then, you had to be aware of what it was you were doing when you struck him down."

"Philosophy on the ways in which people wage war does not help me."

"Does it not?"

"Goddess of war I may be, but no one has bothered to fight one on my behalf."

"I think that perhaps Athena fights for her own self."

"This is me fighting. I need someone to fight with me."

"A sad thing for you that I do not work for free."

"What is it that you want?"

Fear streaked through her. But for all that she could not see the man who spoke, for all that she knew nothing about him, she did not hear the cruelty in his voice that she heard in Mattias's. Perhaps that was crazy, but she trusted her instincts. Her father did business with a variety of people. Many of them were dangerous. Many of them were very bad men. She could sense that. It was a matter of survival.

"It is no matter to you what I want. You are now my part of my collection."

Collection?

She stood, panic rioting through her. "No! I'm not... I need your help. I need my freedom."

"Lass," he said, his voice becoming hard. "No one lives free."

She turned and she ran. She flung herself against the door and it didn't give.

"It won't open," the voice said.

"But..."

"You are mine now."

"Let me go. You don't have to do anything for me."

"I already have. My fire. My food. You have stolen from me. And I need be repaid."

And then suddenly, there was a figure who swept into the room. Concealed by a cloak, his body huge and hulking.

He moved to her, and he swept her up into his arms. It was too dark for her to see his face.

Terror rolled through her as she found herself being carried away further and further from the door.

She struggled, but he was too strong.

He carried her up a curved staircase and kicked open the third door on the left. "Here. You will stay here until I decide what it is I want to do with you."

His voice boomed less so close, but was no less impacting. He was strong and hot and smelled of sandalwood.

She was suddenly unbearably conscious of the fact this was the closest she'd ever been to a man.

He set her down slowly, and she felt…cold. Bereft of his touch. She tried to move to get a better look at him but the room was too dim.

The room was also not quite what she'd expected.

"A…a bedroom?"

"Would you prefer the dungeon?"

"No."

"Then do not complain to me, lass."

And then he stepped out of the room and slammed the door shut. She tried it, but it was locked tight.

Somehow she had leapt from a moving vehicle, right into the enchanted fire.

CHAPTER TWO

"There isn't any time left, Cameron. The launch of the product is next month, and if you can't put on a good showing we're going to lose every investor who backed us through all of this. I am planning something extravagant. It is not just a dry event where investors and buyers will sit in chairs and watch tech wizards speak. There will be food, and dancing. It will be the biggest event in the history of the company."

Cameron looked at the screen and growled. "Why can't *you* put on a good show?"

His business partner, Apollo Agassi, looked at him with dark, deeply concerned eyes.

"Because it's *you* people want to hear from when it comes to technology, Cameron."

"You said it would not be speeches."

"I said it will not be all speeches. This is going to be a hub of all that is to come in smart home technology, self-driving cars… Gunnar and Olive Magnusson will be there and you know she is one of the most captivating people in the tech industry right now. I want them there, they will raise the cachet of the event. I do not want them to outshine us. I cannot accomplish what you can. I can raise money, but you need to cement the goodwill of those who are counting on the smart home system to be as comprehensive as you said it would."

His friend's doubt was an affront. Cameron's face might have been ruined, but his mind was as sharp as ever.

"It is. Believe me. I have a medieval castle wired to do whatever I ask it to do. Fire in the fireplace? Done. Meals of all kinds cooked to perfection? Done. Laundry, comprehensive lighting systems. Every door armed. Security. All managed through either voice, but only the user's voice, or in some cases nonverbal commands accomplished by a device that fits in your pocket."

"A very good sales pitch."

"It hardly needs a sales pitch. It is leagues ahead of all other smart home technology in terms of seamlessness and versatility."

"You say that, but most people—myself included—don't know what that means in a practical sense. Compared to you, we might as well be children when it comes to the depth of our understanding, and that is why you need to explain it."

"Flattery will not move me."

"I will find something that will, by God." Apollo was quiet for a moment. "This is your triumph, Cam. Get out there, and do what I know you can."

"What I *could*," he pointed out.

Apollo suddenly looked weary. "The Cameron I knew would never have sat at home for all these years. The Cameron I knew was a fighter. Against all odds, against ever terrible thing that ever happened. He never took no for an answer, and when he was knocked down, he never stayed down."

Cameron laughed. He had to. Because Apollo's take was so wildly simplistic. So firmly spoken as a man who had no concept of what the accident had meant for him. "The Cameron you knew could dazzle the world with his looks *and* his wits. And that man is dead. There is nothing of him left."

"I don't believe that," said Apollo. "I think it's a neat story that you tell yourself."

"It does not matter whether it is a story I tell myself or the reality. Short of dragging me out of the castle yourself…"

Apollo's face went hard. He knew that look. "Don't think I won't do it, Cameron. I have so much money tied up in this…"

"And it is everything I have, so don't you think I care even more?"

"You don't need anything. You sit in that moldering wreck day in and day out. You have no need of money. You might as well redistribute your wealth."

"Careful," Cameron said, his tone dry. "You're beginning to sound like a radical."

Apollo laughed. "Once upon a time we were both quite radical."

"No," Cameron growled. "Once upon a time

we were a pair of selfish assholes. Once upon a time we left a swath of destruction so great that it was bound to turn into a reckoning. And it did. Perhaps not for you. Your jaw is as sharp as ever, your smile as winning. So perhaps, you should do as I say and spearhead this endeavor."

"You are grim, Cameron, and I find I have no stomach for it."

"Tired of looking at my face?"

"You never even show me the whole of it. You sit there, shrouded in darkness."

So he did. Cameron had gotten used to moving about in darkness. There was not a single mirror in the castle. It was by design. He did not need the reminder. Not ever.

And now... She was here.

She was so beautiful. It was nearly painful to look directly at her.

Athena.

Goddess of war.

And he had felt that war ignite inside of him from the moment that he had set eyes on her. Liquid dark eyes, hair black and shiny. Her lips were full, her curves generous.

He could remember what he might've done, Once upon a time. How quickly he could've seduced a woman so clearly and thoroughly built for sin.

He could have had her underneath him in minutes, crying out for release.

And so what had he done? Kept her captive. For now he had to do it with locked doors, so terrifying was his visage.

Not that she had seen him.

Had she seen him, she would have fought much harder.

Since moving onto these grounds he'd started a collection of beautiful things. What came to him here, remained.

She had come to him, and she was beautiful, so he had taken her.

There was a part of him, somewhere, in the back of his mind that recognized that as…insane.

There was also a part of him that wasn't entirely sure he wasn't insane, so why fight it?

Either way, she was here with him now.

He'd always felt that when he found something, it was fate in some small way. And he had not thought it wise to deny fate, so he kept the thing to see if he ever needed use of it.

Athena was no different.

"The truth is," he said, "Apollo, you do not know the extent of my life. What I choose to share or not share with you is my concern."

"Well, you could make it my concern, considering I'm bound to you professionally."

"That is exactly why you don't know."

"Cameron," Apollo said, sounding weary. "At one time you considered me a friend."

"And I still do. As much as I have friends."

"I have not seen you face-to-face in nearly ten years."

"No one *needs* to see anyone face-to face, not these days."

"Sadly for you, they do. They need to see you." Apollo sighed heavily. As if he was resigned, when he made every rule that he lived by and had no reason to be resigned to anything. "I'm giving you an ultimatum. Either you do this, or I will engage in a hostile takeover of the company."

Cameron's lip curled. "You bastard. You just said that the company would be worthless if I didn't engage in this launch, then what good will it be to you?"

"I will have to galvanize you, perhaps. And don't think I won't do it. Do not think I won't cut off my nose to spite your face, Cameron McKenzie, because we have known each other too long for you to think that I will swerve when I have given my word."

He growled. He knew that Apollo wasn't lying. He knew that he would do exactly as he said.

"I will not be forced."

"You will be whatever you need to be. The time for licking your wounds has ended. They are scars. They will not heal, deal with it."

"You say that now, but when I stand before a room and investors looking as I do, you will perhaps change your tune. Lights."

He treated his friend to the full effect of his face, for the first time in a decade.

And he was satisfied to see Apollo react.

Satisfied enough to smile. Which he knew only made him look all the more fearsome.

"Don't tell me it isn't that bad," he said. "We both know that for a lie."

"Cameron…"

"What?"

Apollo looked…thoughtful rather than horrified. "I think it will be effective. To have you show your face."

"Why?" His smile became a sneer. "Do you suppose we might engender the pity of the investors?"

"I do not think that. I think perhaps they will appreciate your strength." Did his friend pity him too? That was unbearable.

"My *strength*," he bit out. "My strength in overcoming an accident that I caused? An accident that killed an innocent woman?"

"The facts are the facts. We cannot change them. But we can spin them. You're supposed to be a genius. In technology, in business. In people, once upon a time. Create a story for yourself. Or I will make the company mine."

And with that, Apollo ended the call. Cameron dimmed the lights. He did not like sitting in full brightness. It made him feel exposed.

He thought of Athena yet again.

His prisoner. His beautiful jewel.

It was not even unprecedented for him to take living things from the grounds.

He had tamed a stag who now visited him in the gardens and took apples from him.

There was a horse who had wandered onto the property, looking emaciated and dull, and he had claimed him. The only time he went out was to ride Aslan across the moors. The black stallion was now beautiful and glossy and foul of temper.

He was the only thing Cameron loved.

His life was very different now than it had been a decade ago. It was easy for Apollo to talk as if there was a life he could step back into. Apollo did not understand.

He and Apollo had been given to the same excesses, and they had experienced the same ease in their lives once they had become rich and successful. Because they were handsome. He had taken his looks for granted, as he knew his friend did as well. He had not been a vain man, rather they had simply been another tool with which he could accomplish what he set out to accomplish.

And he had used them. Shamelessly. And well.

It shamed him to realize just how much he had depended on his looks. For it was no small thing. That had become apparent after the accident. He could not stand to look at himself.

It was deeper than that, though, the reasons he needed to stay away from people.

It was the pity he could not stand. And he had seen much of it when he had been in the hospital. Doctors and nurses had looked at him as though he was a monstrous thing, and they ought to be used to seeing people altered by accidents.

To realize that you had the look of a man who should not have survived... To realize that you, a man who had been successful, who had been envied by all, was now pitied was...

He could not stomach it.

But he worked in technology, so he had fashioned for himself an aura of mystery, and had made his reclusiveness part of the mystique.

If he were truly honest with himself, he could see why Apollo thought it was time for him to reappear. It would create waves. It would say volumes about the smart home system.

He sat there in the dark, and asked himself truly if he cared at all.

If he did not do this, if he let the company die, what did it matter to him? That he could live out his days here, alone, did he truly care if everything else crumbled?

He thought of Apollo.

Apollo was the only person who cared for him. His lifelong friend, who he had met at fifteen when they had both been school dropouts living on the streets in London, because it had been an easier place for them to scrape by then their home countries.

Never mind the ways they had gotten there. They had shown each other their internal scars back then.

And they had found their strength together.

But even now, Apollo was willing to hurt him for the sake of his own survival.

Of course he was. Survival was what they knew.

Apollo still had his looks. Apollo still had a legion of sycophants.

Without him, Apollo's life would still be full.

But his life? Without Apollo his life would be completely desolate.

Apollo was the only person he spoke to with any sort of regularity. Everyone else he spoke to through messages. He did not speak to them.

His house was stopped by people he never saw. Cleaned by people he never saw.

His whole life was orchestrated from behind a shroud.

And Apollo was his only connection in the world.

The truth was, had his friend given him time to think about it, he wouldn't have even needed to blackmail him.

Because very few things scared Cameron. But falling all the way into the blackness of his own soul was one of them. And his only link to the light was Apollo.

He would do this. He would find a way.

He paused for a moment. Athena.

Athena was the key. The stag had taught him that he did not frighten everyone.

Aslan taught him that he could still have connection.

And Athena? Like the other two, she had been brought here for a reason. If there was one thing he had begun to believe in these years of isolation, it was that there were forces in the world that would give you what you needed when you were connected.

He had become disconnected in his years of access. All he had cared about was money. Drugs. Sex. When he had lived on the streets he had to be rooted in the signs of the universe. For he had needed them to survive.

He had gotten back to that here. Athena was a sign. Something that had been brought to him for his use.

It was why it seemed logical to keep her.

Now he only had to decide what to do with her.

CHAPTER THREE

ATHENA LAY SPRAWLED out on the beautiful bed, unable to sleep. There was a glorious bathroom adjoined to the bedroom, and she could only admire the way technology blended seamlessly with the ancient architecture of the place. She was quite accustomed to luxury. Her father's home had been filled with the finest of things. But there was something different about this place.

And then she thought of the man who occupied it, and she shivered.

You are part of my collection.

She had no idea how she was going to get out of this.

Collection, what a strange word.

It meant prisoner, though. Just as daughter had really meant prisoner for all of her life.

But she would think of something. She had not spent all of her life a prisoner only to become one yet again.

She would think of something. She was resourceful, if nothing else. She was not stupid. She was not weak.

That was what everyone thought of her. A doll. A toy for her mother. Not a woman of any sort of substance. That was what her father had thought.

As for her mother? Athena had never been able to quite measure up to Naya.

No one really saw her.

They looked at her and they saw what they wished to see.

Now, that would benefit her.

She kept telling herself that. Over and over again.

"You may go down to the kitchen for dinner."

She scrambled off the bed. *"Who is this?"*

She knew it was him. But his voice wasn't coming from outside the door. Rather it felt all around her.

"You know who I am, Athena."

She didn't know why his voice made her stomach go tight. Only she remembered his strength. The smell of sandalwood.

She had never been as dainty as Naya—one of the things her mother had often told her.

She had felt tiny held in this man's arms.

What a silly thing to think of.

"The voice of God?"

"Or the devil, more likely." When he said devil, he practically purred.

"I am not afraid of devils," she said. "I grew up surrounded by them. It took me years to figure that out. That my father was not a good man. But… I know now. And I know the men that came and sat at his dining table were monsters. I have sat at dinner with the devil and smiled. Why should I fear you?"

"I did not ask for your fear. You offered freely. You can try to pretend that you do not but…"

"Do you have cameras in here?"

She was actually used to being under surveillance. It was something that she accepted as part of her life, but she did not know him, and she did not have to accept it here.

"No," he said. "It is simply an intercom system with which I can speak to you. The common areas of the home have cameras, but not the private spaces."

"But you can hear me at all times."

"No. Only when I have the conversation opened up. I have no desire to hear you at all times. If I wanted that kind of distraction I wouldn't live here."

"Perhaps, if you are so attached to your solitude, you should set me free."

"Back into the woods?" He paused for a moment. "You must have been hiding from someone who truly frightened you, my goddess, to have scrambled out into the forest and curled up in a shack such as that."

He wasn't wrong. And it alarmed her how that insight curled its way through her stomach, and felt warm. Nearly felt like care.

"You asked for my protection," he continued. "I can offer it to you."

She looked around, as if she could see him when she knew she couldn't. "How?"

"Go have some dinner first."

"Will you be joining me?"

He laughed. The unkind, hard-edged sound filled the room. And cut her like a knife. What had been warm and sensual a moment before now felt frightening.

"No. And you will not thank me if I do."

"H-how do you know I won't thank you? You cannot simply make assumptions about me. You don't know me at all." And she was tired of people assuming they could speak to what she wanted or needed.

"And *you* do not know *me*."

"You say that you don't wish me to be scared of you, and yet you do seem to go out of your way to engage in intimidation tactics. To make yourself as mysterious as possible. You call yourself the devil, and yet you have not hurt me. I know more about you than you might think."

"So you think. Go and have your dinner. We can speak like this."

She huffed, but found the door to the room unlocked.

"The castle is still locked," he said, his voice following her. It was disconcerting. She had wondered if he could read her mind, but realized that it was a natural thought process to have, when she had been previously kept in the room. So it wasn't as if it was a reach for him to guess that she was wondering about her range.

"You're headed the right way," he said.

"This is really annoying," she responded.

"I'm sorry that your prison isn't to your liking."

"You say that as if I should expect to be in a prison. I believe this is quite a high price to pay for a croissant and a cup of tea."

"So you say."

She didn't know why the conversation verged on enjoyable, he was being ridiculous.

"So would say *most* people."

"And what do you know about the world?"

He had a point, she couldn't deny that. "Very little. I have been kept in my father's compound for all this time. But… I have had the chance to observe the way people behave when they are jockeying for power. And so, I think in some ways I know quite a bit. I know that you can be surrounded by luxury, and yet, the people around you can be craven. I know far too much about things like that."

"And what else do you know?"

The question, so simple, made her breath catch. Perhaps it was because she had never really conversed with a stranger—not freely anyway—or perhaps it was simply him, but speaking to him without having him in the room didn't seem as strange as it should.

And even more strange it felt…good to have him ask. About her. About her life.

He wasn't really asking. She knew that.

But she felt connected to him all of a sudden in the strangest way.

"I know how to smile prettily through all of it." She grinned then, looking up, though she had no idea where his cameras were.

"An interesting skill, I should think."

"No one has ever found it particularly interesting before."

"No?"

"Someone would have had to realize it was a skill. My mother never much considered me, not as myself. It was always…me as compared to someone else. My father barely ever looked at me at all."

"Many people grow up in isolation," he said.

"Yes," she agreed. "I assume so."

"Your father was having you marry a business associate of his?"

"A kind way to describe him. He's a man my father owed money to. And he was selling me."

"I see. Not an ideal situation."

"No."

She walked into the dining room, and saw that there was a meal set out for her. "Did you do this?"

"Just enjoy the magic," he responded.

She looked around the cavernous room, candles in gold candelabras all lit, the chandelier above the expansive table glittering. The place setting was fine china and silver, the chair elegant and finely carved. It made a mockery of this idea that she was a prisoner. Or it tried.

She was well familiar already with gilded cages.

"This is very strange," she said.

"It's normal to me."

"I'm not sure that that means anything. But then, I'm not sure that strange to me means anything either."

"Perhaps it doesn't."

She stared out at the spread before her. "Why don't you join me?"

"I do not join people. In anything."

He was hiding himself, and yet it was hard to imagine such an authoritative-sounding man would hide.

"Why?"

"You are not in a position to ask questions."

"I never am." She sighed. "Is this because if I see your face, you'll have to kill me?"

This time when he laughed, it wasn't cold.

This time, it was booming, and it made her feel…electrified.

"No, little goddess. No. Just accept that I…keep my own ways, however strange you might find them. And this line of conversation is done."

Dinner, however, was not strange, but it was very delicious.

Lobster and mashed potatoes, and steamed vegetables. She could not complain.

There was also a glass of wine. She looked at it, but was afraid to touch it.

"Do you not like wine?" It was the first time he'd spoken in a moment and she found it a bit jarring.

"I'm not allowed to drink it," she said, a bit disquieted by how easy it was to transition into speaking to this disembodied voice.

"That is not a condition of your imprisonment. I have offered you wine, and therefore you can have it."

"Imprisonment?"

"Go on," he said, his voice taking on a quality she had not yet heard. It was different. Silken.

It did not possess the growl she had become accustomed to in only these short hours of conversation.

She had never had to pay such close attention to how someone spoke.

"All right," she said slowly. "But only because I want to."

She had the opportunity to try something new, and so she would, though she didn't want him to think it was because she had his *permission*.

"I would not dream of having you try it under any other circumstance."

She took a sip, and blinked.

"And what do you think of it?"

She wrinkled her nose. "I don't know."

"Tell me," he urged. "Tell me what you taste."

There was something about the edge in his voice that made her feel…excited. Determined.

"Grapes, I suppose. But something more. There is a tartness to it, like citrus. A sense of something smooth. It's rich. Buttery. Yes. That's it. Sharp, and very crisp."

"You are very attentive to detail," he said.

"My life, for all these many years has been quite small. Relishing the small details is what makes it interesting. The taste of food, the feeling of the fabrics that I wear. The way the sun feels against my skin, and the smell of the sea air."

He made a strange sound, humming perhaps in the deep part of his throat. "I have not seen the sea for many years."

"But it isn't far from here."

"No indeed it is not."

She wondered at that. Marveled at it in fact.

"But you could go and see it. You're free. No one is keeping you here."

"No, it is true. My exile is self-imposed. But that does not make it less real."

"I do not understand why you won't take dinner with me." She thought she'd push there at least once more.

"Because this is not a dinner party, lass," he said, firm, uncompromising. "And I am not… I am not your host."

"No indeed. You are my captor."

She only drank a bit more of the wine, because it began to make her feel fuzzy, and she did not wish to be fuzzy in the surroundings.

"There was dessert," he said. "In the kitchen. A tart."

"Well, I shall have that."

She got up from the table and walked into the kitchen, where she saw many modern conveniences, and a glorious-looking fruit tart sitting in the center of a stone countertop.

The pieces were already sliced, and she took one and put it on a crystal plate that was sitting there beside the serving dish.

"This looks wonderful."

"Yes. All the food here is."

"Do you make it?"

"Yes. I do."

She hadn't expected that.

"I…"

"I also have a garden on the grounds, which I tend myself. That which I do not grow is brought in for me once every few months by helicopter. But there is a joy to self-sufficiency. Or if not joy, perhaps a deep practicality to it that I appreciate."

"Oh."

"This castle is run entirely on a combination of wind and solar panels."

It was so cloudy here she couldn't fathom that. "How can it possibly run on solar?"

"The panels are not here. But they are directed here by a grid."

"Oh. That is... Interesting."

"Like I said, I do strive to self-sufficiency. Now, I have enough money to have made it so. Though I envision a future where it will not take access to the resources that I have to live the sort of simple life."

"You consider this simple."

She picked up her fork and took a bite of the tart. "Oh. This is delicious."

"Thank you."

In spite of herself, she smiled. He had thanked her.

"I have never shared this with another person."

There was something raw in his voice then. Just a hint of something less...controlled, and she felt it resonate in her like a low note vibrating through a song.

"You've never cooked for anyone?" she asked.

There was a pause.

"No. Never."

He was a strange man. But then, she could only assume that a man who lived out of the woods like this, had no one else in an entire castle with him, and communicated by intercom, could be nothing other than strange.

She began to move around the kitchen while she ate, poking around the fridge, a bread cabinet. And there were many baked goods in it.

It was clear that food was important to him.

There were gourmet cheeses, and an abundance of fruits and vegetables.

He enjoyed the simple pleasures in life. She could see that. Because she understood. She herself had lived a cloistered existence, and knew that it was details such as the food you ate that made it all worthwhile.

"And what else do you do with your time?"

"Everything in this house is my invention. The intercom system, the different automated features."

"Oh. That is… It's what you do."

"You have not an inkling who I am, do you?"

"No," she said. "I don't. Why would I?"

"I had thought that you might have a guess by now. I'm Cameron McKenzie."

He waited for her to respond to that. To respond to his name.

She did not. Rather she simply sat there, a considering look on her face as she chewed another bite of his tart.

"I'm sorry, if that's supposed to mean anything to me, I am hopelessly ignorant. I have never been one to follow the outside news, because I can only follow what my father allows. He does not approve of pop culture or concept."

"So you know nothing of me?"

"Nothing."

What a rare creature she was. She would have no concept of who he had been before. No preconceived idea of how he would be or how he should look.

The more he thought about it, the more the plan he was forming began to make sense.

He would never touch her, of course. She was… She made him think of a rare gemstone. Something spectacular.

Singular.

The more he had watched her, the more he had been transfixed.

She was a sensual beauty. And yet he could see that she was innocent.

The way that she had tasted the wine and carefully considered the complexities of the flavor had been fascinating.

The way she spoke of things…

He wished to listen to her speak for hours.

A novelty. But then, he had been alone here all this time. His only real contact in the outside world was Apollo. And that was different.

She didn't know him. She was a true stranger.

"Tell me, Athena. What do you want to do with your life?"

She tilted her head to the side. "Do you care?"

"I am interested. Whether or not I care remains to be seen."

"I don't understand."

"You were running. From your father. From

an arranged marriage. Were you simply running *from* him? Or were you running *to* something."

She considered it for a moment. "No. I was running toward whatever life I could grasp. Whatever life might be of my own choosing. My own making. You see, I have never had the luxury of choosing anything. Even though I might choose what I wear on a given day, the clothes were all chosen for me. Choice is an illusion."

"One might argue that it always is."

"Perhaps. But for me, even more so. For they are all set out before me. It is not for me to decide who I am, not truly. And so I was willing to go toward an unknown life. I was willing to run into the unknown. Perhaps I would wait tables. Perhaps I would be desperately poor. But I would be free."

He laughed. He could not help it. "That is spoken like a person who has never experienced poverty."

The corners of her lips pulled down. "I haven't. But isn't making your own choice higher existence?"

"When you must fight for every meal you seek out, you do not feel as if you are living a high existence. I personally have experienced this. I feel you have no concept of what you will sacrifice to survive. You break off pieces of yourself in order to live. There is not a part of yourself you will not sell if you do not know how you will make it through the day otherwise. There is no dignity in that sort of poverty."

"I see. I feel… Even now, I feel that at least this is a prison cell I walked into on my own two feet. I'm certain that you might find that hard to understand. But I would prefer the cell to the one my father chose."

"And why is that?"

"Mattias Hamilton is a cruel man. You can see it in every line of his face. He looked at me, and I know that what he saw was something that he could easily break. I have been so protected all my life, all anyone thinks is how soft I am."

They were wrong, he could see that. She was soft. But there was a strength to her, a steel, that was surprising. Anyone who underestimated her would be doing so at their peril.

She was also intelligent, and stunning. She would make a glorious accessory to his triumphant return.

He was beginning to think that there was only one way that he could reenter the world and not garner pity. There had to be another story. A story so compelling that no one thought to pity him.

Athena was that sort of story.

"Tell me more of your past."

"I don't… I don't know much more of my past. I came to live at my father's compound when I was eight. I have no memory of what happened before then. There is a sense of fear. Of sadness.

Loss. I can only assume that I was an orphan. But I do believe that the trauma of it… I did do some reading on this from some psychology books that were in my father's library. I believe the trauma of whatever happened to me before I came to live at the compound was overwritten by better memories. By easier things. It is blank and dark and I think it might be for a reason."

"You think it is to blot out a loss?"

She nodded. "That is my theory. It seems to make the most sense."

He wondered.

"And this man, this father of yours, he was going to marry you off to a man who you believe to be cruel. Does he believe this man to be cruel?"

She tilted her head to the side, her jet-black hair sliding over her shoulder like a shimmering waterfall. "I don't believe he thought of it at all. I believe that he saw it as a means to an end, and did not consider even the slightest bit what would befall me after he sent me to Mattias. He knew only that it would solve his problem. He thought nothing of whether or not it would create problems for me. I do not believe he has the capacity to care deeply. I was…" She cleared her throat. "My mother had a daughter. A daughter who died. She was an adult then, she died in a fire. Her husband… Everyone was grief-stricken, is my understanding. But especially my mother, and her husband, Ares. My father gave me to my mother. And only recently he gave Rose to Ares."

"Who is Rose?"

"She was another girl who was brought to the compound, around the same time that I was. That was the beginning of the end. The beginning of me truly seeing what was around me. My father was going to sell Rose to settle his debts, and then Ares demanded her. He could not deny Ares. He was his former son-in-law, after all. And he's very rich and very powerful. He sold her. Like she was a commodity. I am… I could not be unmoved by that. And then it became my turn. And I realized that no matter that I was treated as a daughter, and she as a servant, we were the same. A commodity. Now I do question my past. With all of these revelations."

"Do you exist in the outside world?"

She shook her head. "I don't. I am not real. If I am married off to a man who is cruel to me, if he crushes me, if he takes what he believes to be a doll and plays with me to his own ends and leaves none of me behind, who would ever know? And no one would seek justice for me. Do you see? Do you see why I had to escape, no matter what?"

If he were a different man, he might feel some measure of guilt for his treatment of her. But he did not feel guilt. He only felt fascination at the evidence of her strength.

"So now I know where you came from. I know

you had no plans for your future. But what are your dreams?"

Her expression softened. "I would see the world. Everything that was kept from me all this time. I would watch whatever I wanted to on TV. And read whatever books I chose. I would use the internet. Without anyone watching me. And I would... I would have romance. And I'll find Rose. She is my friend. My real friend. I would choose what I wore, and I would probably try different kinds of wine. And perhaps a drink with an umbrella in it."

It was such a charmingly innocent list. There were some things on it he could not give her, but many that he could. And what he could not himself offer... He could set her up for a life where it would be possible after. Not because he was a good man. Because he was a fair man. And because there would be no more women who were used as his victims.

Yes, he had decided to keep her. And yes, he was going to leave her no choice when it came to going through with his plan.

But she would be less a prisoner, and more an employee. For he would offer payment.

"What if I told you I could give you that life?"

"I would be very skeptical of that. For I have never seen charity on that scale being handed out freely."

"And I already told you I didn't engage in charity."

"Yes. You did. And here I am, having eaten a lovely meal, eating a glorious dessert, and all I have done in exchange for it is remain trapped in a bedroom. And so I do deeply question what the cost of this offer will be. I had a very expensive cup of tea earlier, surely this has cost much more."

"Yes. Because, Athena, I need you to marry me."

CHAPTER FOUR

ATHENA WAS STUNNED. She dropped her fork down onto the counter. It clattered loudly. "What?"

"I need you to become my wife. And when our marriage is over, I will set you up with enough money to live whatever life you choose."

"But..."

"Freedom, Athena. I offer you freedom after a time. Real freedom. The kind that comes with having the financial assets that you require."

"Marriage..."

"Is likely the only thing that will keep you safe from Hamilton. If you are married to another man, particularly one of my status, then you will exist. And you will exist out of his reach."

"Are you a man of status?"

"Yes. Or at least I was, once upon a time, and with you on my arm, I will return to that place."

"You need my help," she said, because she knew he was not asking out of a sense of altruism, this man who had called her part of his collection.

"Less than you need mine. But yes. But as my wife, you will see the world. You will choose your own clothes. You may eat whatever you like. You may watch whatever you want. You can read whatever you want. I will not give you romance, lass, but I can give you many of the other things on your list. And when I am done with you, you will be free to go out and seek whatever you wish."

"That sounds…" She stopped. She had never even seen this man. "I need to see you."

"You will. In good time."

There was a reason he would not let her, and it…it was disquieting to say the least.

"But before I agree…"

"There is no agreement or disagreement, Athena. The question, my goddess, is whether you agree happily, or angrily."

"I could cause a scene, and let everybody know that you've forced me into marriage."

"You could. And give your current fiancé opportunity to play the part of rescuer. It would end up being the perfect sort of void for him to step in. However, if you step out with me for all the world to see as though you are dazzlingly in love with me, we will both benefit. It will be a story that the media will adore, and it will leave no space for Hamilton to step back in to claim you for his own."

"You make it sound as if it's so easy."

"I know how the media works. I know how public opinion works. There was a time when I knew how to spin these things better than you can possibly imagine. I may not have been outside these castle walls in ten years, but I still understand the way of the world. I have been watching. Believe me when I tell you, this is the best way to ensure your safety. Your freedom."

"And what do you get from it? Because there must be something. More than something."

"I need this for my reentry into the world. This is for the launch of the very system I use here in the castle. It will be available to the whole world soon. But my business partner has decided to make a whole spectacle of it. A gala, dinner, dancing, speeches. As I said, I know how public opinion works. Better for me to come back into this world with someone on my arm."

"Because you have been here. Not out in the world?"

"Clearly."

"Why?"

"Something happened. Something…terrible, and I had to go away for a while, and now I must go back. All will become clear."

"I would like it to be clearer now."

"Do shiny rocks and old coins talk back?"

She blinked. "What?"

"The rest of my collection does not cause me such problems."

"Uh… The rest of your collection hasn't been asked to marry you."

"I do not recall asking."

He was so arrogant. How could a man who never showed his face be so arrogant?

"How long will we…?"

"It depends. On how long you are required for my purposes, and how long it takes for you to feel safe that your father will no longer come for you. Again, it is your legal marriage to me which will make you impervious to another man's reach."

"But we…"

"I will not give you romance, Athena. That will come later. With someone else. Ours will be a marriage in name only."

"Oh."

Of course it would be. Anything else would be absurd. She had never even set eyes on the man. It was only that… Truly, she had not imagined he would offer her marriage without also wanting to lay claim on her body. He was a mystery, Cameron McKenzie. And not simply because she had never seen his face.

She knew that he was tall.

She knew that he was heavily muscled. And smelled of sandalwood and made her feel safe and small. That his voice could be fire or ice. It could cut, or it could warm.

She knew that he had not left these walls in ten years. What she knew made him even more confusing than what she didn't know.

What she did know, was this mess, this…business of being part of his collection, was related to choices she'd made. She had made no choices at eight, when she'd come to live with the people she thought of as her family. She'd made a choice when she'd jumped out of that car.

She had suddenly been more than that doll. She'd been Athena, and this was where that choice had led her.

So she would see where this led her too.

"Yes. I will marry you."

The next day, breakfast was waiting for Athena when she got up. And still, there was no sign of Cameron. It wasn't until she was having her second cup of coffee, that he spoke to her. Still through his intercom, and not face-to-face.

"In one month, we will make our debut as husband and wife."

"Oh!" She jumped, sloshing coffee over the edge of the cup.

There was a long pause. "My apologies. I have forgotten certain things about interacting with people."

"Yes. *Why* is it that you don't interact with people?"

Something had happened. He'd come here.

But why cut everyone off? Why see no one?

"That is a story for another time. Until then, I wish to tell you the rules of the house. You may go anywhere you wish. The library, the gardens, the stables. You may eat whatever food you wish. If you need something, you simply need tell me over the intercom system, and I will procure it for you. Anything can be brought here by helicopter from the outside. You can have whatever your heart desires in less than an hour."

She was overwhelmed by that. "Oh. Well, that's…"

"You are never to go to the north tower. It is my domain. And you are not allowed. Am I clear?"

There was the ice again. It should repel her, and yet it only made her more and more curious about him. Who he was. Why he hid. Why he collected things.

And why should she care?

Was it only that he was the first person she'd been able to truly get to know in years?

"I… Yes. You made yourself clear."

"It does not give me anything to be cruel to you, lass. It would bring me no joy. I do not make rules for my own amusement. But you will remember who is in charge."

"Yes. How can I forget."

"You will be given whatever you need to be comfortable. All I ask is that you respect the boundaries that I have given you." He made an attempt to warm his voice, and she was disappointed with herself for caring he had done so.

"Yes," she said, feeling frustrated. "I wish that you would…"

"It is not up to you to decide how this arrangement will play out. Tell me. What is it you want? What is it you *need*."

She felt increasingly frustrated by the distance between them, and she knew she shouldn't think about him at all. He was offering her protection so she could get out into the world safely. So she could be free. So she could find out who she was. If she had a family.

She should care about that.

Not that she had grown attached to the man's voice, and yet somehow felt lonely for having not been in his physical presence since the day he'd picked her up and…

"Nothing," she said. "Nothing now."

"Good. I will be making arrangements behind the scenes as needed to. Until then, make yourself comfortable. Neither of us is familiar with what waits for us outside. It has been too many years for me, and a lifetime for you. We must be ready."

"In that case, I need something to watch TV on. I must familiarize myself with the culture."

"Whatever you wish, as I said."

She decided to test him. "I should like an assortment of chocolates. To choose from whenever I wish. And I would also like a horse. I am an accomplished rider, you know. It was a skill…it was a skill that my mother prized."

Naya had been excellent with horses, and so should Athena be.

"It will be given to you." He paused for a moment. "You test me. You think I am not as good as my word."

He knew exactly what she was doing. The bastard.

"I shall also need a trousseau," she sniffed. "Fit for your bride. I shall put in my order when I have the chance to gain access to the internet and look at what I wish."

"That you cannot have."

She spread her hands wide. "Why not?"

"Because you can't."

"You're maddening." She had to stop herself from stamping her foot. "You said that I could. You said that I'd…"

"And I have changed my mind. You do not make the rules. I do."

"You are a petty tyrant," she said.

And what she resented most of all was how conflicted she felt. Angry with him one moment, intrigued the next. Missing him, of all the strange things, and then ready to find him and attack him with her bare hands.

"I," he said, "have been called much worse."

"And yet you have no desire to reform?"

He laughed then, a dark, unsettling sound. "Oh, I have been reformed, little goddess. On that you will have to trust me."

Cameron sat down at his desk and called Apollo. "I have a plan."

"Why do I not like the sound of your tone?"

"These days it seems that you don't like anything about me, Apollo. It seems strange that we still consider ourselves friends."

"Don't take it personally. Or do. It is of no concern to me."

"In one month I will be in London for the launch of the new product. I promise you that. But I will not be alone."

"You won't be?"

"No. I will be bringing with me a wife."

CHAPTER FIVE

HE GOT HER a horse, as promised. Over the intercom he told her to go outside one afternoon, where he had the animal waiting for her.

He watched from the shadows as she lit up with glory, pleased over the appearance of the creature.

Then he slipped back into the passages that he used in the house. The ones that carried him through secret halls so that he could move around as needed and remain unseen.

He had historically used them when the staff had come to clean the house, but now he used them to navigate around Athena.

He would face her. When he was ready.

Or rather, when she was.

He wondered what the girl would think of him. She was cosseted.

She would never have seen anyone who looked as he did.

He told himself that this was not about his vanity. He also told himself it had nothing to do with the fact that this was the closest he had been to another person in a decade.

There was no room left for tenderness inside of him. Had it ever existed?

He and Apollo had always been jaded playboys. He felt in many ways that he had been born one.

Growing up on the streets both he and Apollo had sold their morality and their bodies and had thought little of it. If you were closed off completely inside then nothing could touch you.

It was easy to sell yourself. It was a renewable resource, after all.

But there was more money in being brilliant, and thankfully, he and Apollo were that as well.

Finding an old computer had changed their lives. It had just made sense to Cameron. And his natural ability with programming had sparked something else in Apollo.

"You know, we use what we were born with to make money. We should use this. Your skills. You're a genius."

"I don't know about that."

"No doubt you can change the world with this, most people would need the most cutting-edge technology and a college education."

"Instinct. Just like sex, I suppose."

"For you, maybe. This is our change. You don't want to earn money like we do now for the rest of your life. What's sadder than a whore, Cam? An old whore."

He'd laughed at that because it was true enough.

Apollo had always been the marketer. The master at getting them the meetings. Getting them into the rooms they needed to be in. He was also the one who knew how to dress. A wealthy lover of Apollo's had provided them with custom suits back in the day. They had been nineteen, maybe, ready for their first product pitch. Apollo had been the one that said they must dress at the level with which they wished to achieve someday.

Thankfully, Apollo's lover had agreed.

It was Cameron who had been the inventor. Always. Had he not looked as he did, he might have been called the computer geek. But no one could ever accuse him of such standing as he did at six foot five and with the face of a fallen angel.

Of course, his face had been a casualty of his excess.

He was still a hulking brute. In fact, only more so now. He had nothing to do beyond care for his fitness. His body was no longer decorative in any regard. All that mattered was that it was able to accomplish exactly what he wanted. His mind had to function more sharply than it ever had, and he prized his physical strength and agility. His endurance. Because those things he could control.

And that, he felt was the real issue with this present moment.

He could not control the way that Athena reacted to seeing him. There had been a time when he had known precisely how his every social interaction would go.

His masculine beauty had been an asset that he had not appreciated at the time.

And now...

Likely, he would frighten her.

He did not mind being frightening, but he preferred it to be because of something he had done, and not simply because he had walked into a room.

One of his security cameras flagged that Athena had come back into the castle. She was wearing the cloak that she had arrived in, her cheeks flushed, stained a glorious rose. She had been riding, he could tell. She had that look of joy that she had when she was out galloping on the back of the horse, and he recognized it, for it was the same sensation that he felt when he did the same.

"Did you have a good afternoon?" he asked.

She did not even react to the sound of his voice. Hearing from him in this way did not seem to shock her anymore. "Yes. Thank you."

"There are scones. In the kitchen."

A smile tugged at the corner of her lips. "Have you been baking in the middle of the night?"

"Perhaps."

"Well, I thank you. Your hobby has benefited me greatly."

"Is this the sort of thing you expected living in your father's house?"

She had a thoughtful look on her face as she moved from the entry down the hall into the kitchen. He followed her every movement on the cameras. "It sounds strange to hear him called that. Though I don't know what else to call him."

"My apologies."

"None necessary. But he did not care for me.

And I do not think he ever saw me as a daughter. My mother did." Though there was something hollow in her voice then, as if even that had not been simple. "I will continue to think of her that way." She sounded resolved then, determined. "I believe that she loves me, in a fashion. I also believe that she is firmly underneath the thumb of my father, and she does not possess the wherewithal to seek her freedom." She shook her head. "That isn't fair. As you pointed out, poverty is not something a person should readily race toward. She would have no way to take care of herself."

"Have you learned so much lounging about my castle?"

"I have been *thinking*. And while this is not a wholly different existence than the one I had before, it is also entirely separate in many ways. I do not feel so much a decoration around here. And it is… Wild. Gloriously so. It makes me feel the same."

"Good."

He found that he meant that.

He was fascinated by her. By his opportunity to observe such a beautiful creature without inserting himself in her path directly. Without his face impacting their interaction.

"The scones look lovely," she said, taking one off the plate. He had left jam and cream out for her as well, which she spread on with much relish. He enjoyed watching her eat the food that he

provided her. He had not realized that he was…
Hungry for such things. For this matter of interaction. For the ability to share something with
another person.

It made him appreciate, truly, the connection
he had to Apollo for most of his life. Without each
other, they would have been truly alone. And he
had never fully considered what that would be
like. Even in his concealment in the castle, he'd
still had access to Apollo.

There was something about Athena that made
him extremely conscious of what he'd not had all
this time, and what he had.

His desire for her was…

He shut it down ruthlessly.

He had gone a decade without sex.

It was an appetite. Like any other. Not special
or unique in that regard. Except, unlike sleep, or
hydration or nutrition, you did not need it to survive. It could be denied. He'd had enough sex in
the first twenty-eight years of his life to last him.

First he had sold it as a commodity, and then,
the ultimate excess had been the ability to give it
away for free. To anyone he chose.

And he had.

The drive could be denied easily enough now,
and when it could not, he handled it dispassionately and alone.

But she was… She was glorious. And even

just gazing upon her over the cameras was intoxicating.

"I do feel that it is a bit of an unfair advantage," she said softly. "That you can see me, and I have not seen you."

"And yet it is not a new development."

She must've been able to feel his gaze on her. So bright that his desire for her burned.

He wondered...

Did he truly fear her response to him... Or his own to her?

He had no idea what thwarted desire was.

If he wanted a woman, she had always wanted him in return.

The power of being desired had always flowed his direction.

When his focus had been for sale, he had taken satisfaction in the fact that people were willing to pay handsomely for a chance to have him. If he could not find desire for the person buying his services, he could at least manufacture arousal from the rush of power he felt at their desperation.

But to want someone who looked at him and recoiled...

He never wanted to be one of those people. The one so desperate for the touch of the person they desired that they would beg. They would pay.

It could never be him. Never.

He would live a life alone. He would live a life of celibacy before he debased himself.

And perhaps that's what all this was. A fortress to avoid that level of debasement.

His refusal to leave until he had secured himself a bride whose beauty far outstripped his own was certainly evidence of that.

"There are things about me that are far more interesting than how I look," he said.

She seemed to consider this. And then she looked up, her eyes unerringly finding a camera he knew she couldn't actually see. And yet...

She was looking at him.

Like she could see him.

It sent a shock down his spine to have those large, dark eyes staring right into him.

"Is that so?" she whispered. "Tell me one of those things."

He shook off the feeling that had overtaken him, that had left him frozen.

"Your father wished to sell you to pay off his debts," he said, the words more caustic than he intended. "Mine never knew me."

"Never?"

He did not know why he was compelled to answer that challenge, to share himself. Why should he? She was merely a shiny rock. A new trinket.

And yet a rock does not have eyes, no matter how shiny. She is one who will see you.

Soon, all the world would see him, so what did it matter?

Yet he found it did.

And he found himself replying to her.

"No," he answered. "I was with my mother, off and on until I was fourteen. We lived in Edinburgh. Times were very hard. Sometimes, my mother was bright and happy and looking forward to a clean future. In other times, she was mired in her addictions. I loved her very much. She died of a drug overdose when I was sixteen, but I had not been living in her house for two years at that point. I met another teenager named Apollo. Two years younger than myself, he had been out on his own since he was ten. After my mother died we managed to get ourselves to London, we made money however we could. Eventually, we were able to take our ill-gotten funds and transform them into something legitimate. The foundation will always be made of those hardscrabble years. And I do not regret them."

"Oh. I don't know why, but I always imagined you in this castle."

"No. I bought the castle ten years ago. As a refuge."

He waited for her to ask why he needed a refuge. But at this point, she seemed well versed in what he refused to answer.

"How did you make money?"

"Do you really wish to know the answer?"

"Yes."

"Petty theft at first. We were very good pickpockets, and Apollo has always been a great distraction. He was small for his age for a time." It was hilarious now to think of his friend who was well over six feet as the small, scrawny boy he'd been with wide dark eyes, but he had been the sort of creature to ignite the pity in every passing woman on the street, and while he had sold a hard-luck story… Cameron had been ripping them off.

"Of course, that only got us a pittance. And we quickly realize there were other ways to make money. Elaborate scams take a long time to set up. The easiest thing to sell is sex."

He watched her closely, to see if she was disgusted at the revelation.

"You… You sold yourself?"

She said it gravely, and yet he heard no judgment there.

"Yes. Easily. At that point we were hardened. It was of no cost to us. We were able to make quite a bit of money that way. Especially if you added a bit of blackmail on top of it. There are very few people who want to expose that they are paying for sex with teenage boys. Trust me on that."

"That's awful."

She did pity him. But not his looks. His past.

What a strange creature. Where had she learned feelings such as this in the life she had lived?

Perhaps it was a testament to what he already suspected to be true. Life had to steal the softness from you. As it had done to him.

He had disconnected himself from his feelings to the point he could not find them if he tried.

When he'd found that guilt over Irina...

He added that to his collection. Like a dragon might hoard gold.

He was a monster, it was true.

But he felt that guilt. And that seemed significant.

And now he felt the echo of her pity across the space.

"It is utterly no consequence to me," he said. "I felt nothing about it then, and I feel nothing about it now. It was just another con. We never felt anything beyond disdain for them. We walked away with their money. We always had the power. And that is the important thing, Athena. You can sell anything but your power."

"That is terribly cynical."

He leaned back in his chair, all of his focus on the screen. On her. "*I* am terribly cynical. Life has given me no reason to be an optimist. I have had successes, and I have had failures. For all that life gives you, it will be standing in the wings waiting to take something away. There is no use getting attached to anything. And I have found these years spent here have at least been... Mine. I am in control of all around me. The first and only thing to ever defy that control was... You."

"But you didn't have to come get me from the hovel. Why did you?"

He looked down at his hand. At the thick scar tissue there. "I wanted you."

She looked up, her face in full view of the camera. "For what?"

"I didn't know. When I find something beautiful here on the grounds… I often take it back with me. I am isolated here and… I look for things to pass the time."

He had some ideas of what to do with her. Certainly. But he had known, even then, that he would never seek his body's ultimate desire with her. But he had gotten a great deal of pleasure from simply having her near.

"I need to know more about what's to happen next."

"All in good time. When I decide."

CHAPTER SIX

ATHENA RODE LIKE she was being chased. By her father. By his men.

She rode until the breath left her lungs.

Until the green around her blurred together into a rush of velvet.

She had no idea what she was doing here. No idea what would happen next. And it was beginning to feel... Unbearable.

One thing she had taken for granted living with her father was that at least she understood what her day-to-day routine would be.

At least, prior to his determination to marry her off.

There had been a sameness. A deeply expected ebb and flow.

She had risen from bed, she was prepared for the day. Her mother provided her with an excess of beautiful clothes and each day she would be outfitted several times. Her hair combed until it was glossy. If her mother wished to have spa treatments, they would have spa treatments. If she was in the mood to read by the pool. They would read by the pool.

Her doll...

Not a daughter, perhaps.

Just a hollow thing to fashion as she chose. No choice, no mind of her own.

Not here.

Perhaps here she was breaking out of that plastic mold. Perhaps here she was finding who she was.

And though it was not answers about her past, she felt that it brought her closer.

Cameron spoke to her often. Throughout the day. There was always a different sort of treat setting out for her on a plate.

She could not decide if it was a gesture of care or not.

She was somewhat ashamed to admit that she was beginning to have... A strange sort of attachment to this man that she had only ever spoken to remotely.

His story about his childhood had left her feeling raw. Sad.

He was... An extremely tragic figure, that much she knew. She couldn't remain unaffected by his story, though why it should feel like grief she had no idea.

Why she should feel compelled by his dark voice and tragic circumstances when he had told her she was an object, she could not say.

Any more than she could understand why he wouldn't face her, when it was inevitable.

If they were to be married...

The word made her take a swift, indrawn breath.

She also realized that he moved around the grounds much more often than it seemed.

He had to. He had arranged for her to get the horse. He seemed to observe things that would be outside the purview of his tower.

He went to the kitchen, obviously, though she could not figure out the pattern of his movements.

And whatever his voice came over the intercom, her heart gave a little jump.

The sound of his voice was soothing. It made something warm expand in her chest.

My goddess.

She should not like him calling her that, and yet she did. She rode harder, faster, to get away from herself. To find the edge of this cage.

It was only another cage.

She should not allow herself to have grown so content here.

She should not let herself feel anything for him.

This was not the world. It was just more walls.

On and on she rode. Until she saw the edge. Until she came to the wall.

At the far end of the grounds. Kilometers away from the house.

It was vast, and tall.

And yet… She took the horse down to the other side of the perimeter, and saw that there were loose rocks.

She would be able to climb over that. It would take hours for her to get here without her horse but...

It would be possible. For some reason, her own line of thinking frightened her, and she turned the horse and raced back to the castle.

She was surprised when she came back in and Cameron didn't speak to her.

"Cameron?"

She said his name, and received no answer.

Was he gone?

It seemed nearly impossible.

He didn't leave. He'd said so himself, and yet...

Hours went by, and he did not greet her. He did not contact her.

A strange sense of disquiet started to fill her, and for the first time, she felt as though she might actually be alone.

The feeling of abandonment, stark and upsetting, shocked her. To her core.

He could not be gone. The very idea was a loss, deep and aching.

It went beyond her need for him to protect her. It went beyond anything rational. It had nothing to do with what he might do for her when they left here, or how her marriage to him would insulate her.

The idea of not seeing him, not ever, made her feel devastated. The idea of not hearing his voice...

Of Cameron McKenzie remaining a mystery she could never truly unravel.

That all but destroyed her.

And something called her. Beckoned her. Toward the north tower. The place that she wasn't allowed to go. She was curious. But more than that, she was compelled, as if by his very voice. Why did he not wish for her to go there?

Because it's where he is.

And she was propelled by that.

She began to walk toward that tower. Cautiously taking the winding stairs that would carry her up, up to the very top.

A strange sense of unease filled her as she moved slowly up the staircase.

Surely he had cameras. He would see her if she was approaching.

He would stop her. Call out if he needed to.

But he didn't. So she kept on going.

At the very top of the stairs was a door. She pushed it open slowly. And she sighed… Everything.

Cameras. Video screens filled with different views of the property. Everything that she already knew he could see. And, true to his word, her bedroom was not present.

"At least there's that. At least he's… Well he's not a pervert."

She turned around the space, trying to find some identifying feature. But the place was

Spartan. There was nothing to be gleaned from it. There was technology, but she already knew that. About this place, and about him. It was other things, about him as a human being, those were things that she didn't know.

And she could not find…

She turned in a circle, and then she saw a huge piece of metal, twisted and set up on a shelf, underneath a glass case. And then, on the other shelves…

Rocks. Coins. Gems.

His collection.

The thing he said she was part of.

She reached out, curiosity directing her movements before she could think it through.

"What are you doing?"

She turned around and jumped back. Because there he was, standing in the doorway, his hood over his head, casting a shadow over his features.

Her heart contracted, then leapt into her throat.

"I told you never to come here." That familiar voice was so close now, and it was all ice.

"Cameron… I…"

She was stunned at the sight of him. He was so much taller than her. So much larger than she remembered or realized that moment he'd carried her to her room. She was frozen. And he was thunderous.

"Leave," he said, his voice a low growl.

A shaft of light fell across his eyes. Only his eyes. They were bright, electric blue.

Beautiful.

Terrifying.

"I…"

"Get out!"

His voice vibrated through her, not low now but thunderous.

"I… I'm sorry… I didn't know…"

"You knew *exactly* what you did," he said. "I told you never to come into the north tower, and here you are."

She took a step back, fear and something…else, spreading through her.

He was so large, so imposing and terrifying. The threat felt…she did not think he'd hurt her. She felt almost drawn to him, even in his fury. Like a magnet.

He was here. He was outraged.

But…

He was in front of her.

"I was looking for you," she whispered, taking half a step toward him.

"Enough," he said, halting her movements. "Do not blame me for your deception."

"It was not a deception, I…"

He took a step forward, and the cloak fell away from his head, as he reached out and took hold of her wrist. He drew her toward him, and she was frozen completely in shock.

The first thing was the scent of him. Sandal-wood. His skin.

Then his strength. His heat.

It stole her breath, made her feel bound up in him. In his intensity. He was more than a man, he was something altogether much more dangerous.

Much more compelling.

And then…

He had long dark hair and a heavy beard. And his skin was…

Ruined.

Twisted from scarring. His forehead was rough, a gash causing a dent on his right cheek where it looked as if he had not only been cut, but broken. His nose was crooked, like a prize fighter who had taken too many blows. Three bare slashes crossed his left eyebrow.

Whatever other damage was on his face was covered by the beard, save one spot, another slash of bare skin, where hair did not grow, down one side of his face. And the hand that held her wrist had more thick, heavy scar tissue.

Whatever had happened to him… It had been horrific.

It was the reason he didn't leave this place. It was the reason he only spoke to her over the intercom.

"I…" she tried again.

"Leave," he said, flinging her back, releasing his hold on her.

"Cameron, please…"

"I said, get out!" And he turned over the table with the video screens on it, they went crashing to the ground. "Do you think I'm serious yet?"

Fear overtook her then. Because he was a beastly sight. Hardly a man. But it wasn't the scarring.

It was the rage. Red and violent, terrifying.

"Out!"

She fled down the stairs. And out the door.

She ran. Ran to the fields, ran through the grass until she couldn't breathe. She knew exactly where she was going.

To the wall. To the weakness in the wall.

She couldn't stay. Not with him. Not like this.

That man couldn't be reasoned with. And she would not ever put herself in danger. She was not a prisoner.

She told herself that. Repeated it over and over again as she scrambled over the fields, making herself breathless, fear and desperation dogging her every step.

When she came to that spot in the wall, she scrambled up, climbing over the top and flinging herself down to the ground below. She kept on running. Running and running.

Only to come to the edge of a cliff. Overlooking the sea. The sea was this close? And he said he hadn't seen the sea in years…

And then she heard a sound.

A growling.

She looked up, to the left and saw a dog. Feral and skinny, his lip curled. He was a huge, rangy hound, and fear shivered through her as she stood and faced him down.

"Don't… I'm not going to hurt you. I'm not…" She took a step back, the water behind her, the animal in front.

And then she heard a sound. The pounding of hoofbeats, and the dog heard it too. He paused and looked up, behind them, his muzzle still a snarl, his body still oriented toward her, ready to pounce.

But it was Cameron. On the back of a black horse. Riding with his cloak billowing behind him. "Athena!"

The dog turned away from her, looking at him.

He jumped off the horse and ran toward her, but the dog leapt at him, clamping its jaws around his forearm. Cameron growled, and shook his arm violently, the beast flying away from him. But crimson red bled through the fabric of Cameron's shirt.

She gasped in horror. "Cameron…"

He was not a monster.

He bled.

He was bleeding now because of her.

She felt slapped, confronted with the consequences of her actions.

And overcome by his presence. So grateful she wanted to weep.

So overwhelmed by the sight of him she could hardly sort through what the feelings meant.

Fear? Certainly.

But something else.

He picked her up off the ground, his grip firm and strong. "You little idiot." And then just as he had done two times before, he carried her as if she weighed nothing. But this time, he put her up on the back of his horse. And then he got up behind her, one strong arm clamped around her waist as he began to guide the horse at a flat-out run toward the castle.

The heat pouring from him was something like rage and another thing altogether, and she was locked against it by the strength of his forearm, trapped between that arm and his solid chest.

"You're mine," he said, that familiar voice in her ear, along with the heat of his breath on her neck, she shivered helplessly with it, unable to understand what was happening to her. "We have a deal."

"You're bleeding," she said, looking down at his arm.

"I've bled far worse than this. Or have you not yet come to understand that?"

"Cameron..."

"I know that you needed to flee my hideous visage, but this is why you were told not to go poking your nose in places where you're not allowed.

This is why I told you we would wait to see one another, but you didn't listen."

"You *frightened* me," she said.

"You did not do as you were told."

Neither of them spoke for the rest of the ride back to the castle. They did not go back in the way she came out, but rather rode through a gate that opened automatically for them.

She wanted to lean against him and struggle against him at the same time. She knew that the stirrings in her stomach, and lower, were related to desire. She was not stupid. She might be innocent in some ways, but she had explored her own body. She'd had spare little else to do in the compound.

She understood sexual desire.

She simply didn't understand it here.

Now.

"Does it recognize you?" she asked, desperate to think of something other than the strange ache between her thighs.

"Yes, it does."

"Facial recognition?"

He laughed. "Yes. I get a great deal of pleasure from that. From the fact that I have forced it to learn to recognize this face."

"Your face is not why I ran." He didn't say anything, rather he growled. And she could feel it vibrate against the back of her shoulder blades. She was so distressingly conscious of how large he was. How broad. And hard.

"Go inside," he said.

"No," she said, getting off the horse along with him.

He began to lead the steed toward the stall.

"Do not argue with me."

"You are hurt," she said, taking the lead rope from the stallion. "I can take care of the horse."

"He answers only to me," said Cameron, refusing to let go of the lead.

"Perhaps he will do just fine with me," she said, maintaining her grip on it as well.

"Why must you test me so."

"You're bleeding," she said.

Finally, he dropped the lead rope, and she knew that it was not a gift, but rather he was trying to teach her a lesson. She snarled to match the growl he had given her earlier and went toward the stables. She took the horse's saddle and blanket off him. His bridle. She checked his hooves for stones, then patted his flank as she set him back into the stall.

"You see," she said. "He tolerates me just fine."

"A very brave lass."

"Perhaps he likes everyone, Cameron, it is only that no one else has ever been here."

And much to her surprise, his ruined mouth twisted upward into a smile. "I cannot argue with that, though I might try."

"I have a feeling you might try to argue with anything. You are extraordinarily hardheaded.

I asked to see you two weeks ago. Another two weeks until you claim we are to be presented as husband and wife."

"We will not just be presented as husband and wife. We will marry."

"You thought that hiding your face from me was the only way to do that?"

"I had thought…" He cut himself off, and then his voice went hard. "I thought it best you know me first."

"I do know you now. Except, I don't, do I? Because the moment that I saw you face-to-face, you showed me an entirely different side of yourself. Your anger. You ruined all the monitors in your office. And to what end? To frighten me? That was a silly thing to do."

"It is not for you to decide whether or not my actions are silly," he said.

"And yet I have. I refuse to be a prisoner. Not anymore. We are partners in this endeavor. In your protection of me, and in my aid of you. But I am not your prisoner."

He gripped her wrist again, moving closer.

He smelled of sandalwood. Of the moss here in the Highlands. Of clean skin.

He was incredibly tall. Powerfully built.

There was a strange hint of something… Power? It reminded her of someone, from long ago, but she couldn't quite say who. Or how or why.

It made her mouth dry and her heart pound heavily.

"I am angry. That is why you saw my anger. That's why I'm here. That's why I keep myself away from the world. I do not know how to have a partner."

"You said you had a friend... Apollo."

"Yes. But if Apollo had met me now, we would not be friends."

"Apollo could not have met you now. Unless he fell asleep in a hobble in the woods and you carried him to your castle."

He growled. Releasing his hold on her.

"You still cannot have access to the internet."

She was right back to being frustrated with him. But the awareness of his presence didn't ease.

"Why?"

"You will... You will find things about me."

"Things that you don't want me to find?"

"I simply wanted us to find one another first. Our own rhythm. I wanted you to know me without knowing who I was before."

"How can I know you when I had never seen your face?"

And she meant more than just the way he looked. She meant so much more.

She looked down at his arm. "You're going to need to see a doctor..."

"We will call one in," he said. "And get the necessary shots."

He looked pained, but resigned.

"Come inside," she said, finding it her turn to take hold of his wrist.

He looked bemused as she tugged him toward the castle.

"Go on," she said. "Call a doctor."

"I do not see people."

"You just agreed. You need vaccinations, among other things. You've been bitten."

"Fine. I do have a doctor I use."

"You're a liar then!" she said.

"No," Cameron growled. "He does not count."

"Why not?"

"Because I decided he did not."

"Well call him now," she insisted.

She pushed him down into the armchair by the fireplace.

"Magic some fire," she commanded.

"Fire," he said.

The flames erupted, and she looked critically at his wounded arm. The shirt was stained, and there was a hole in it where the beast's tooth had punctured the fabric. So she decided rather than pushing the sleeve up to go ahead and simply tear it. She rent it wide, exposing the deep wound there.

"Oh," she said. "I'm sorry."

"You should not have run away."

"You shouldn't have *chased me*. You shouldn't have…" He leaned in closer to her and her breath caught and released tremulously. "Frightened me."

Yet it was not fear that made her voice shake as she looked into his blue eyes.

"You should have stayed where you were told you could be. I gave you the entire run of the property, the one place I told you not to go…"

"And why not?"

"Because it is mine."

She looked at him, at the ferocity in his gaze. "I'm not afraid of your face," she said again. "What happened?"

"And this is why I delayed our face-to-face meeting, little goddess. It is the only conversation to have when one beholds this."

"Call the doctor."

What he did was send a message to his chief of staff to have his trusted physician sent to the castle.

He would be brought by helicopter quickly, Cameron assured her.

"I do not count Dr. McCall as a person. He is a tool for my use," he said.

"Like part of your collection?"

"I was badly injured after the accident and even after the initial recovery there were complications to watch for and the man saw to them when I had a need."

"Practical. You know, Cameron, I am realizing I was merely an object to my mother. Something to represent what she lost, not really who I was. It is painful, to treat a human being that way."

"Many things in life are painful, lass."

They lapsed into silence for a moment.

"Tell me," she said. "While we wait."

"It was a car accident," he said.

"I'm very sorry," she said. "It must've been a terrible one."

"You have no idea. It was… A horror."

"It looks as if it was a miracle you survived."

"It was. My passenger was not so fortunate."

"Oh… I'm sorry."

"There is no need for you to be sorry. I am. I will be. Forever. Irina's life is over. And mine was spared. There is no justice in that. I was driving at a high rate of speed. It is my fault."

"Was she… Was she your girlfriend?"

He laughed. A cold, hollow sound. "She was my lover."

"Oh, I'm so sorry. It must've broken your heart."

He looked blank then. "No. It didn't. And that, little goddess, is the very worst thing. I was not in love with her. She was merely an amusement. It might've been any woman in the car with me. But it was Irina. Beautiful, vivacious, with all that life ahead of her. With parents who loved her very much. She was a model, she was about to be in her first movie. She had everything in her life to look forward to. She would have eventually married, she would've had children. I was simply a detour along the way for her. She should have had that life. She had sisters. She had a family. I do not have that. So many people are alive who miss her."

"And so you have to live as if you died?"

"Is that not justice?"

"No. It is not justice. It is just... I don't even know what it is. Needless punishment."

"And what would you know of it, Athena?"

"I..."

He moved all of a sudden. "He's here."

"I'll get the door."

She jumped up and went to the doors, which Cameron opened by voice. The physician was an elderly man, who took one look at Cameron's arm and began to work without saying a word. He got out his medical bag and vigorously scrubbed at the wound before stitching it dispassionately. And then he took out two very large needles and gave Cameron shots. He did not explain what they were.

She had to wonder if that was the bargain Cameron had made with the man. Care for him, but never speak. As if they really weren't sharing the same space.

The doctor left quickly after that, with Cameron sewn back together and a bottle of pain pills left on the table. Cameron took the pain pills and threw them in the trash.

"You can grow dependent too easily when you're in constant pain," he said, his voice rough, speaking of hard-learned experiences. "I have trained myself, all my life, to not feel pain. I learned to extend it to the physical so that… I did not live a half-life on these pills."

All of the things that had happened since he had found her, his anger had ebbed.

And she was beginning to grow accustomed to him. More than that, even.

She reached toward him, and he jerked back. "I'm fine," he said.

"Oh. You seem… I…"

"Do not worry about me. I'm not worth your concern."

"You're not ready for this," she said.

"Who are you to tell me what I'm ready for?"

"The woman who has been living in your home these past two weeks. Do you remember how to dance? There will be dancing, you mentioned that."

"Do you know how to dance?" he asked.

"I do," she said. "My father made certain that I was apprised of all the necessary social graces for… Well I suppose it was for me to become somebody's wife when the time came. It was just beneficial to me to ignore it."

None of that life had been for her.

She had felt privileged. To not be like Rose. To not be a maid.

She had not been occupied with doing work, her life had seemed easy, and it had seemed indulgent. But it was never for *her*.

Much like now.

She had been collected, and she might have been anyone.

For some reason that hurt. Sharp and painful in her chest.

"I'm certain that I remember how," he said.

"And will there be a dinner? You will be expected to sit and make conversation."

"That's why I have you."

"I cannot make all the conversation for you. How will you tell people we met?"

"That I found you in a hut on my property."

"You can't do that," she said. "I have only ever been one place in my entire life, and even I know that you can't do that."

"You make too many demands," he said.

"I have been made your prisoner. How is it that I'm too demanding? You're the one who decided everything needed to be difficult."

"Fine. Then we will prepare. Your way."

"One thing you prove to me for certain today is that you need more practice dealing with people. Turning tables is not going to help win you any favors whether you show up with a wife or not." She frowned. "Why do you need a wife?"

"Look at me," he said.

She tilted her chin up and looked him full in the face. "I am."

"Be honest with me. Do you think anyone

would look at me and see anything but an object of pity?"

"Perhaps it's because you were yelling at me, but I do not pity you."

"Perhaps it is that you need to see me before."

"Show me."

He took his phone out of his pocket, and very quickly pulled up the photograph. The man in the picture was unrecognizable. His brown hair was short and pushed off of his forehead, he had no beard, and he was… He was so handsome he verged on being beautiful. His blue eyes bright as gemstones, his jaw so sharp it could cut glass. His features were perfectly symmetrical.

She looked at him. His eyes.

To recognize those eyes.

"That's you."

"It's me. So you can see… You can see."

"You…"

"Be honest with me, little goddess. Do not lie."

"You were very…beautiful."

"I was. Understand, I was not a vain man, but I used my looks to my advantage. And when people hear my name, that is what they see. I have not shown my face to the public."

"But they know."

"Of course they know. They just do not know the extent of it."

"And you thought…"

"By showing up with a wife, I am showing up

at the suggestion that I have done more than simply sit in this castle for the last decade. I will have proven that I am not simply an object of pity."

"Then we will make sure they know that. We will make a story, one that convinces everyone. One that sweeps them away. If you're going to take control of it, then take full control. It will be a story unmatched. And there will be no way for my father to come for me, because we will be so well regarded as a couple, that my disappearance would create alarm across the world."

"There you have it, Athena. You are indeed the goddess of war. This is what you look like riding into battle."

She felt… Strong. Resolved. Like he had seen her. Like maybe…it did matter that she was Athena. Not a rock or a coin or a doll.

Not Naya.

She had started the day by running away. But she wasn't running. Not now.

"And a war we shall have. But first, we will dance."

CHAPTER SEVEN

HE DID NOT know how she had so effortlessly up-ended his control. It did not seem rational or reasonable. It did not seem *possible*. He had pursued her today out on the moors, and he would have said he would never pursue another person.

Already, she had forced him to contend with a lack of control that he found unacceptable.

The dog bite on his arm was… It was inconsequential. But that she had seen him face-to-face, that she had made demands of him…

He called Apollo.

"Things did not go as planned today."

He relayed everything about Athena to his friend.

From the moment that he had carried her out of the hovel, and to being viciously attacked by the dog, to her demanding that they dance.

And of course, along with that, her seeing him.

"It sounds as if you have met your match."

He laughed. "Apollo. There is no match for me. No match for *this*."

"Not in your looks, friend. In your spirit."

"In what sense?"

"You are a stubborn asshole. This Athena sounds like she has a backbone made of steel. And how? Do you not marvel?"

"Marvel at what?"

"If everything that you've told me about her is true, her father spearheading her off to be married to a stranger. The fact that she has never left her family compound before these past couple of weeks… She is extraordinarily self-possessed."

"Yes. She is that. But it is only irritating. For she does not do that which I asked."

"Good. You deserve that."

"She is beautiful," he said. "And I am pleased with that. Because when I present her to the public, it is all the better that she is stunning. She will make a triumphant prize. A tale as old as time, don't you think?"

"Obviously. And yet you do not sound pleased with her beauty."

A smile curved his lips. "Look at me."

"I am. I have. These past ten years. But you don't trust me to see you face-to-face. I have seen you."

And yet he could not shake the fact that it felt as if Apollo had not seen him. They had the ability to have a screen between them. He could control the setting, the lighting. How long he was comfortable with the interaction.

It was different, to be seen. Really seen.

To have Athena look at him, fully look at him, with those dark, liquid eyes was almost more than he could bear. He felt as if his skin was being flayed away from his bones. And he knew what that felt like. He had actually experienced it.

It was a strange thing. The bite from the dog had felt like nothing. But Athena's gaze? That had been nearly unbearable.

"I want her."

The words nearly cut his throat.

"Unsurprisingly," Apollo said, the word brushing Cameron's statement away. "Have you been with a woman these past ten years?"

Cameron laughed. *Laughed* at his friend.

With all the rage and bitterness in his soul.

What did Apollo think he had been doing here?

"*Of course* I haven't been. I've seen no one."

"Truly no one?"

"What did you think, Apollo? That I was playing games with you?"

"No. I didn't. And yet I could not quite believe that you had actually concealed yourself to that degree. I had thought that at least you would…"

"That I would pay for sex?" he said, flatly. "That I would become one of those sad men or women that we mocked mercilessly as we took their money, as we took their desire? No. I would die celibate before I debase myself in such a fashion."

"I did not mean to suggest…"

"But you did," he said, hard. Ruthless.

"I meant that you might see it as a practicality. If you order food, you might as well order sex."

"I learned to cook. Apply that how you will."

Apollo laughed. "All right. Point taken. But your right hand can hardly be a true substitute for physical passion."

"I've had enough to last a lifetime."

"Obviously not, if you have a desire for her."

"It is inconvenient. And I've no wish to act on it. I just do not wish to feel it either."

"It must be galling for you. To want something you cannot have."

"I am very familiar with the feeling."

"Not in this context," said Apollo.

"You certainly know nothing of it."

Apollo laughed. Bitter. Hard. "Oh, you think you know everything about my life? About what I feel. About what I can have. When you have not been a part of my life, not really in all these years." His friend shook his head. "You have no idea what I want."

"No," he said, feeling somewhat shamed. "I don't suppose I do."

"She wishes to dance with you?"

"Yes," he said through gritted teeth. "And I have no wish to put my hands on her."

"Your mistake is believing that the only thing anyone ever wanted from you was your face, Cameron. You have other attributes. Focus on those and find her charm."

"My money?"

"I believe the gentler ladies would call it your manhood, Cam."

He gritted his teeth. "Thank you."

"Of course, I'm assuming that everything is fine there... I feel as if you would've told me."

"Enough," he said, waving his hand. "Everything is fine there, thank you."

"Charm her. Anyway, you need to figure out how to look as if you are doing so when we are at the product launch. And by the way, I have begun marketing it as an event not to miss. One with a very special guest."

"You are very good at what you do."

"As were you. So figure out how to become good at it again."

"I don't know how to be who I was. It feels... Wrong somehow."

He sighed heavily. "Irina is dead. Whether or not you get on with things."

Then Apollo hung up, and left Cameron to contemplate that. He dug into his closet, and took out a suit. It had been a long time since he'd worn one.

Then he went downstairs, where he knew Athena would be waiting in the old ballroom. He had not—for the first time—looked ahead at her.

And the moment he walked into the room, he regretted that choice. For he was not prepared. Not for the devastation of her beauty. Not for the way the yellow gown she was wearing conformed to her curves. Soft and draping around her breasts, highlighting the subtle golden glow of the supple mounds. The waist was corseted, the skirt flaring out in a soft chiffon followed her hips.

Her black hair was swept up into a bun, curls trailing down and framing her face. She had no makeup—he'd provided none, it had not occurred to him—but she glowed all the same.

She was like a sunrise.

And he had been in the darkness for far too long. She stepped forward, her eyes grave. And then she extended her hand.

He could only look at it. Soft and perfect. Like the rest of her.

It felt as if there was a barrier to touching her. As if doing so might break this. Might break her.

The last time he had held a woman, her body had been broken.

The last time he had held a virgin woman, there had not been enough regret or anguish in all the world, in all his soul, to make the moment endurable. He felt... As if touching Athena now would be compounding his sins, and that was something he would've thought was impossible. How could his sins possibly be more than they already were. When they were so... Unforgivable.

Perhaps that was the real justice in the world. That he wore the truth of who he was outside now. Before it had been concealed.

His brokenness. His ugliness. And now... All the world could see that he was a monster.

"Is there something wrong?" she asked.

"No," he said, his voice hard.

He reached his hand out, and pulled her to him.

And they were more than face-to-face. They were so close they could share the same breath.

Today he had seen her, and a doctor. Ten years of not sharing space with anyone, and in the weeks since she had appeared, there had been two.

And then there would be countless more. Because he was resolved. He would go forward, and he would do as Apollo asked. He would see his friend.

But all of that was drowned out by the feel of her hand against his. That soft, enticing skin, the soft press of warmth that bled into his body. Into his soul.

And then he pressed her body against his, held her close as he had done long ago, and yet it was not an echo of things familiar. It was like something else entirely. Something new and sharp. Something enchanted.

He had never believed in such things. Not in the past. But things had changed in these last ten years.

He had learned to watch the grass grow. To marvel at the simple magic involved in rising bread dough.

He had changed.

Even if he had changed far too late to prevent the greatest tragedy he had ever been a part of.

That was the real trick of it.

His ego, his selfishness, his insides had shifted. But it was too late now, for he had earned a visage that matched who he was.

But for now, he would focus on the magic inherent in holding Athena in his arms.

"Do you remember how to do this?" she asked, her eyes downcast.

He reached down, placed his forefinger beneath her chin and tilted her face up. "You never forget such things. The simple pleasure of holding a woman in your arms, carrying her over the dance floor."

Although, it was not the pleasure he was thinking of now. And he did not deserve to have that thought. He did not deserve to allow that desire to take root in his soul, for even the need of it was more pleasure than he had experienced in all these long years.

Even the ache of desire felt better than the decade of cold that he had lived in. For him, desire had been nothing more than an inconvenience to satisfy. Something that he resented, and certainly not anything he reveled in.

If he had to, he would ruthlessly dispense with the need in a matter of minutes. He did not allow himself the chance to luxuriate in fantasy. And he did not allow himself to think of it as pleasure, rather a simple release.

But this... This promise of something. The suggestion contained in the brush of her fingertips against his shoulders, that hint of questioning in her dark eyes, the curve of her lips.

No. You are misinterpreting.

There was no desire there.

He was acting as if he was the Cameron that he had been.

A man who easily called up the desires of women the moment that he entered the room.

A man who was sought after by all.

No, he was the man who had lived alone in a castle for ten years with not but his right hand to keep him company.

He was a man who had only hours ago chased this woman from the room with nothing but his face and a shout.

He was maimed.

Ruined beyond measure.

But it had been true always. It had been true before.

It was just now he could not fool anyone.

"One, two, three," she said, urging him on. And then he instinctively began to lead as Athena counted.

"Thank you," he said, "but I do know how to count."

"You weren't moving. I thought you might have needed some help."

"How nice for you, to have found a husband the world will think a brute."

"Better a husband who appears to be one than a husband who does not, but will create devastation in private, don't you think?"

"I am capable of devastation."

"You speak of the loss of Irina."

"I was carefree then. I thought that I had beaten the game. I was born into nothing, and I had become something. And I made the mistake of believing that I might very well be everything. I thought that I might be God. I had created a world from nothing. And who else does that? I fancied myself all-powerful. Not subject to the rules of anything. There was nothing but what I wanted in the moment. I loved fast cars and fast women. I loved being able to choose where I went and what I did, what I ate, what I wore. Who I took to bed. It was all intoxicating. I had, up until that point lived a life where everything was dictated by need. Need in the most basic, survivalist sense of the word. And then it became about want. And I got lost in that."

"An accident is an accident."

"Yes. Of course it is. But when you drive at a high rate of speed, and you are both distracted..."

"It sounds as if you were both along for the ride."

"But I was not God, was I?" He smiled, and he knew it was a bad imitation of the expression. "Yet I could not bring her back to life. That's a lesson for you. Creating things is not the ability to create life, Athena."

She moved her hand up his arm, where he gripped her at the waist, past his bicep, to his shoulder. The touch was so unexpected, so sensual, and he had to grit his teeth against the effect of it.

"Men can create life. I don't even think creating life is what makes you particularly special."

"And what is then?"

Her eyes met his, luminous and unafraid. And he wanted to draw closer to that light. "What you *do* with that life."

He ached to draw closer to her and yet he knew...

The accident with Irina had been his reckoning. His curse. The moment his outsides had transformed to match his insides, so he could no longer snare anyone into his toxic circle by convincing them he was an angel, when he was instead, a devil.

He did not draw closer to her.

"I suppose you don't consider sitting in a castle for a decade to be a worthy use of life," he said.

She shook her head. "I have been forced to hide. Forced to stay put. To stay concealed. You can leave whenever you want to, and yet you don't. I have a hard time understanding that."

"Even with what you have now seen?"

"Yes. Even with that."

She didn't say it wasn't that bad. She didn't say no one would notice.

He appreciated the honesty.

"You are beautiful. What would you know of it?"

She lifted a shoulder. "I don't know what good my beauty does. I can't say that I've never thought much about it. I was protected, all that time, from the gazes of men, and when my father saw fit, he decided to use my beauty as a commodity. I have no idea what my beauty might do or work against out in the real world."

"You will know soon enough. The headlines will scream of it. Especially when you're on my arm."

"Will it hurt you?"

"No." And without thinking, he lifted her hand and put it to his neck. "Many places on my body feel nothing." He dragged her fingertips down to his collarbone, just to the very edge, where he began to feel touch. Where all the nerves had not been severed. But by God he would swear he felt it anyway. Burning him down to his soul. He had not expected to be so undone by her touch, least of all when he'd been dictating her movements. "It is a metaphor," he gritted out. "For what you will find inside."

She looked up at him, and the confusion and questioning he saw in her eyes, made him step back.

Hunger.

This touch that had transcended medical science and made him *feel* had created a reaction in her. And God above it was unbearable.

"Don't look at me like that."

"Like what?" she whispered.

"Like you want answers to primal questions. Because you do not want me to be the one to teach you. You don't even know what you're asking for, do you?"

She shook her head.

Because she was reacting to him only because he was a man she was in close proximity with. Judging by what she had said about her life, about her childhood, it was a rarity.

It had nothing to do with him.

"Tomorrow we will be married." She swayed slightly in his arms when he said that. "And we leave for Europe in two days. The event is in London. We will go first to Paris."

"Why?"

And he decided on honesty. Because what else was there?

"Because I have always loved Paris."

CHAPTER EIGHT

THE WEDDING WAS arranged quickly after that. She still felt terrible about his arm. About the fact that he had been bitten coming after her. She didn't know why she should feel terrible. He had taken her captive. And then he had frightened her.

Because in actuality what he's offering you is protection. And you know it. Because in actuality, without him, you would be in trouble.

That was true enough. Without him, she would be on her way to marry a madman.

He had taken her prisoner, initially, it was true.

But still, the wedding, the thought of it made her tremble. He had made it very clear that he wanted nothing physical from her. She saw a flash of his face in her mind's eye again.

He was... He was terrifying.

Would he kiss her?

The thought made her stop and press her fingers to her lips.

A kiss...

She knew what it was like to be held in his arms. She knew what it was like to feel all that power clinging to her...

What would a kiss be like?

It made her shiver, but not from cold.

She put on her cloak and wrapped it tightly

around her as she went outside, the early morning air heavy with the scent of dew.

She looked around, and found flowers. She wanted flowers for her bouquet. This was her wedding, after all.

What was it about him that compelled her so?

He wasn't beautiful. But then...

Weren't the mountains here in the Highlands beautiful without being soft or symmetrical? They were wild, craggy and dangerous and lifted her soul and filled her lungs all the more for it.

She thought back to the girl that she'd been, just a couple of months ago. The girl that she had been who had wanted a wedding. Who had almost been willing to be okay with being sold into marriage for the adventure that might come along with it. This would not be romance. But it would be her wedding. Surely that had to mean something. She would not let it go by without there being something real to mark it.

So she clipped flowers, and a matching one to put in his suit jacket.

The thought made her smile. Because she knew he would scowl.

How did she know that? She had only just seen his face for the first time. How did she know that he would scowl at her.

She just did. She could hear scowls in his voice often when they spoke. Just like she could hear amusement, though she could not imagine him smiling.

She had gotten to know him these past weeks.

And even though he had frightened her, he had also come for her.

He had rescued her.

She had gone off into an unfamiliar place and gotten herself into trouble. He might have been angry, but he had kept her from coming into harm of any kind. Her dress and cloak were wet from the dew on the ground by the time she made it back to the palace. Breakfast was waiting for her.

A smile touched her lips.

Of course, the man himself was nowhere to be seen. He had simply made her a gorgeous stack of waffles with fresh fruit, and vanished.

She wasn't really hungry. Not with anticipation of the day. But when he made her food, she always ate it.

She frowned. She didn't know why. Perhaps because he was a hard man, and this was something of a gift.

She knew that it was. The way that he could show feelings of some kind.

Or maybe she was attaching too much meaning to something that was quite basic.

She went up the stairs to her bedroom, and stopped.

There was a white lace dress hanging from the

top of the wardrobe, the train fanned out across the floor.

Had he brought this? Had he brought it and set it out for her?

With shaking hands, she undressed.

There was a necklace with the dress. A beautiful necklace, with what looked like a large gold coin. She looked at it more closely. It was Athena.

The goddess of war.

She had her sword brandished, her hair flying wild in the wind. Around the perimeter of the coin in flowing script it said: *Have courage. Take heart.*

She smiled, rubbing her thumb over the gold pendant, it was perfect.

He did see her.

She was not just any woman.

She was Athena.

She slipped the dress on, and was surprised how well it fit. It had long sleeves, and conformed to her body perfectly. She looked like a bride. She took some of the flowers that she had picked and braided them into her hair, and then she used some of the makeup that had been provided for her recently to put gold on her eyes, and red on her lips. She found a ribbon amid some of her things and tied the rest of the flowers into a bouquet. Except for his.

She nestled his into the center of the bouquet

to make it easier to carry, and then she put on the necklace.

Have courage. Take heart.

She took a breath and headed down the long spiral staircase. And there he was. Waiting. Looking imposing in his dark suit.

Imposing, but stunning.

He was not a man who could be accused of being handsome. And yet there was something about him that drew her. Would it have been so if they had not spent those weeks talking? If he had not saved her from the dog? Would it have been so if she had not seen him bleed for her. If she hadn't been eating his cooking, if she hadn't felt his care in that way?

There was no way to know.

But he was incredibly tall. Six foot five at least, with broad shoulders and a broad chest. He was like a warrior of old. A man who was scarred by battle.

A man who would go to war with her. *For* her.

"It suits you," he said, looking at her with dispassionate blue eyes.

Except there was something there. A banked ember she sensed had the potential to become a whole wildfire.

She swallowed hard.

"Thank you," she said.

"Let's go."

"Wait," she said.

She moved toward him, and plucked the flower out of the center of her bouquet. She looped it through the buttonhole on his lapel.

She patted his chest. "There."

He frowned. "What are you doing?"

"I thought that it was right. For a wedding."

"I see."

He did not thank her. He turned and began to walk away, and she caught up to him, and draped her arm over his, almost without thinking.

But it *did* just seem right. It was their wedding, and she was to be his bride. Shouldn't they walk together? Shouldn't he hold on to her?

He looked at her, a question in his eyes.

"It also seemed right. For a wedding."

"Come on, lass."

They walked out of the doors of the castle, and down a quiet path. The birds were singing and she felt something lift inside of her soul. She hadn't expected that. She expected none of this.

She gasped when they came around the corner and there was a little stone chapel.

"Oh," she said. "How lovely."

"There was a whole village here once. And it had everything that people might need."

"Is that why there was that little place that I stayed in?"

"Yes. Very standard hut that the villagers would've lived in back then."

"And this was the church."

"For all the good it did them. They clung to life here for as long as possible, but… Well, that's a history lesson for another time."

"It must have done their souls good," she said. "A church like this. I've never been in a church."

"Really?"

"No. As I said. I've never left the compound until recently. I have always thought they looked beautiful. Serene."

"My mother took me to church on Christmas. For all the good that it did *her*. She was no better than those doomed villagers, was she? And she certainly didn't manage to do any work saving *my* soul. Much less her own."

"Perhaps you have to meet God halfway." He stopped walking, and she kept on. "Come on."

He shook his head, but said nothing, and they continued on into the chapel. There was a priest standing there, collar and all, waiting for them.

"Mr. McKenzie," the man said. "Very good to meet you. And this must be your lovely bride."

"Yes," said Cameron, his voice hard. "Let's make this quick."

"Of course," said the older man, slightly taken aback, clearly, but his gentle demeanor was not disrupted.

They approached the altar, and the priest opened his Bible.

He read a Scripture, and then from the Book of Common Prayer.

The vows were very traditional, the kind of thing she had seen in movies and read in books. But it felt utterly unique. Utterly special and wonderful, as they spoke the words. As if no one had ever spoken them before. And she knew that it wasn't real. He was not genuinely pledging to love her. They were not going to stay together.

But with the stained-glass window casting fractals of color around them, she truly felt like she might be experiencing romance.

That this might be what they wrote songs about. That this might be what people started wars over.

She was not immune to getting swept up in it.

Though Cameron look swept up in nothing. He was stoic, that ruined face of his completely flat and unreadable.

"I now pronounce you husband and wife. You may kiss your bride."

Her stomach dropped, her heart giving a great thud against her breastbone. They would kiss. He would take hold of her and lower his head and…

"No kissing, thank you," said Cameron.

And she felt the sting of that. Of the rejection. Why does it feel like a rejection?

None of this mattered. It wasn't real. They would never see the priest again after today. There was no one else here to act as a witness.

And when it was all over, they stood there with legal documents in front of them, and Athena only looked at them.

"I don't know my last name," she said.

"Yes, you do," Cameron said. "You're Athena McKenzie."

And it took her breath away. Because he had not only given her this. He was not only protecting her. He was showing her to the world, making her real. And he had given her a name. She knew, right in that moment, that whatever happened between the two of them, whether they parted ways after this, and she never saw him again, she would keep that name. She would.

And she signed the paper.

Athena McKenzie.

"We will have documents made for you eventually, in that name. It will make things easier for you."

"Thank you. How…"

He shrugged a shoulder. "Money accomplishes many things. And it most certainly buys an identity if you've need of it."

"Thank you, Cameron."

When they finished, they walked back down the path together. There was no wedding party. There was nothing. Just the two of them.

And they were married now. Husband and wife. She felt it. Felt connected to him.

And she felt compelled then, by something, to reach out and put her hand on his forearm. "How is the bite wound?"

He stopped walking and looked at her. "It's fine. I have been injured much more severely than that."

"But you were injured protecting me. And I am very sorry. I'm sorry that I ran."

"I *did* yell at you."

"Yes, you did," she said. "But I didn't have a plan. I had seen that vulnerable spot in the wall and I thought that I might exploit it to my own ends if I needed to. And then I… I didn't give you a chance. You did tell me not to go there, and I did."

"It's true."

"Why did you want to keep me away from there?"

"Because it is where I stay. It is mine. And I don't allow anyone there."

"Because…"

"Because there is nothing in there but old artifacts and memories. And none of it is worth showing to another person."

"I'm sorry."

"And I did not wish to encounter you until I was ready. I told you, I have not seen another person face-to-face for ten years. I knew that I needed to do it. I knew that. And now I have seen you and the priest. These are all *necessities*."

"Yes, because you must see people at the launch. And it's important to you, isn't it?"

"I have been perfecting this technology for ten years. People will be able to adapt it to their own homes. To their own needs. I am working on a system that can be intuitive enough for someone who uses sign language. For someone who needs an adaptive home. For someone who just wants convenience, certainly, but... I know and understand what can happen in life, to change the course of things for you. There are many ways that technology can improve the quality of life for anyone."

"It has for you. It has allowed you to keep contact with the outside world in some ways, but keep separate from it."

"Perhaps."

"I think it has," she said. "And you're going to be telling investors about this?"

"Yes. And potential buyers. Big clients, who will buy these systems for resorts and large companies. For housing developments. I do not want the system to be prohibitively expensive, rather what I want is for people who have a need to be able to access it. And for those who perhaps want something that is simply frills, then that will be more reasonably priced. But, I feel that it is not so much to ask for those who want frills to pay more."

"You do have a bit of altruism and you."

"Nothing that was not forced upon me. I would never have given a thought to have somebody else live. I clawed my way up from the gutter. That has given me less compassion in most situations.

Let me assure you. Because I lived a life where it was all about survival of the fittest. So those who cannot keep up fall behind, and that is the natural order of things. It was not until I had to face my own mortality, my own frailties, that I had to perhaps acknowledge that people are trying a lot harder than I give them credit for. And that perhaps it is not so bad to offer a hand up."

"It has changed you."

"Obviously." He looked at her, and the gaze was pointed.

She wanted to roll her eyes at him. She didn't. "Yes. I understand what you mean. You mean physically. That isn't what I mean." She paused a moment. "Can I see the north tower now?"

"Why would you want to see that?"

"Because I have seen you," she said. "And I am your wife now."

These words felt every bit as much like vows as the ones they'd spoken in the church.

He laughed, low and hard, and doused her certainty. "You are not my wife in any real sense of the word."

"I am your wife in the *most* real sense of the word."

They'd said vows in a church and signed papers. It was real.

"You know, back when this village thrived. We had something called handfast marriages. And they were not real until they were consummated."

A riot of heat assaulted her. And she imagined him wrapping his arm around her waist and drawing her toward his chest. She imagined that kiss that he had declined to give her. She imagined...

She drew slightly closer to him. Then she reached out and plucked the flower out of the buttonhole. She held it close, and twirled it in a circle. "I see. And so without consummation it is not real to you?"

"No. It is not. I believe the Catholic Church would agree with me."

"And yet it must be real enough to deter my father's men, or Mattias from ever coming after me."

"Yes. But they do not have to know whether or not the marriage was consummated."

"Consummated. That's a very cold and clinical way of putting it."

Yet she did not feel cold.

"Do not spin fantasies. The act itself is cold and clinical."

She frowned. "I would hope not. I intend to have a life after this. And so I will find out one way or the other."

"Good for you." He didn't sound like he meant that.

She wanted more of him and she wasn't going to get it here. This conversation was making him cruel, and she didn't know why, but she felt... tender.

"Show me the tower?"

"There is nothing for you to see." But he didn't say no. And when he began to walk into the castle, she went after him, and then she saw that he was leading them toward the north tower. She wondered if this was his way of apologizing.

She trailed after him, up the stairs, and back to that place, which was still upended from the tantrum he had thrown the day before.

"Oh, all of your things..." She moved to the collection, which was the only thing still righted.

"They don't matter."

What he meant was he could easily replace them. She knew that.

The collection though... That long bar under glass. Because this was not a room for anyone to see.

"Is this the collection I'm part of?"

"Yes," he said, hard and offering no explanation.

"Why do you really collect things?"

He looked...embarrassed, almost. He looked away. "A habit. One I didn't indulge in all the years after Apollo and I made success but something about this... I used to pick up whatever I found. I had no money, and one never knew what one might need. If you could find something for free, you kept it. And you held on to it."

Her heart squeezed tight. "You started your whole career that way."

He nodded. "When you are poor, simple objects can change your life. I suppose out here, bankrupt of all the trappings of the life I once I had, I slid back into that mindset."

He had thought he might need her, and so he'd kept her.

He hadn't even been wrong. It made her want to laugh. And cry.

"It's a rather Spartan room," she said.

"I live a fairly Spartan life. It is simple. And I don't mind that."

"Are you not lonely here?"

He looked at her, his face hard. "Loneliness happens when you let yourself want something. I want nothing. I wake up every day, and I follow the direction my mind needs to go. I need to create things. To invent them. If there are problems, my brain wishes to solve them, and I do that using technology. It is my only real drive. The business stuff… That was never me. That has always been Apollo. I simply want… I need to fix things. And that is all. Personally, as a human being, I require very little. I'm not driven by the need for material wealth. The pleasures of the flesh no longer appeal to me the way they once did. Even then… What I wanted was control. What I wanted was to spend the years taking back what I felt had been taken from me. Empty, useless pursuits."

So, he didn't feel *nothing* about prostituting himself. He had felt very deeply about it for a time.

She chose not to say anything more about that either. More good sense on her part.

"We..."

"We shall leave tomorrow."

"Oh." She felt disappointed by that, and she couldn't even say why. Perhaps because he was refusing to acknowledge that they were married.

Perhaps because you want him?

That little voice inside her felt nearly *dangerous.*

She needed to leave him, and all of this, behind, once he helped her. She needed to find out who she was and find her family. She couldn't afford to be so...beset by him.

And yet she was.

"What?" he asked, and she knew embarrassment over the fact he'd witnessed her inner turmoil.

"It is our wedding day. And it will be our wedding night and..."

"You will have dinner as you always do. I will take dinner as I do. Do not spin stories about me. How could you, anyway? Do you not see?"

The problem was she did see. Perhaps deeper than he wanted her to. And she did not find him repulsive. Rather she found him compelling. Rather she wanted to draw nearer to him.

"I'm not spinning stories. I'm just getting to

know you. Thank you. For the necklace. Have courage and take heart."

"I didn't even know what it said. I simply found a necklace with the goddess Athena on it, it seemed appropriate."

He was lying. She did not know why he was lying.

"It's a good thing you never get lonely. Because I think most people here would. How nice it must be to want nothing."

He looked at her, his expression remote. "It is the only thing I know."

She left, her steps echoing on the flagstone floor. Husband and wife. Husband and wife. She heard it every time she took one step, then another.

But it was not real. None of it was real.

She had been fooled before, into believing she was a daughter when she was simply a convenience.

She couldn't let attraction, gold necklaces and the lies of her own heart blind her to the fact this was no different.

Not a wife.

A convenience.

She had to do her best to remember that.

CHAPTER NINE

WHAT SURPRISED ATHENA the most was the manner in which they traveled. And she didn't think that it should surprise her. It wasn't as if Cameron was going to get on a commercial plane. But for some reason, it seemed odd that this man who went nowhere, procured a private jet to take them to Paris.

It was luxurious, not unlike the private plane she had flown on for the very first time with her family only a couple of weeks ago.

It occurred to her then, that she was about to be out in the real world for the first time ever.

And that she had no idea if her family was looking for her.

As the plane descended, her anxiety began to mount.

"Are there news stories about me being missing?"

He looked at her. "There must not be. Apollo would've said."

She nodded. "That speaks volumes to the fact that my father does not know how to put out such information. I really must *not* exist to the outside world."

"All the more reason this is important."

He had tied his long hair back away from his face,

and it gave her an even better view of his eyes. She was struck again by how beautiful they were.

When he had spoken his vows to her...she had grown... Lost in them. In him.

And when they had been dancing...he'd asked her...

She felt a flush of embarrassment.

She was not stupid. She was twenty-eight years old, she might never have had an opportunity to be held by a man, but she did understand desire.

She'd been too shocked, too ashamed to admit it.

That being held by him, that the feel of his large, warm hands on her curves, the scent of him, the way that he was so solid, like a wall of granite, had begun to create a stirring sensation between her thighs.

And he was hers now. Her husband.

Her husband...

Not real.

And yet her attraction to him was. So didn't that matter?

She had to remember that she had jumped out of a moving car to start a new life, and while she knew this... Cameron, was not her final destination, did that mean she couldn't want him?

Did it mean she couldn't have him?

The door to the plane opened, and out there on the tarmac was a limousine.

Suddenly, she was frozen. Because here she

was, on the precipice of something much bigger than she was.

"I don't have a passport," she said.

She'd only just had a name change. There was no way he'd gotten her the papers she needed yet. It was one thing to have no documents in a country church with a priest who was likely on Cameron's payroll. But here?

He laughed. "Everything is taken care of. You've no need to worry."

"We won't be... Traveling through immigration? My father made sure that I knew that I couldn't get far without him because I was not in possession of my own documents."

"As I said. It is handled. Do you think billionaires wait in lines to have their paperwork pored over? Of course we don't. And neither will you."

"How does that work?"

"I declared you."

She wrinkled her nose as they walked off the plane and got into the limousine. "Declared me? Like... Like I am an *apple*?"

"Yes."

She huffed. "That's vaguely demeaning."

"Little runaway beggars who technically don't exist in the system should perhaps not be choosers."

"Basically men who have not even spoken to another person face-to-face in ten years should perhaps not think so highly of themselves."

He laughed. "Oh, I don't think highly of myself, little goddess, but I certainly know what I'm about."

"And that is?"

"Getting exactly what I came for."

And then it was difficult for her to banter with him because she was so focused on the scenery around them. The majesty of the buildings, the architecture. She felt something in her spirit move. She had been affected by the Highlands this way, by nature. Not things built by men.

But this artistry, this triumph of humanity called out to her.

In the same way that a mountain did, or a flower.

People didn't have to make things beautiful. They only had to make them functional. But they made art instead, simply because they could.

"What do you think?" he asked, his voice sounding rusty.

"I am an awe. This is more beautiful than any book ever suggested that it could be. This is…"

"Yes, it is."

She watched him closely, for some sign that he was having an emotional reaction. It was impossible to say. He was remote. The only indication that he was moved was the tightness of his jaw, the way that it tugged on the scar tissue on his cheek.

"Where are we going?"

"Apollo has assured me that accommodation has been arranged for us."

"Thank you. For taking me to see this. It's… Important to me."

"I know. I told you, there are things on your list that I can give you. A chance to see the world and comfort is one of them."

"You also said there were things you could not give me."

"Romance, Athena. I have not ever had one bit of it in my soul. Even less of it now."

"I don't believe that. A man who wishes to return to Paris before doing anything else must have a bit of romance in him."

"Or he likes a croissant."

She couldn't help herself. She laughed. Because it was true, he did like a croissant. And he made them with the expertise of someone who had been trained in fine French pastry.

She may not have been very many places, but there had always been fine food at her father's compound, so she was educated on the subject.

The food that Cameron made surpassed anything she had had her father's world-renowned chefs make for them.

"All right. Perhaps that's all. But do you not like the art here? The architecture?"

"Of course."

"What is that if not romance?"

"Just an extension of lust, I would think."

That made her heart hit hard against her chest.

"Are you particularly lustful?" she asked, whispering, her lips suddenly feeling full. Obvious. She swallowed and shifted in her seat.

"That is not a road you want to go down."

"It isn't?"

"No. You did not listen to me when I told you how it was, because you don't wish to believe me," he rested his elbow on the window, his chin on his knuckles. "You should, I have seen many things, and done most of them. When you spoke of experiences you wished to have, you said romance. You did not say sex."

She felt edgy, embarrassed. Her heart was thundering and she knew her cheeks were pink, so she determinedly looked out her own window. "Don't they go together?"

He laughed. Hard and bitter, and she did not know why it made her feel hot.

"No, little goddess. They don't. Lust is selfish. It is all about satisfaction. It is all about the fulfillment of a very base, rough need. It can be over in seconds with no fanfare at all. It is not romance. Its neighbor is greed, not love. Make no mistake of that."

She did not know why she was pushing the subject. Except she couldn't get the way she had felt when they danced out of her head. Couldn't get the way she'd felt speaking those vows to him from echoing in her soul.

She felt confused. By all of this. Because she had escaped her father's compound, and had gone from one cage to another, and yet here she was now, in Paris, in the next phase of that. And she did not feel like Cameron's prisoner. She had gotten to know him these past couple of weeks. She did not feel like his prisoner at all.

He was the first man she had met outside the compound, surely, she should know that meant her feelings were skewed.

He was monstrous. His scars were not something that could be called minor, nor could they be considered something easy to overlook.

He was not handsome. He was not beautiful. He had been once. But his looks were gone. Ruined. Twisted.

And yet.

She had heard the term sex appeal before. She understood it now.

He was feral. Strong. Large.

All things that appealed to her. There was a rugged masculinity to his being that ignited the femininity within her.

His hands were rough, and the way they held her could be gentle.

The paradox of it intrigued her.

She knew that her feelings were improbable. She knew that they would lead her into trouble. She knew that it was impossible.

She knew that she should stop pushing him.

Except, while there was the aspect of him being the only man she knew, which in many ways should deter her, there was also the aspect that… She had him as a resource.

She wasn't making up the way her body felt when it was close to his.

It did not need to be forever to be good. She felt certain of that.

And some would argue that it would be a waste of an opportunity…

He was staring at her.

"What?"

"You are a strange creature," he said.

"A side effect, I would think, of spending so much time in my own company."

"You said you had a friend."

She nodded. "Rose. As I said she… Well, she was a maid. My father decided he was going to sell her and… His former son-in-law rescued her. He's not unlike you."

"In what way?"

"He is scarred. From a fire. It killed his wife. It was years ago, it was… The daughter that I replaced."

He nodded slowly. "I see."

"Yes. Well. I guess they felt that they owed him something. Ares has never seemed like a cruel man to me. He's frightening, certainly."

"The god of war," he pointed out.

A smile touched Athena's lips. "Yes. I suppose so. That's funny. I hadn't thought of it."

"So Rose was your friend."

"Yes. But we were both quite sheltered, so neither of us could really teach the other anything. And neither of us really remember life before coming to the compound. Rose had to work. In contrast, I never learned how to do anything. I can't cook. I've never cleaned. I'm… I'm spoiled in many ways."

"And yet you were willing to jump from a moving vehicle and escape the fate you did not care for."

"Yes. I am not as soft as they think I am. It makes me wonder, again. What exactly happened to me in my years before going there. Because there's something…some connection that I might not know about but…"

She shook her head. "It doesn't matter. Not now."

When they arrived at the glorious marble building, the limo pulled smoothly against the curb, and Athena stood in awe. She was used to luxury. But this was an old-world beauty of a different sort that she had never seen.

When they walked into the building, they drew stares. People looked away quickly, but she could see that they were transfixed by Cameron.

Athena began to speak loudly and quickly in French. Whatever she could think of. Silly things, laughing and doing her best to draw the attention. She looped her arm through Cameron's as they headed toward the elevator. The doors opened, and they got inside, and once they closed, he turned to her. "You speak French?" he asked.

"Oh, yes," she said. "We spoke Russian as a...a family. I speak Greek and English, French, Italian, German...a bit of Japanese."

"Why?"

"Why not? I had little to do, and so I learned when I could. As I said...my mother wanted me to be frivolous, I think. Malleable. She didn't want me to want anything, and yet I did. I wanted more. I suppose that in and of itself is a triumph when you have been trained to not want at all, and are given every luxury to keep you from ever doing so."

It made her feel stronger than she had a moment before.

"And why exactly did you do all that out there?"

"Because you were uncomfortable. And I didn't like it."

It was honest. That was what struck him. Her honesty.

And her desire to do something for him.

He moved away from her, to the far side of the elevator. "Athena," he said. "Do not mistake me for something better than I am. Many people would be deterred by the scars. But you... You see a project. I am not your project. I am not a victim for you to pick up and make whole."

"I consider myself warned."

"I am who I have always been. And that is not the kind of man that you should involve yourself with."

"I consider myself warned," she repeated. "Do not make the mistake that everyone else has. Do not make the same mistake the man who called himself my father made. I am not soft, and I am not foolish. No matter that men have tried to control me all my life I know my own mind. I know who I am. I chose to do what I did because I care about you. You cannot stop me from caring."

Everything in him went hard. "And that is where you're wrong. I can. With time."

She withdrew, but he sensed that it was not a retreat. Rather, a calculated move. She would be back. At full strength. One thing he knew for certain about Athena. She was formidable.

The goddess of war.

He would do well to remember that.

It was easy to take her as soft. Because she was so beautiful. But perhaps that was what had made the Athena of mythology equally formidable.

The elevator doors opened and revealed the penthouse. Athena didn't look at any of the surrounding furnishings. Rather she went straight for the open windows that faced the incomparable view below of Paris. The Eiffel Tower. The

Seine. She put her hands against the glass, her eyes clearly hungry for the site.

And he felt… Hungry for her.

He recalled what she had said in the car, and knew she had been testing him. The question was why?

He knew why he wanted her. What he could not fathom was why she might wish to test out her sensuality with him.

The man he'd been would have taken her up on that. Without question. Without care. He would have taken her admiration of him as his due and demanded that she worship him on her knees singing his praises with her lips. Her tongue. Yes, he would've done all those things. He was not that man now. And perhaps he should rejoice in the change, or see it as some sort of redemptive moment.

But he did not feel redeemed. He felt as dark and lethal as ever. And she…

She is a goddess of war.

Yes.

"I wish to go out," she said.

"We were just out."

"I know. I know we were. But could we… I will need a ring."

He had no idea how he had neglected to realize that. She would, of course. Agreeing to show all the world that she belonged to him.

They had not exchanged rings in the ceremony and it had not struck him that it was missing.

It felt a glaring error now.

"And perhaps it wouldn't hurt for us to be seen prior to your big unveiling. There could be rumors," she said.

"I thought that you did not know anything about popular culture."

"The man who called himself my father actively discouraged me from participating in such things, but aren't all teenagers rebellious? In whatever way we can be. Obviously I was hungry for whatever information I could glean. It was difficult living where I did, but there were always ways to find a magazine here and there. One thing I do know is how hungry culture is for gossip."

"You are a funny creature."

"So you said. And I know."

"What *is* your last name, Athena?"

She looked blank then. "McKenzie. Or, it is now. The only one I know. I would have claimed my father's. But that is not real. It is not real. None of it was."

"I will help you. I will help you find the truth of your past."

He paused for a moment. "If that is what you want. You must understand that the answers might not be what you want them to be."

"Spoken like a man with a dark past."

"It is. There is no happy secret behind me.

There is nothing but tragedy, desperation and debauchery. Nothing but pain."

"And yet it made you who you are."

He laughed. "Yes. It did. The man you see before you is little more than a monster. Why do you think what I have been made could be positive in any regard?"

"Because. I see many positive things in you. You're brilliant. You're very strong. And you are an excellent cook."

"I am not."

"Let's go out. We can ease in. How many years has it been since you were in a restaurant?"

"Ten years."

"And I have never been to one. Please. Let us go out in Paris. We're still no one. No one and nothing."

"But with all the resources in the world."

"A boon for us. Let us enjoy it."

She looked at him, and something mischievous lit her dark eyes. "Put on a suit."

"Why?"

"Because I think you look rather... Dashing in a suit."

"And will you dress for me?"

"Yes."

"Then wear red."

CHAPTER TEN

ATHENA ZIPPED HER dress up with trembling hands.
It was skintight and only went to the middle of
her thigh. Much more scandalous than anything
she had ever worn while living at the compound.
It showed the curve of her waist, hips, left nothing to the imagination when it came to her back
end. And as far as her breasts went... It molded
to them perfectly, her golden curves pushed up
and revealed to a near indecent degree.

But he would appreciate it. She had seen the
way she looked at him when they had danced.
He looked hungry.

And you wish to encourage him?

She did. She couldn't explain her connection to
Cameron. Except she was beginning to feel that
she had not run into that cabin in the woods out
of simple desperation. But that perhaps something
had guided her there.

He was a man set apart. A man who had not
had anyone come into his home for a decade. So
why had she happened upon him? That seemed
to be the real question.

Maybe she was silly. She could accept that.

But her whole life had been positioned outside
the ordinary. Why should she expect to be any
less now?

She didn't know how to fix her hair in terribly complicated ways, so she had left it hanging straight and glossy down her back.

She had put on a bit of makeup, which had been part of the trousseau she had demanded.

And beneath the dress... Beneath the dress was underwear as crimson as the dress itself, wispy and see-through.

The idea of him seeing her and not made her pulse race.

She came out of the bedroom, and there he was. Standing in the center of the room, the beautifully lit city of Paris behind him. He looked severe in a dark black suit, his long hair tied back, his beard trimmed a bit more neatly now.

He was... A glorious contrast. Beastly in part, utterly sophisticated on the other hand.

It was those seemingly incompatible things that made her pulse race. That made her feel giddy with excitement.

His face...

She could not find it hideous.

It was compelling. As was he.

It was painful to look at, in the sense that it spoke of the pain that he'd been through.

And yet.

She could not look away from him. Because there was nowhere else she wished to look more. Not even in Paris.

"Shall we go?" he asked.

"Yes. Are you all right?"

He laughed. "You are no more experienced than I and going out into the world, and you ask if I'm okay?"

"I'm less experienced than you. And I think perhaps that makes it easier. I have no preconceived idea about how anyone might treat me. I have no expectations. You lived a whole other life." She stopped herself. "You lived two other lives."

"Come," he said, his voice gruff.

They went down to the street, where the limousine was waiting for them. She wondered… She wondered if he had driven at all since the accident. She chose to wait to ask the question until they got into the car.

"Have you…"

"No." Like he knew what she was going to ask. "I've not had occasion to drive," he said.

"Does the idea bother you?"

"The idea of driving *you* anywhere does."

She nodded.

"You don't know how to drive, do you?" he asked.

She shook her head. "No. That was definitely not part of my upbringing. Nothing that would give me any sort of independence. It was for my own good, of course. Of course no one in the compound had any idea who I was, so how could it be for *me*?"

"I am familiar," he said. "With such things. And also with how you can find pleasure while also remaining unsatisfied."

The words cut deep. She knew he meant when he'd sold himself. Of course he'd found some pleasures, but it hadn't been…

Whatever he said, that was not the true intent of sex, she was certain of it. She felt more when he looked at her than he seemed to have felt about whole paid encounters.

It was a perversion of something meant to be more.

Just as her whole life had been a perversion of family.

Yes, she had felt joy. Connection.

But they were only slivers of what was meant to be.

She understood him. In this, she understood him.

"It is costly," she whispered. "Taking those sorts of small pleasures. Because on the other side of the wall is a whole world. A feast you sacrifice for the crumb before you."

"Sometimes the crumb is all you can see."

"Yes. So too with freedom, I suppose."

"There is a freedom to driving, yes. But then, that freedom can be easily accomplished with enough money as well. As you can see."

"Provided you're the one in control, yes."

"Perhaps that is the problem," he said, and she

sensed the change in subject. "The amount of lives I have tried to live. Maybe the problem is a man can only jump to so many. And this last one… It is what I will not be able to find my way out of."

"I don't believe that. I've had three lives too. The one that I can't remember, the one in the compound, and now this one. I need to believe that I can change again, Cameron, otherwise what will happen to me after?"

He looked at her. Long and hard. And she found herself looking back. Unflinching. Unwilling. "You will do just fine, my goddess. You are a woman of exceptional strength, and there is nothing that will compromise that."

"I don't know that I believe it. It would be nice if I could. But I have no evidence to suggest that I will be all right when I'm out and left to my own devices."

"Perhaps you will make mistakes. Perhaps you will sample all the things that have been withheld from you, and you will find yourself drowning in the excesses. I'm familiar with that. But there's something different about you, Athena. It is your warrior heart, I think. It grounds you. I lost myself. Because I never knew who I was. Except angry. I took joy in manipulating others. Because I felt that somehow they were withholding something from me simply by existing. You do not have that same spite in you that I have in me."

"I don't know. The spite is beginning to feel

real. I spent a great many years believing that I was simply spoiled. Protected. I spent a great many years not thinking about how many years were passing. And then I had to wake up. It was like a bucket of cold water being dumped on my head. And I find that I am angry. Because here I am, twenty-eight years old with no real idea of how the world works. And no idea at all where I fit in it. I was not a fit for the life at the compound, not really, because it was not for me. And what is? I do not know. Perhaps I will discover my roots, perhaps I have a family, and I will have no place there either. You're assuming that I am measured because that's my nature, but I believe it is simply because it is all I've ever had the opportunity to be. I'm angry. Because the whole world is out there. All of this before me, and it was denied me. And why? I may never have the answer to that."

"You may not. And so what will you do with that? I let it twist me. The people around me were selfish, and so I let myself become equally so."

"Could I be selfish. Just for a while?"

"Of course you can. When we part, you can live for yourself. Take the money that I give you and spend it on clothes. Go to clubs and dance the night away, buy yourself a luxury car. Take as many lovers as you please."

She watched his face when he said that, and was satisfied to see it darken with something unreadable.

"Is that what you think?" she asked. "That I should take many lovers? I thought that you decided I needed romance."

"It is what you said, not me. But it would likely benefit you to seek something other than romance for a time. Something that is simply light and free."

"Did you find those interactions light and free when you had them?"

He laughed. The sound cynical. "No. If you want the honest truth, I've never found sex to be anything more than a weapon. Used against the other person, or used against my own demons."

"And yet you enjoyed it?"

"Physically, it feels good. But I was dark and twisted long before that car accident. And so the dark and twisted always served me. I took great joy in using beautiful women who begged to be with me. Because I was important and handsome and all the things they prized. Because I was no longer poor, where people would just pay for my services, pay to have a handsome man on their arm, or a secret, shameful night in bed. Yes, I took great pleasure in that power shifting. All the women who graced my bed were symbolic of that. A salve for my rage. Except they were human beings. And using them was wrong. And nothing brought that into sharper clarity then Irina dying in my arms simply because she had the bad misfortune of being my lover for that couple of weeks."

She swallowed hard. "It hurts you. The harm you've caused."

"Yes," he said. "And once Irina died, once the accident happened, I let every bit of harm I ever caused hurt *me*. Cut me. Down to the bottom of my soul. Because something had to give. Because something had to shift. Because otherwise it's all… Because otherwise it's all so ugly. It is all so ugly."

She moved her hand to brush against his thigh. The suit pants were luxurious in quality, soft, his thigh hard. And she could feel a large dent in the muscle there, more evidence of trauma from the accident.

"You are not ugly. Just so you're aware."

He gripped her wrist and pulled her close. "Don't lie."

"I'm not. I don't have any reason to lie. You have told me that you want nothing from me physically, why would I…"

He released his hold on her, and her heart began to thunder hard.

"Let us go choose you a ring. I will not touch you, Athena. And you will thank me for it later. I am nothing more than a curse. Make no mistake. If it weren't for my loyalty to Apollo I would never have agreed to any of this."

"I don't believe that. Because I don't believe

that you do a damn thing you don't *want* to do. You are pretending that you had no choice and I cannot for the life of me fathom why. Why you need to believe that."

"It will do you no good to try and peer inside the darkness."

"Blah blah blah," she said, feeling irritated. "So terrifying. As if I didn't live with a crime lord for most of my life."

"Do not push me."

"Somebody has to."

They said nothing, and when they arrived at the jewelry store, he took her hand, but she thought that he pulled her a bit roughly from the car. The only way that he could express his irritation. And in kind, she made sure to bump against him a bit harder than necessary as they walked into the store.

"It seems as if it would be after hours."

"Apollo made a call."

"How handy to have a charming billionaire for a friend. Perhaps I like him."

He turned to her, and he did not touch her, but his eyes pinned her to the spot.

Those blue, electric eyes. "You will not."

"You told me I could go out and have however many lovers as I want to."

She was goading him now and she knew it. It thrilled her. Filled her with that same delicious fear she'd felt at the castle. Was it wrong there was a thrill to it?

She didn't care. She didn't.

Her whole life had been somewhat wrong, why could she not have the wrong she wanted?

And the wrong she wanted wasn't Apollo, but she did like making Cameron go fierce.

"*Not* him," he growled.

"Why not?"

"Because if I have to know a man who has seen your naked body, I will not be held responsible for what I do to him."

He walked into the shop, and left her standing on the sidewalk, the breath pulled from her body. She scurried along behind him quickly.

"Mr. McKenzie," said the elderly man attending to the display counter. "We were told to expect you. We were also told not to allow for any onlookers."

The windows behind them were suddenly covered with black curtains that fell from the ceiling.

"Thank you," said Cameron.

It was funny, to watch him attempt to interact with other people. To watch him make an attempt at politeness.

"And who is this lovely lady?" the older man asked.

"Athena," she said.

"My wife," he said. "We married so quickly we had time to find a priest, but not the rings. We are about to make our debut as a couple, and I wish for her to have something stunning."

"Because of our love, of course," said Athena. She looked at him and smiled.

She wondered if he would smile back.

So rarely did he smile. Once, she'd seen him do it once.

He remained stoic.

"Yes," he said flatly. "Because of our love."

He was maddening. And amusing, even though she had a feeling he was not being amusing on purpose.

The older man pulled out a small tray, with a selection of four different rings.

He was very good at his job, Athena could see, because she didn't need the choice of the whole store. No, these four were all perfect in their own way, and she knew she didn't need to see anything else.

But it was one that was shaped like a pear, glittering and brilliant, with two sapphires on either side, that was the one that truly caught and held her attention.

The sapphires were like his eyes.

"That one," she said.

"Excellent taste, *mademoiselle*," he said.

He gestured toward Cameron. "Put it on her finger."

Cameron took the ring out of the velvet case.

It looked comically small in his giant hands.

He was such a large man, imposing, and she imagined that it was the beauty of his face that had once softened him. And there was nothing to soften him now. Nothing to make him less formidable than he was.

She appreciated that. Not that she would have ever wished the scarring on him, but there was an extreme quality to him now.

Something that she knew most men didn't possess.

He was unique. And terrifying. Marvelous.

And when he slipped the ring on her finger, she lost her breath. It was as if the ring sliding onto her finger was a kiss, another vow. An intimate touch even though it was nothing more than gems and precious metal.

It felt real. Even though she knew it wasn't. Even though she knew nothing could be further from the truth.

It felt real.

She felt like she might be his.

What's the matter with you? You should want to be your own.

She knew that. She shouldn't want to go from the ownership of one man to another. She looked up at him, and their eyes met.

It wouldn't be ownership. The kind of claim that Cameron had staked on her was different.

Except he didn't want that claim.

"Perfect," she whispered.

"We'll take it," said Cameron.

"Wonderful. Mr. Agassi said that he would set-tle the account."

"I'm certain that he did," said Cameron. "But I will not allow it."

"Something to take up with him. I will not defy him."

"And get you to find me?" he asked the man, who was so small he only came up to the middle of Cameron's chest.

"Mr. Agassi spends quite a bit of money here. On mistresses. He is a valued client."

Cameron laughed at that. Bitter.

"Of course."

They walked back out of the store, and he took her hand. "Down here. There's a small café that serves very no-frills food. But of the highest quality. I think that will be a good experience for your first restaurant. Neither of us needs anything overly formal."

She was still processing what had just hap-pened.

She was wearing his ring. They were walking down the Parisian street together. He was hold-ing her hand.

His hands were so rough.

"Why are you so angry?" she asked.

"Right now? Or in general?"

"Well, start with right now and work your way back," she said.

"Apollo is being heavy-handed. I don't need his charity, and he well knows it. I'm frustrated with him because he strong-armed me into the situation anyway."

"Except he didn't," said Athena. "You were ready. You were ready to leave, and perhaps, Apollo knew that and decided to give you the push you needed. Be honest, Cameron, no one could force you to leave if you didn't want to. You never would've danced with me if you hadn't wanted to, and you certainly wouldn't be here," she said, sweeping her arm wide, "if you didn't want to be. You are a stubborn, beastly man, and you certainly won't be told. So why you are hell-bent on acting as if this is all because of your business partner, I don't know."

He looked at her, and for the first time, she thought she might have succeeded in actually shocking him. His eyes went fractionally wider. "Are you... Are you telling me that you think I know why I have done this?"

"No," she said. "I don't know. But I don't think you do either."

"That makes no earthly sense, woman."

"I think it does. You want this." She stepped in front of him, and she put her hand on his chest. She was shocked to find that his heart was raging there. "You want to be away from there. You do... You don't actually want to be alone you..."

He gripped her wrist again, and pulled her hand

away. "Stop toying with me as if I am not dangerous."

"What will you do? Will you devour me? Or will you kiss me?"

"Athena…" he growled.

"Cameron…"

"You do not want this," he said, his voice low. "You have been captive all of your life. You need to go and experience the world. You do not need to kiss the first man you meet."

"Why are you afraid to kiss me? Are you afraid you won't stop?"

"You don't want me."

"I do. I do want you. How dare you tell me how I feel."

"You are being a silly girl. Let us go eat."

And she found herself being hauled into the café, where she was seated unceremoniously. She tried to appreciate the fact that they were in a restaurant. That she was experiencing something new and different. That it was like something out of a movie, and such a simple thing, such a normal thing for other people, and yet so different for her.

Because she was still focused on what it had felt like to touch Cameron's chest. To feel his heart raging beneath her palm.

The din of the restaurant was a foreign sort of thing to her, and she kept checking with Cameron to see if he was affected by it, but it was as if he was protected by a granite wall. But it closed her out too, and she didn't like it.

He ordered their food. Croque monsieur and a croissant with an egg in the middle. Crepes honey and lemon.

There were baguettes, and other glorious breads. And very strong coffee.

He did not ask her preferences, but there was no need. He'd provided everything.

"Thank you," she said, softly.

"Are you angry with me, or are you happy with me? Make up your mind." And it was like the wall had dropped, his annoyance a way in she was happy to take.

"I'm everything," she said. "All at once. I am so gloriously grateful for this experience. That you're the one who found me. And yet you aggravate me."

"Tell me. More about you."

"There's nothing to say," she said. "Do you want to hear how my father barely spoke two words to me? And how I didn't know that could be considered strange? Do you want to hear about how my mother needed me for emotional support at all times, but didn't know how to offer any in return? People think that I am soft and cosseted because I have never had to do any work. Because when it comes to my physical safety and comfort, that was always managed, cared for. What no one realizes, is how I had to fortify myself. And when

I look back on that time, it is like a hollow, dark pit. Because it was never for me. I was a shrine to Naya, not a human being. And I can never go back. I can't. I have been more alive, more real in these last weeks than ever before. And I know that I was your prisoner. But it wasn't the same. I was still able to be more myself. I am still now able to be more myself. So yes. I do find you maddening. Utterly." She laughed. "But I also find you compelling. I find you… I want to help you. I want to…"

"You can't. You know the piece of metal that you saw in the north tower."

"Yes," she said, remembering clearly that large, twisted piece, which he had had under glass.

"That was in my leg. My right leg. That I can walk as well as I can is something of a miracle. That it missed my artery is another miracle altogether."

"Cameron…"

"I have been given an inordinate amount of miracles. I have done nothing to deserve them. Not ever."

"Shouldn't you do something to pay them back, then?"

"I don't know what that would be."

"Maybe that's why you're here. Because you're trying to figure that out. Maybe it will start with Apollo. Your friendship. But it can't… You lived. Your life cannot stay so small."

"Most people would never tell me what to do in the manner that you are."

"Most people haven't lived a life like me. I've never had the opportunity to do anything." She sat there for a moment, and suddenly she felt guilty. She was passing judgment on him. Without really being fair. He had felt as trapped in his life as she did in hers.

The accident had been the thing that he felt had taken away his choice. She had no right to act as if he was simply lightly choosing to stay in isolation. He had not thrown away his freedom, it felt every bit as ripped from him as hers had from her.

"I'm sorry. I have been hideously insensitive."

He laughed. He really laughed. And there was a smile that accompanied it. They drew stairs in the café, and she found herself grinning even though she didn't really know what he was laughing at, and she had a feeling the laughter was somewhat unkind.

"Do you think I care if you been unfair to me?"

"I am the only friend that you've made in the last decade."

"You are not my friend, little goddess."

"Yes, I am. We talk every day. We have for weeks. You have shared your food with me. We are now out to dinner together. You bought me a very nice gift."

"If you mean the ring, that was Apollo."

"Fine. But even so, we are friends, you ridiculous beast."

"I do not have friends. Except Apollo."

"Why is that so important to you?"

"You are a little she demon."

"Maybe so." She bit happily into her sandwich, because she could take joy in the fact only she could have provoked him like this. She was certain. She was satisfied that she had gotten a reaction out of him. One that had simply been anger. "But I am right about you. You left the castle so that you could do something. So you should do it."

"And what is it that I want to do?"

"I don't know. But you told me an awful lot about the tragedy of Irina dying so young. You told me a lot about the tragedy of your upbringing. You have billions of dollars. Perhaps there is something in that. Perhaps there is something that you're supposed to do. You do have another life. Another chance. And you have the perspective of a man who has lived… All of your lives. What is it that you think needs to change? What is it that you think you need to bring to the world?"

"And what is it that you need to bring to the world, Athena? Are we now going to compete in philanthropy?"

"Maybe I'm a missing person," she said. "Maybe that's what I need to do. Maybe I need to help find people who are missing. Like me. People who are being locked away, hidden away.

Maybe I need to help fix that. So that women like me can't be sold into marriage. So that women like Rose, my dear friend Rose, can't be sold to pay off debts. I will take the money you give me, and that is what I will do."

"I will match it. You don't need to spend all of your money."

"And what need do you see?"

"No child should sleep on the streets," he said.

"Good."

"It is that experience that creates monsters like me. Perhaps I can at the very least stop more of them from being made."

"Maybe that's why you're out. Maybe that's why you're here."

"You are difficult," he said.

"I never said I wasn't. Or rather, I suppose I'm just discovering that. Which is a bit exciting. Because I spent so much of my life being forced into being biddable. And I have never really thought I was. I have always thought that there might be more to me than that."

He looked at her, and she could not figure out exactly what the expression meant.

"A productive day. Your first time at a restaurant, and a glancing bit of insight into what you're meant to be."

"I think you're mocking me, Cameron."

"I would never mock you, little goddess."

"I don't believe that. I believe that you're mocking me because you find my sincerity uncomfortable."

"You know what's uncomfortable. Having eighteen inches of metal stuck in your leg. And no, that isn't the euphemism."

"I wouldn't have thought it was," she said, wrinkling her nose.

"Did you enjoy your meal?"

"I did. Perhaps we can take a walk?"

She smiled at him. And had the feeling that in his world that smile was waging a war. But that was just fine by her. She was the goddess of it, after all. And he insisted upon calling her a little goddess. So she would not let it go. She would not release hold.

She would instead be the conqueror that he had named her.

Even if it began with a walk.

"Looking for romance, Athena?"

The way his accent curled over her name made her stomach tighten.

"You were quite clear on your opinions regarding that subject."

They paid at the café, and then walked outside. It was a warm evening, couples were strolling down the well-lit sidewalk, holding on to each other, gazing at each other lovingly.

Perhaps that was romance. So soft, so easy.

He did not take her arm.

They walked, with a healthy bit of space between them. It was dark now, and they were performing for no one.

She wondered if either of them actually knew how to perform. Or if so many years left to their own devices had made them…

Perhaps they were too much themselves.

Those people that walked together seem to blend into one. To curve around each other.

Perhaps there was an element of training in that. In learning how to bend.

Athena was a bit like a hothouse flower, if she thought about it. She had been left in the corner of the greenhouse, and left to grow on her own. She had never touched the elements. Had never truly been tested, but she had grown rigid, in her way.

Cameron on the other hand was a hearty thistle you might find out in the Highlands. Too remote, too stubbornly wild to be tamed. Too prickly for anyone to draw near.

She could curve herself around him, just maybe, if she could get herself to bend that way. There would be no way to miss all the thorns.

"This is beautiful."

"Yes." His voice was hard then.

"Is this better? Walking in the dark like this?"

He made a musing sound. "I suppose. I did not think I would ever see Paris again."

"What did you like about Paris? The first time you were ever here."

"That I was a man with means of my own. That I was never a whore here. I liked that about it."

He spoke of that time as though it meant nothing. He spoke of selling its body as though it was something that mattered not at all.

She could tell that it did.

And she remembered the way that he had spoken of sex. How it was not romantic. And yet, she saw the way these people walked together. These people who undoubtedly went back to a bed somewhere and made love. It was physical, certainly. But surely connecting to another person like that was also romantic.

And yet, this man, for all of his experience, denied the existence of any romance whatsoever.

As though his body and soul were two completely separate entities, and what his body engaged in, his soul left the room for.

But now he had been sitting alone in his castle all that time. And she wondered. She wondered if it would be the same.

Or if now maybe that he had been so connected to his thoughts all these years if… If he would find it different now. If those things would align for him.

"You didn't like being up…"

"You can say it. I was a whore. I sold myself."

"You say that to degrade yourself. I don't like it."

"I cannot say anything to degrade myself. I am

degraded under my soul. There is no more that can be done."

"And yet you try. Every time you open your mouth. Every time you say things like that. You try."

"Perhaps you should listen."

"I don't see why I should."

"Athena…"

"Tell me. Tell me really, how it started. Tell me."

"No. There is no need to speak of it. We are walking down the streets of Paris, and you wish to speak of my time as a rent boy?"

"I don't know that I wish to, but it keeps coming up, and I feel the way that you use it to try and distance me."

"I shouldn't have to try to distance you. If you recall, I took you prisoner."

"Please. You took me prisoner, and then offered me the world. You took me prisoner, and then offered to take care of me. What I want to understand is why you were so married to the idea that you were the worst person on earth."

"Ask Irina."

"She's dead, so I can't," said Athena. "And before you say that's the point, I will remind you that you are alive. So perhaps you should find a better tribute than sitting around talking about how you're beyond redemption."

"How do you even give attribute to a woman

you felt nothing for? When I tell you about my time as a rent boy… When I tell you that I am… Do you really want to know how it started?"

"Yes. You told me you made more money, but you had to discover that at some point."

"All right. There was a woman. Older. I was seventeen. Every bit as tall as I am now. Not as broad, mind you, because we did not have enough food on the streets. I was quite lanky. But I looked older than I was. Apollo was still working his charm, distracting people while I went in and stole their purse. We stole this woman's purse. We ran. Later, she came to the door of our storage unit that we stayed in. She had followed us. Seen us go in.

"She said that she was sorry to see boys taking to the streets to fend for themselves. She said she wouldn't call the police. She asked me to come to her house. She fed me a meal. It was…"

He had a terrifying, detached sort of look on his face. In his voice. "I thought perhaps she was caring for me. For the first time, I thought perhaps someone was caring for me. Just because. And then she asked for sex."

"What?"

"Yes. She was an older woman, attractive enough. She was lonely, she said. And I… I was too. I had seen her as a mother figure, feeding me dinner, taking pity on me even though I had stolen from her. But she did not see me as a son. She offered me the entire contents of her wallet plus two hundred more dollars for sex. I said yes. Because I'm not a fool. I said yes because not only was she not calling the police on me, she was offering to pay."

"That's... That's very..."

"It's unsavory is what it is."

"Yes," she said, honestly.

"That's the kind of man I am."

"You were a boy. Was it your first time being with anyone?"

He nodded. "I wasn't concerned with sex. I was concerned with survival. So... You don't judge me, because you feel that I did it out of desperation. For food. For money. That is true. But the worst was the small, needy part of myself that wish to be touched. That wish to be close to another person." His lip curled. "I learned. As I went on. I learned not to think of it that way. You can't. You might feel something good for a moment, but the shame of it afterward, and the pieces of yourself you leave behind... It isn't worth it. So you go somewhere else. And watch her body do all those things. It's much easier that way."

"Oh."

That told her more about him than anything else ever could have. He went somewhere else. It was how he had survived so many things. She wondered if he had ever found a way to come back to himself.

She wondered if he even wanted to.

She had thought that maybe he separated his body and soul on occasion. But she wondered now if it had been something more final than that.

"I'm so terribly sorry for what the world has done to you. And I am sorry... The way that I spoke of my willingness to leave my family, the way that I spoke of being poor, as if it was a Charles Dickens novel, and not something that is harrowing. Attending to your own survival that way. I am sorry."

He had not grown thorns for the sake of it. He needed them. She wondered if there was a part of Cameron that remained untouched, unspoiled by the world. And she felt desperate to reach down and find it.

She felt like it might be essential to her. To testing her own strength and to...being needed for herself.

For perhaps she had been specifically sharpened and honed to attack the demons that lived in him.

Perhaps she was the goddess of a very particular war. One that lived in him.

Perhaps it was not so wrong to hope that she could be what he needed here, just for a while.

"Do you have any idea how many women have wanted to fix me, Athena? I laughed at them. While I made them mine in bed. I changed them, they never changed me."

"Did you go somewhere else inside with them?"

"I didn't have to. Eventually, I learned to take pleasure in my power. Do you know, it can be quite intoxicating to have a man filled with shame begging for your body, offering you money, saying no one can ever know. They debased themselves for *me*. And later, they kept on doing it. All these rich socialites. Beautiful women. And they would gladly give their bodies to me, and I could afford to give mine in return for free. And I took great pleasure in feeling nothing but their fingertips on my skin, in feeling nothing but pleasure in my body. Discard them, never think of them again. Not even remember their faces. What did it matter? All those rich people who used me, and I got to use them right back. It's heady, the power in that."

He said those things, so cold. And yet, she knew he wasn't cold. This man who enjoyed good food, who was walking with her now.

This man who had offered to save her. Who had asked nothing of her in return. Not really.

"It begs the question," she said slowly. "Why won't you touch me? If it means nothing."

"Because if I am to learn one thing from what happened to Irina, it will be not to inflict myself on another person again."

"You were not a punishment."

"There are those who would beg to differ."

She looked again at all those couples, walking together. Melting against each other.

She had the strangest sense that whatever was happening between herself and Cameron was somehow deeper. For all that it wasn't an easy stroll. For all that they didn't touch. She had never known another person. Not really. She and Rose had known each other as well as they could. But they did not remember their lives before coming to the compound. Their friendship was often marred by the disparity between them, by the fact that Rose had to work, and Athena was prevented from helping her with any of her duties.

Athena couldn't let Cameron know her as well as she wanted to. Because there was a limit to what she remembered. But she could know him. As much as he would share. And it didn't matter that he was trying to shock her. Trying to get her with those thorns. Keep her from getting too close.

There was intimacy in this. The kind that she had never shared with another living soul, and he didn't shock her. He did not appall her. Instead, she felt honored.

He had hidden away all these years, and she had seen his face first.

And now she had his story.

"There is one thing that you and I can both fully appreciate," she said.

"And what is that?"

"Here we are. Walking. Free. Nobody's telling

us what to do, or where to go. We could leave if we wanted, or we could stay forever."

"Little goddess, I fear that you are spinning fairy tales."

"I'm not spinning fairy tales. The truth is, this is the most that I have ever seen. All in one day. I am… Overwhelmed by it. But it isn't just the place. It's everything that you've told me. This is the deepest I have ever been able to know another person."

He stopped moving. "You should take it as a warning, not as a novelty."

"I don't care what I should and shouldn't do. I am not your prisoner. I'm your partner. And I have spent far too many years kowtowing to what others want from me. I spent too many years in the back of the greenhouse, left to my own devices, in the most lavish of settings, but there was no attention paid to my deeper needs. Talking to you… That fulfills something in me."

"You are a romantic, Athena, which speaks volumes to the differences in our upbringing."

"Yes. I would not say that my life has been normal, but it certainly shielded me from a great many things. You were right. As I said. I did not have an appropriate level of respect for what it meant to have the resources that I did. I feel differently now."

His voice suddenly went hard. "Tell me. Tell me when you first realized your life was not normal."

"I was ten. We watched a cartoon. The little girl went to the zoo. She got a balloon. She got an ice cream cone. I asked to go to the zoo, and my mother said no. I threw a tantrum, I begged, I cried. Screamed about going to the zoo. The next day, a bunch of balloons, a tray filled with ice cream cones, and a lemur appeared in the courtyard. Just for me. Just to make me happy. And I knew that it wasn't the same. It was somehow more, but not at all what I had asked for. If I can have a lemur brought to me, then why would it be beyond my parents' reach for me to go to a zoo? It made no sense. And it was always like that. I would ask for something outside the walls, and they would bring it to me. That was why when... I'm ashamed of this."

"Tell me," he said. "I should have some of your shame since you had all of mine."

"When my father first said that he was having me marry Mattias I was excited. I didn't know the man. But I was... Ready. I was ready to leave. I was ready for something new. For... I wanted romance. Yes. But I wanted sex as well. Do you have any idea how difficult it was growing up in a compound surrounded by grim-looking guards. With your hormones raging like that. I had fantasies about them. But if any of them touched me my father would've killed them."

"And why didn't you run away?"

"Did you not just hear the part about the

guards? No. It was unspoken. If I ran away they would come for me. I just always had the sense that if that happened, I would break something. And the consequences of it would be unpleasant. Like I said. I began to have a sense that all was not normal when I was about ten. There were just some things that I knew. When I realized what manner of man Mattias was, when I realized this was not the fulfillment of any kind of fantasy, that was when I decided that I had to run. That was when I decided that it had to happen, no matter that it was frightening or unpleasant. It was worth whatever consequence to get away then."

"You had fantasies about the guards?"

"I might not have been allowed free rein to everything, but there was a library. I am quite educated on what occurs between men and women, even if I've never experienced it myself. Yes, there were always strong handsome looking men looming about. And I was a teenage girl. Of course I did."

"But none of them ever touched you?"

"No. Because that's how terrifying my father is."

"A pity."

"You're telling me. I could've passed the time quite nicely."

He laughed, and she felt buoyed by that.

At least he found her amusing. The subject of

her childhood seemed to have eased some of the tension surrounding his.

"I was given nearly everything except what I wanted most. Freedom. The very definition of a gilded cage, I know."

"Do you suppose it was better, better than what I had to endure?"

"Yes. Because here I am, escaped now, on the other side of it, and certainly more innocent that a person my age should be, but also protected, in many ways. I wouldn't have remained so. Because in the end…" She smiled, though there was nothing amusing about it. "I would've been turned into a horror as well. That's the way of it. The world sees people as commodities and when you don't have any power agency of your own, someone is always waiting for the opportunity to sell you."

"I sold myself."

"Only because somebody was a very insistent buyer."

"Well, that is the truth of it."

They looked at each other, it was dark, and his face was mostly hidden in shadow, she imagined hers was as well. She couldn't make out the scars on his face. She couldn't make out his expression, or much of anything at all.

"We go to London tomorrow."

"I will be pleased for that."

"You will like it."

"I will."

She wanted to stretch up on her toes and kiss him. She was nearly dizzy with her need to draw closer to him. But he had been very clear that he didn't wish for that to happen. He said it was to protect her, but she had a feeling...

So much of his past, his trauma was tied to the things that people had taken from him. From his body.

She couldn't walk with him, talk with him, hear the story that he told about that woman he had thought cared for him, and then asked him for sex, and then kissed him.

She would mean for there to be feeling behind it, but she didn't think that he would be able to do more than that. She wouldn't be any different, really. It would feel like she was using him. Like she had offered some sort of emotional balm only to turn it into something base.

She wouldn't do that. They walked on, and her knuckles brushed his. She caught her breath. And then she deliberately wrapped her fingers around his hand, the rough warmth a comfort, a need and a deep pain all at once.

In the darkness, they held each other's hands and walked back to the penthouse.

CHAPTER ELEVEN

WHEN HE WOKE up the next morning he was in a foul temper. They would be having dinner with Apollo tonight, and the following night would be the product unveiling.

He had no patience for any of it. The first thing he remembered was the way the soft skin of Athena's hand had felt against his own.

He growled, sat up and looked around the bedroom. It wasn't big enough. Not sufficient enough for all the rage that poured through him. He wished to ride Aslan across the moors.

That was the only way to exorcise the demons that hounded him.

This was the *real* reason he had stayed in the middle of nowhere.

Because with Athena next door, the way that he really wanted to cope with the need that was coursing through his veins was to crash through her bedroom door and…

He would not.

The very idea made his stomach curdle.

There were competing, terrible needs inside of him, and he did not care for them at all.

He knew all about the physical release that came with sex. He had honed his own need to be only that. It was why he was so able to ruthlessly and efficiently find release on his own.

Because it meant nothing. Yes, he liked the softness of a woman's body. He had enough experiences to know exactly what he would choose when he was in control over the selection of his partners, and he preferred women. He liked the way they looked. The way that they smelled. The shape of them. It was certainly an added pleasure to have a partner. But he did not need it. He had gotten rid of that need. That yawning, ridiculous need that he'd still had at seventeen. That had made him so naïve and hopeful. That had made him think perhaps...

He had extinguished that. He was not a better man for it, but he was a man who had survived.

He did not wish to introduce Athena to his brand of sex. It was cold. It was transactional. And now... It would be far too rough. At least now. While he was so close to the edge.

And never. The bottom line was never.

He got in the shower, and turned on the cold spray. He gritted his teeth. And then he went to the fridge and took out some eggs and cream.

He got out some flour. There were fresh strawberries in there as well, and he quickly made crepes.

He was just finishing making some very strong coffee in the French press, when Athena appeared.

She was wearing...

Next to nothing.

A silken robe, with a lacy garment underneath. Her black hair was tousled. She looked… Much more appetizing than the breakfast that had been spread out before them.

"Good morning."

She smiled, and her smile looked wicked. "Good morning."

She took a tentative step into the kitchen, and looked up at him again. "I've never seen you in the act of cooking. I hoped to catch you quite often at the palace, but I never did."

"And why do you look sheepish this morning?"

She looked away. "I do not wish to make you uncomfortable."

He laughed. He could not help it. The very idea this little creature could make him uncomfortable.

His laughter, though, seemed to provoke her outrage. "I have a rich fantasy life, Cameron," she said, as her cheeks turned a deep pink. "A woman has to do something while she tries to go to sleep."

"You are a vixen."

"You have pushed me to be."

"It is probably for the best that you were kept under lock and key all those years if you are so easily provoked. You would've been trouble."

She laughed., though it was not an easy sound. "I would've been. Yes. I would've been. Because believe me, those guards would've all been mine."

"Big talk."

"Who's to say my big talk isn't true. None of us can prove it."

He gritted his teeth, pushing back against the idea of Athena fantasizing about him before she went to sleep. She was being deliberately provocative. She had been that way ever since they had arrived.

But then… She'd been testing the waters with him since she had first come to the castle. Going into the tower when he had told her not to. And now pushing him physically after he had told her no.

But he had held her hand last night. And there was no earthly reason for him to do that. It wasn't a sexual gesture at all. It was something more. And he shouldn't have allowed for it to happen. But he had enjoyed the feel of her skin against his far too much.

So much for your grand declarations that you would never touch her.

Well. That was never going to work in a literal sense. Not when they had to make their debut as a couple. Not when they would absolutely have to touch in that venue. But he did not have to touch her last night. And he had anyway. It was an indictment against his soul.

What was one more?

"This looks delicious," she said. But her eyes were not on the food.

He had no idea what game she was playing. But

then… There was a chemistry between them. A magnetism. That she felt it in spite of everything was perhaps not as unfathomable as he had initially told himself.

The basic human desire to mate was not unique. And was typically not sensible.

And as she had said, she had been cloistered, and kept away from exploring her sexuality.

A pity she would not be doing it with him.

He set the crepes out before her, and put fresh cream and strawberries on the top.

Then he poured her a strong cup of coffee, and watched intently as she took her first bite. She hummed, the sound sensual. And then she took a sip of the coffee, closing her eyes for a moment before looking up in meeting his gaze.

"Thank you. For sharing this with me."

There was something unspoken then. The way she curled her lips up spoke of something intimate.

She was thinking that eating his food was tantamount to sensuality.

She wasn't wrong, unfortunately. Because he felt her enjoyment.

He was giving her something that gave her pleasure, and he could not remain unaffected by that.

She had brought his body to life in a way that he had found untenable from the moment he had first seen her.

General arousal was one thing. The desire for another person was...

Unprecedented.

Even before the accident he had never wanted one person with the ferocity he wanted her.

"It is a very short flight to London."

"I figured. Geography being what it is." She was being salty with him. And was clearly unrepentant about it.

"You need to stop being a brat. I was explaining the itinerary to a woman who has never been anywhere before. Many would find that helpful."

"You were speaking words to fill the space without having to acknowledge the tension between us."

Everything in him went hot and sharp.

"Let's acknowledge it then. I could take you in the bedroom and have you. You would enjoy it. It doesn't matter that it's been years, I know what I'm doing. I could kiss you, bare your beautiful breasts and suck your nipples into my mouth." His own words started to make him hard. Her breath hitched. And he realized he had miscalculated. He had attempted to frighten her. But she was aroused. Yes, this girl was aroused.

"Then what would you do?" she asked, the words a breath.

She was pushing, and he was through coddling her. If she wanted to push, let her see where it went. Let her see who truly held the power here.

Let her see he could unravel her without ever once putting his hands on her, because sex and desire were simple alchemy, and he knew the ingredients and wielded them well.

He growled. "I would put my hand between your legs and see if you were wet for me."

She nodded, the shining curiosity in her eyes stoking his need. Pushing him further. Making him want to push and push. He could feel his sex grow heavy with desire, his heart thundering as he saw, vividly, in his mind the picture he painted with his words.

"And then, I would stroke you. Pushed a finger inside of you while I rub my thumb over your clit. Push one finger inside of you, and then another, give you a taste of what was to come."

"Yes," she said, her eyes going glassy.

He gripped the edge of the counter, and looked across the space at her, his eyes meeting hers directly.

"I would kiss my way down your stomach, between your legs, where my tongue would slide over all that wetness. The taste of you… It would be better than this cream. I would devour you. There is nothing that tastes so good as a woman in need of satisfaction, and I bet that you are the sweetest of them all. I would eat you until you begged for me to stop. Until the pleasure was far too great. I would make you insane with it. Cry out my name."

She was shifting in her chair, her desire clearly building.

And he felt himself slipping.

Losing the intention of this little exercise.

Losing himself in her eyes.

In the way her skin went rosy and her lips parted.

"And then finally, I would take you. It would hurt the first time. But I would thrust into you hard, and take us both over the edge."

She let out a shaking breath, and he could see that she was on the edge of release without even being touched. And this was dangerous, he knew it. This was everything he should have avoided. This was…

It was words. It wasn't bodies. He had had so many words with Athena. And somehow it was different.

"Touch yourself," he gritted out.

She obeyed quickly, pushing her hand between her thighs, over the top of the robe, so she didn't reveal any part of herself. But she pressed her palm expertly against her mound, and let out a short, sharp cry. And then she slumped in her chair.

"Oh."

"That's what I would do," he said, turning away from her.

"Well let's do it then," she said, her voice sounding thick.

"No. We have business to attend."

He was affected. Shaken by what had just happened. He was so hard he was in pain. He needed another shower. Not a cold one this time.

"Why would you…? Why would you…?"

"Enough," he said. "To show you. That you are playing with me, and you don't know what you're doing. I can make you come by talking to you. I can make you feel all kinds of things, but I would not feel any of them in return. Be grateful that I refuse you the thing that you ask for. Be grateful, you stupid girl."

And then he turned, and left her sitting there, but he was not unaffected.

Not at all.

CHAPTER TWELVE

SHE FELT SHAMEFACED, on the flight to England.

She almost couldn't even enjoy the sights of Big Ben and Westminster Abbey, the London Eye, Buckingham Palace.

Almost.

He had not shamed her past the point of all enjoyment.

But she couldn't… She could not believe that she had *done* that. That she had let him spin a story that had created such a deep arousal in her that she had responded without ever…

And she supposed, that was the point of it. The lesson. Proof that she was much more naïve than she cared to admit. Much more naïve than she thought.

Yes. She supposed that was the point. He had effectively used his experience against her.

But she was not going to weep. No. She was too strong for that.

He might think that he had gotten the upper hand. But he…

He had felt something. She was sure of it. He hadn't planned that. It had just… Happened. She was nearly almost entirely certain.

She needed to believe that. Because otherwise… Otherwise, he was in much greater control of all this than she was.

Does that surprise you? You don't know anything about men. You don't know anything about life.

That wasn't true. She knew about life. She knew about what she wanted. She knew that he… That he called to her.

She could talk about the hands of guards at the compound all she wanted, and she enjoyed it, because she could see that it put him on his back foot. But none of them would have ever been able to bring her to orgasm simply by speaking.

She had *touched* herself in front of him.

Through her clothes, but the fact remained that she had done so.

She felt scalded by that.

And yet…

It had certainly been one of the more adventurous things she had ever done.

In some ways, she was proud of herself.

Because she felt as if it could only have ever been them. She was a replacement for nothing, in fact he was actively trying to resist this, which made her feel like it could only be here creating this need, and bringing him to the edge.

They arrived at the London penthouse, equally glorious to the one in Paris, with a fantastic view of the Shard.

She knew that she should be soaking in the

iconic nature of the view, but the only thing that felt iconic to her was Cameron.

She felt slightly nervous at the idea of meeting Apollo tonight.

Apollo was Cameron's only friend.

Except for her. She would not allow him to diminish the connection between them. They were friends.

Friends who had... Who had had a very charged sexual encounter this morning.

There was chemistry between them. She was clear on that.

He was the one who seemed to take issue with it.

It was tied up in him, in his own baggage, she knew that. But that didn't make it any easier to try and sort through it all.

She hadn't asked for this. She had wanted freedom. She had gone and gotten herself tangled up in possibly the most damaged man on the planet.

But he was a good man. She was sure of that.

That was... There was that at least.

But it didn't help her now. Didn't help with all of her attention.

She busied herself, getting ready for their dinner tonight.

She put on a blue dress, sleek and like midnight.

She rather enjoyed seeing her body in such provocative clothing.

She enjoyed it even more when she stepped outside and stood face-to-face with Cameron, who clearly enjoyed it as well.

"Excellent," he said. "I see you readied yourself."

"I did consider wearing a burlap sack. But I wanted to make a good impression on your friend."

"Good."

She looked at the tension in his jaw. "Are you nervous to see him?"

He turned to her, his blue eyes sharp. "I am not nervous. I do not get nervous."

She laughed. "You're a liar. You are nervous. Of course you are. You've been hidden away in a castle for the last decade. All of this is extremely new to you."

"None of it is new to me. There are no mysteries yet remaining in humanity for me, lass. People are selfish, greedy, filthy creatures. And stepping away from them for ten years will have done nothing to change that. They are also shallow and vein. I will no longer challenge their vanity, but I will engender discomfort. That's because of the shallowness. You can't win everything, I suppose."

She tried to read him. Tried to look deeper. The shock of his blue eyes, of the need she felt when she was near him made it nearly impossible. "But it won't be like that with your friend."

"Difficult to say."

"Is it only Apollo tonight?"

"Yes. He felt that it would be best."

"I agree. It is nice to know that your friends know you so well."

He growled, and she suppressed a smile.

"You don't like that. You don't like having it pointed out to you that you have friends."

"You are not my friend."

"I am. Who else have you spent this much time speaking to?"

"Of the things we have talked about? No one," he said, his voice suddenly honed to a fine blade.

She searched his face.

He was accustomed to using sex as a weapon. And of course, this was no different. The fact that he had talked to her, and not touched her even once, the fact that he had kept his distance, the fact that he had not taken his own release, all of that was part of it. Him taking control. Because he was afraid. He was afraid that she would test his control.

He didn't like it. More than that, he loathed it. She had the power to challenge him. Whether or not he wanted to admit that. He wanted to pretend that he was immune. To everything. But he wasn't.

And she was… She was learning something. How to knit herself into another person's life. How to develop a relationship. And yes, she supposed in many ways theirs was built on forced proximity in the same way her relationship with Rose had been. But it felt different also. She didn't have to befriend him. He hadn't had to talk to her. They were a means to an end for one another, and yet for some reason, in spite of all that, they had gotten to know each other. It felt real. And it felt like it mattered.

They rode in the limousine to a large manor house outside of the city.

"Does he live here?" she asked, breathing out and in.

"Yes. Sometimes. Apollo goes wherever he wishes."

"It's amazing."

"He will preen if you show him that sort of appreciation when you meet him. He loves to impress."

"Well, I am suitably impressed."

And she could see that statement put Cameron in a dark mood. She would be lying if she said she didn't appreciate that. That she had roused jealousy in him.

For that was what it was. She was impressed with his friend's house, and he didn't like it.

They walked to the front door, which was opened for them ceremoniously.

She held on to Cameron's arm as they were ushered into a grand foyer that was every bit as grand as the exterior had been.

Robin's-egg blue wallpaper and gold details created a clean, stunning site. But it was the restored gold chandelier hanging from the ceiling that truly stole the show.

"This is *glorious*," she said.

And then, a tall, dark-haired man in a suit walked in. His jawline was sharp, clean-shaven. His brown eyes were nearly black, his skin golden brown. He had broad shoulders and large hands. He was truly one of the most beautiful men she had ever seen.

It was an easy sort of beauty.

It reminded her of the easy romance that she had seen while they were walking in Paris.

Cameron did not have an easy beauty.

But it compelled her.

He compelled her.

She wasn't sure what it said about her that she didn't want easy. That as beautiful as she could see Apollo was, he did not appeal to her in that same way.

Goddess of war...

Perhaps that was it. Perhaps she was destined to be at war. Perhaps it was what she craved.

She knew for certain that she didn't want soft. She knew for certain that she didn't want to bend easily, nor did she want anyone to easily bend around her.

All those things became clear when she gazed upon the glorious visage of Apollo.

Because many women would have fallen to their knees then. Melted down at his feet.

And she felt absolutely no inclination toward it.

"You must be Athena," Apollo said, grinning widely. "How nice to meet a fellow Greek."

He spoke to her in Greek. She spoke back in Greek.

"I do not know that I'm Greek, though I have learned Greek."

He frowned. "Athena? Your name is certainly Greek. And you speak it as if you have spoken it from the cradle."

"I…"

She was stunned then because…of course. Her family had been Russian, and she was Athena, which she'd thought was a bit of an extravagance, but perhaps it wasn't.

She'd felt as if Greek was a language she'd learned, yet much like English she didn't remember learning it.

Maybe she had always known.

"Sadly for you both, I speak Greek. Because of you," Cameron said, directing that at Apollo and redirecting Athena's musings.

"One of my many sins." His gaze raked dispassionately over Cameron.

"It is good to see you."

"Is it?"

"Yes," Apollo said, and Athena was almost certain that she heard his voice get rough with emotion, even if it was only a slight change.

"You're both ridiculous," said Athena. "You love each other. You might as well show it."

"That's a very strong word," said Apollo. "But we spent a great many years needing each other, that much is certain."

"It is good to see you," said Cameron, his voice desperately flat, which Athena knew meant that he was fighting back emotion of some kind.

"*Men.* Honestly. Is it so terrible to admit that you're friends? And that you have hated your separation?"

"I have not hated our separation," said Apollo. "With Cameron gone I have much less competition for women."

"Are you so simple?" asked Athena.

"Yes. I am." But there was a dark light behind his eyes that told her he was not. And anyone who mistook him for being simply a beautiful face would find themselves at a disadvantage indeed.

She looked back at Cameron. "Are you going to say anything emotionally literate?"

Cameron looked bland. Which was no mean feat. "I've no plans to."

She let out an exasperated sigh. "I suppose we best go in and have dinner. Since we are not going to have the emotional reunion I was hoping for."

"Are you invested in an emotional reunion?" Apollo asked.

"I am invested in Cameron's emotions."

She could feel Cameron's gaze on her. Fierce,

and questioning. He didn't understand why she would freely admit that. But why would she be ashamed? She cared for him. She wasn't embarrassed by that. She was… She was happy about it.

Here she had spent all these years shut away, and now she was friends with him. She was… She wanted him.

She wasn't ashamed at that. She was glad of it.

"Are you? I confess, I was not sure in what manner Cameron managed to convince you to present yourself as his wife."

"He is not presenting me as his wife. I *am* his wife."

Apollo looked between the two of them. "Indeed. How interesting."

She looked at Cameron and treated him to a sunny smile. "He's very noble, actually. He saved me. I owe him a great debt."

Cameron growled. "I did not save you. I took you prisoner."

She patted his hand. "I think we both know that isn't true." She grinned at Apollo.

"You got soft in your time rusticating."

"I am *not* soft," said Cameron.

"You certainly don't look it."

"No," Cameron agreed, his lip curling.

"Let's not get into that." Athena sat down next to him. "Let's just have dinner."

"She is quite something," said Apollo.

"She is *irritating*," said Cameron.

For some reason the exchange cheered Athena immensely.

"You look much more ready for tomorrow night than I anticipated. If she has accomplished that, she has certainly done more than I've ever managed to do it all those years of phone conversations. I applaud her."

"Thank you," she said to Apollo. "It is nice to be appreciated. Cameron appreciates me, he just can't admit it."

That earned her another sharp gaze, but she was enjoying herself far too much to be chastened.

She had been embarrassed earlier. About her response to him.

But she felt... Free of that now. Did it matter she cared for him? If she wanted him. There were other things holding him back, things that had nothing to do with whether or not he wanted her.

It was the same reason he could not cry with joy and give his friend a hug because he had seen him for the first time in ten years.

He was a prisoner to his feelings.

She didn't need to take that personally. And she did not need to be a prisoner of hers simply because he was.

She didn't have to be a prisoner anymore at all.

She heard footsteps, and looked up. Standing in the doorway was a very young-looking woman with wide, luminous eyes. She smiled, and her blue eyes sparkled.

"You didn't tell me that we had guests, Apollo."

"I thought that you would be studying."

"I was. But then I got hungry. Very mean not to tell me."

Athena was confused for a moment about what relationship he might have to this… This girl.

But then she stepped into the room, and met Athena's gaze. "Hello. I am Hannah. Apollo is my guardian."

"Oh," said Athena.

Cameron, for his part, looked questioningly at his friend.

"I don't usually live here," she said. "But I am on holiday from school."

"Yes, and she has a final exam yet to take before she is fully on break."

When Apollo addressed her, she blushed, her cheeks turning a deep rose. "Yes. I do. So… I can't stay for dinner but…"

"You can stay," he said.

She smiled happily, and took a seat next to him.

Athena, for her part, was grateful for the company, even though the girl was quite a few years younger than her. She had actually been to university, so… She knew more about the world than Athena did.

After dinner, the men got up and retired to the study to discuss business. And that left Athena alone with Hannah.

"He's terrifying," she said, clearly speaking of Cameron.

Athena went rigid. "He isn't."

"I didn't mean because… You know, they just both have that… That manner about them. Apollo would terrify me if I didn't know him. He's been very good to me since my parents died."

"I'm sorry," said Athena.

Hannah forced a smile. "It's okay. I mean… It isn't. But they were never very much around when I was younger anyway. I was away at school all through the year, and then even when I was home they were often gone. Off on adventures. When I was sixteen they… They were killed in an accident. They were on a canoeing trip and their boat capsized. It was terrible. But my father was good friends with Apollo, and he… Anyway, Apollo is the manager of my trust. And my guardian. Until I am twenty-five."

Looking at her, Athena guessed that was a few years away.

"And how old are you now?"

"Nineteen." She smiled very prettily, in that way nineteen-year-olds could.

"He gives you freedom?" Athena asked.

"Oh, yes. I'm very grateful to him."

But there was something hollow in the way that she said that.

"And you and Cameron are… You're his wife?"

She nodded. "Yes."

She felt sort of guilty, but she didn't know how far their ruse needed to go.

"It must be quite something. To have all that focus on you."

There was a wistfulness in Hannah's tone that made Athena feel sorry for her.

Then she wondered... If she was any different than this girl. Who wanted a man so far out of her reach he might as well have been on another planet.

No, you know it isn't real. The desire might be, but you know you will have to move on after. You might be Greek. You might have a family. McKenzie is just a name he gave you, but it isn't your name. You have to find your name. Remember that.

CHAPTER THIRTEEN

"ALL THE TIMES we talked and you managed not to tell me that you have a ward."

"It wasn't relevant to any of our business."

"I see."

He stared at his friend hard.

"Don't judge me," Apollo said. "Athena is clearly under your thumb. And you know exactly which way I mean that."

"I haven't touched her. Not the way that you mean."

He hadn't. Even now, he hadn't.

"But you *want* to," Apollo said.

"She's beautiful. Who wouldn't want to?"

Apollo poured himself a measure of scotch, then turned to look at Cameron. "Why the sudden pretense that you're a man of honor?"

"I might ask you the same." He looked hard at Apollo. He only *suspected*, he wasn't *certain*, but when his friend looked away, it confirmed it.

He had a forbidden attraction to his ward. A woman who was substantially younger than him, and under his protection.

"Touché." He knocked back his scotch, his breath hissing through his teeth. "I have done very few things in my life that are worthy of being called honorable. Looking after Hannah is one of the few. I owed her father. He was... He was a friend."

"Friends I don't know about."

"You disappeared for a decade. You don't get to be childish about the fact that I had other friends. It is my job to take care of her, and I will."

And he didn't have to ask Apollo why that meant he could never put his hands on her. Because it was the same reason he wouldn't touch Athena.

They were damaged. Women who had even the slightest air of innocence about them were not for them.

Not in the slightest.

They'd cauterized their souls long ago to keep from bleeding out, and they were bonded over this, but he very much doubted they could truly bond to anyone else. Even their relationship was not...

They were not emotionally literate, as Athena herself had said.

"And you really do intend to let her go once this is all over?"

"Yes," Cameron confirmed. "I have promised her freedom. And my protection."

"Perhaps there is hope for both of us then. Perhaps we can at least play men of honor when we need to."

"I do not give myself so much credit."

Apollo paused. "Do you know anything about where she came from."

"She was the adopted child of a crime lord. Russian."

Apollo looked thoughtful. "That is very interesting. I had an interaction recently with a man called Castor Xenakis and he was recently reunited with his sister. She's married, and free now, has been for a year. But she worked as a maid for a crime lord. Russian, I believe."

The words resonated inside of him.

"Athena told me that her only friend at the compound was a maid, and they were Russian."

Apollo arched a brow. "Interesting. Don't you think? For what it's worth, I believe she is Greek, or at least of a family who is, she speaks the language too well."

"Do I not speak it well?"

"No," Apollo said, simply.

"And where is Castor Xenakis now and how do I get in touch with him?"

"He will be there tomorrow. Perhaps it would do you well to meet him. And Athena as well."

"I do not wish to expose Athena to any sort of danger. If there is even a chance that anyone there will—"

"No. Castor is on a mission to end that man. Whatever he intended for Athena, Castor will help keep her safe if anything. And he may have an idea of who her family is."

"You think she has a family?"

"Well, if the maid did, why wouldn't Athena?"

It was true. If the maid had a family, why wouldn't Athena?

All of this was very interesting. Very interesting indeed.

"Tomorrow," said Apollo. "You can ask Castor yourself."

CHAPTER FOURTEEN

FOR THE PRODUCT launch itself she decided to wear gold.

The dress that she wore was nearly like armor, gold leaves made of metal fashioned into a bodice that clung to her curves. The skirt was a shiny material that shimmered like liquid when she moved. She had tied her hair back tightly, and applied her makeup in a dramatic fashion, her eyes smoky and seductive. If she said so herself.

She took a breath before walking out of the room, and put on her necklace.

Have courage. Take heart.

She pictured what it had been like when she'd done the same in Paris. When she'd seen him standing there in his suit.

It made her smile. That this wasn't the first time. That they were them. And this was something they did.

She walked into the living area, but he wasn't there.

She turned a circle. "Cameron."

He did not answer.

"Cameron!"

He didn't answer.

So she walked right for the door of his bedroom, and without knocking, she opened it.

He had been standing bent over the desk, gripping the edge. Wearing nothing but a pair of dark trousers, his torso bare.

He stood, straightening, his dark hair loose around his shoulders, his blue eyes intense.

His body...

He had scars. His body had not been spared them. But his muscles were... Glorious.

Her mouth dried.

He was perfection.

The scars only enhanced it.

He was like a thing honed from rock. A mountain.

He was power and glory. And while he made her mouth dry, he made that place between her thighs wet.

She barely held back the gasp of pleasure that rose in her throat, but the sound was enough to shake him from his thoughts.

"What?" he asked. It was a growl more than a question, but she was used to that with him.

"We have to go," she said.

She took a step toward him, and he took a step back.

He had the look of a predator, assessing the situation. Knowing that there were only two options. To flee or to inflict lethal damage.

"I am just finishing getting ready."

His jacket and shirt were on the back of his

chair, a tie draped over the top of them. He had upended a chair, she could see. He was...not well.

"Can you admit to me that you're having difficulty with this?"

"It is... I did this many times before. Before the accident. Before I looked... I did this many times before. Many of the people in the room will be people who knew me then. It is... I cannot stand pity. I cannot."

"Why not?"

"Because I'm a *man*. I am not a broken *thing*."

"But surely you have experienced pity before to hate it so much?"

He laughed, hard and cynical. "Yes. I have. Well spotted."

"Why is it so bad?" she asked, her tone a near whisper.

"When they pity you they take advantage of you. When you let yourself be pitied, you begin to feel sorry for yourself. And when you begin to feel sorry for yourself, you embrace that needy, horrid thing inside of you that demands you let them touch you. I do not need pity."

"You're afraid of it. Because that woman..."

"*Enough.* You don't know me. Nobody does."

"*I* know you. I do. You can say that I don't, you can try to be angry about it. You can push back at me all you wish, but I do know you, Cameron. She shamed you. You wanted affection and she used that against you. And you are afraid of having that happen to you again. It is logical. Reasonable. There is nothing wrong with you that you wish to avoid being hurt like that again. But you do have control now. You are not that boy. You have Apollo. And you have me. We won't let you down."

"I don't need anyone."

"And it would be so bad if you did?"

"Yes," he said, his tone caustic. Bitter.

"Cameron," she said softly. "Why is it so bad to have people who care."

"Because it means nothing. In the end it means nothing. People will choose their personal addictions every time over connection and it will never, ever last. And then what are you left with? Nothing."

And he stood there, looking at the white shirt sitting on the chair.

Everything in her felt jagged, broken. And suddenly the necklace around her neck burned.

She walked over to the chair, and lifted the shirt up. "Come on," she said.

He didn't move. But she did. She walked up to him and unbuttoned the cuff of the shirt, maneuvering it slowly over his hand, and up his shoulder. The touch felt erotic, and yet she hadn't meant it to be, but there was an intimacy to this she hadn't counted on. "I have no problem getting you ready to go myself."

"What the hell are you doing?" He was affected, or he wouldn't be angry.

"I'll dress you if I need to."

"I'm not a *child* or an *invalid*," he said, but allowing her to shrug the shirt up over his other arm too, and draw it into place. She looked up at him, so close. She could smell his skin again. She loved the way he smelled. She began to button the shirt. And that made her smile even broader.

"What?"

"I have to say, I've had quite a few thoughts about the buttons of your shirt these last few days. But I never imagined doing them *up*."

He put his hand over hers, and stilled her movements. "You play a dangerous game."

"You keep telling me that. And yet, I find myself consequence-free. I imagine you want to tuck it in yourself."

He did so, and she took his jacket off the back of the chair as well, putting it into place. She left the jacket open, let the top two buttons on his shirt undone.

"You don't need a tie. For the shirt or for your hair. Leave it like this. You keep thinking that you have to step up to the podium and be the man you were before. But you're not. You're the man you are now. Look at you." She moved out of the way so that he could see himself in the mirror, and he lowered his head.

"Look at yourself," she repeated.

He lifted his head slowly, and she could see the moment his eyes met his own there.

Then she moved to him, and she reached up and unhooked her necklace.

"You're strong, Cameron McKenzie. You do not need to be the Cameron McKenzie you were before. I cannot be the Athena I was before I was taken to my family. I don't even remember who I was. I can only be the Athena I am now." She turned him toward her, and put her hands on his chest. She could feel his heart raging there. "I am the Athena that I decide to be. Your warrior goddess. Thank you. For giving that to me." She put her hand over his, then slipped it from where he clung to the vanity, and turned his hand palm up.

Then she pressed the necklace into his hand.

Have Courage. Take Heart.

He looked into her eyes, deep. She felt it like a touch.

Like his words earlier, but different. Sexual yes, but more than that.

Deeper.

This, she thought, was like making love. She knew another person might never understand.

But Cameron had had sex with strangers. All physical, no feeling. What he did not have was someone to piece him together when he was broken. To touch him, just to touch him, and not to get anything back.

To listen to him. Understand him.

He took the necklace, and slipped it into his pocket, then put his hand over hers and held it there, hard. Firm. "You are strong," he said. "Do not let anyone make you feel different."

"So are you."

When he lowered his hand, he kept hold of hers.

"Shall we go then? You have a product to launch."

"Yes," he said, his voice rough. "I do."

CHAPTER FIFTEEN

HE COULD NOT explain what had happened in the room. He could not explain the weakness that had overtaken him when he had been frozen, barely able to bring himself to put the shirt and suit jacket on. He could not explain why he had allowed Athena to do it for him.

Yet somehow, when she did it, it was as if she was putting armor in place for him. As though they were going into battle together.

And now they were standing outside the venue, all lit up with banners hanging down the side, promising the largest product launch in the company's history.

He could explain what he had created effortlessly. Could explain to everyone in the room why they wanted it. And yet...

Was it fear that he felt now?

There had been a time in his life when fear had been a constant companion. He had purposed in himself to never feel it again.

Maybe that was a foolish thing.

When he had nearly died in that car accident, he had felt fear. When he had watched the life drain from Irina, he had felt fear.

Perhaps he had never left it behind. Perhaps, like when he was a boy on the street, it had simply become part of him, and he had not noticed it anymore. Had not been able to call it for what it was.

But with Athena by his side, he felt stronger.

Have Courage. Take Heart.

He had got that for her and then…

Somehow it had been right for him.

He had lost his sense of why he had wanted her there in the first place. It had been about public opinion at first. But that wasn't the case now. Now he recognized that he wanted her there because of himself.

Because he actually… He wanted to do this. He wanted to show that he was capable.

To show that he didn't need pity. They walked up the stairs slowly, and when they entered the crowded ballroom, there was a hush that fell over the crowd.

It was to be expected. And that, he thought, was a better reason than any not to delay the announcement until later. So with Athena on his arm, he walked straight to the center of the room, and right toward the podium.

He stood in front of the microphone, and he could see Apollo standing down there in the front of the crowd, looking at him questioningly.

"I know this was not the scheduled time for the speech." he said. "But let us not pretend that I'm not the elephant in the room, so to speak. I have not been in the public eye these last ten years. And I know there were rumors about why. You can see that they were true. The accident that I was in ten years ago, that made headlines around the world, and left supermodel Irina Sharapova dead, disfigured me. During that time, I went away to heal. During that time, I put my mind to good use, and I have spent all that time making this new smart home system. It is leagues beyond anything that we have ever done before. Leagues beyond anything anyone has ever done before. From facial recognition, to remote access, nonverbal cues and accessibility features, it is the most sophisticated system for any home. I was able to turn an entire medieval castle into a high-tech wonder. We will do a demonstration of the features later on tonight, but I felt that you should know that I believe strongly enough in the product that I've shown my face for the first time in ten years."

"And who is the woman?" The question came from one of the reporters at the front of the room.

"This is Athena McKenzie. My wife. So I guess you could say I have not only worked on product development these last ten years.

"No further questions about my personal life," he said. "The focus of this is the new smart home system, and nothing more."

He gripped her hand tightly, and led her down the stairs.

And then, he took her out to the dance floor. "It is time to put our rehearsals to good use, don't you think?"

"I…"

He brought her into his arms, and the feeling of her pressed against him was more potent now. Now that he had seen her eyes go cloudy with pleasure. Now that he had watched her find her release.

Now that she had dressed him. Now that she had heard his darkest secrets.

She would go on to live brilliantly. She would go on to be the woman that she wanted to be. She would find her family. He would see to that.

But for now, they would dance.

This was all he would allow himself. The only intimacy.

No matter how he wanted her.

Precisely because he wanted her, that was why. That was why he couldn't have her.

Athena's heart was still pounding. Her hands rested on his neck. She wanted to kiss him. How was it they hadn't kissed? It seemed wrong.

It seemed as if she would've had to kiss him a hundred times. She was his wife. Tonight she had buttoned his shirt for him. Put his jacket in place. She had been his support the way that a wife ought to be.

But they had never kissed.

Her lips burned with the need of it. And yet her soul was ignited by the knowledge that she had him in ways no one else ever had.

You are not remembering to let it be only desire...

How could she?

There was no *only* desire.

Not with him.

Not with them.

She was lit up with the knowledge of him in a way she was certain only lovers could be.

They went through the evening, dancing, dinner. Everyone wanted to talk to Cameron. And Cameron was...incredible.

Finally, hours later, they had a moment to breathe.

"Cameron..."

"Cameron," said Apollo's voice from behind them. Athena turned, and they stopped dancing. There was a man, a sinfully gorgeous man, standing next to Apollo, and on his arm, was an equally beautiful woman.

"This is Castor Xenakis, and his wife Glory. I told you that Castor recently found his sister."

"Yes," said Castor. "My sister Ismena—Rose, as you know her, was just rescued from the compound of a crime lord."

And Athena's world went sideways.

"What?" Athena asked, or she thought she did.

Maybe she just screamed it. Inside her own head.

"With Ares's help, that's Rose's husband, I've collected some information that might be of use to you." Castor was still talking. Athena's ears were buzzing.

"I…"

"I think I have information on where to find your family. There was a news story. It was part of my search. I spent years looking for human trafficking victims. There was a missing girl called Athena. Taken from a beach. She and her twin brother were kidnapped. They were held for three months."

"No… A twin brother?" She felt like she was breaking apart. Like something inside of her was being shattered.

"Please don't tell her all of this here," said Cameron, putting his arm around her waist. "If there's somewhere where you can speak privately…"

"I apologize. Do you not remember any of this?"

Athena shook her head. "I don't."

"Let's go," he said. "To the garden in the back."

Cameron held tightly to her as they were propelled out of the venue. Once they were outside, Castor reached into his jacket and took out a file. "It's all here."

And suddenly, something in her mind broke wide open. "Constantine Kamaras. My brother is Constantine. He was my twin. And there was… A baby."

"I… There are some things in that file you will want to look at. Some things that you will need to know. Cameron, may I speak with you for a second?"

Castor took Cameron aside while Athena sat there, trying to catch her breath. He came back a moment later. "We don't have to stay," he said.

"Yes, we do," she said. "It's… It's for you it's…"

"Tomorrow. We will go back to America tomorrow. We will arrange to meet your family. I have already talked to Apollo about speaking to them."

"We can't just… I don't know…"

She was fighting memories, and also reaching for them. She could remember forcing a boy to sit and watch a cartoon with her about ponies…

This is stupid, Athena. But you will do stupid things for me!

She'd grinned at him. Just like she did to Cameron now when she suggested something silly and he reacted darkly.

Perhaps she'd started training to handle Cameron even back them.

She saw more fragments in her mind.

A woman, beautiful and glamorous. Her mother?

A handsome man in a suit, graying. And an older man who was completely gray. A father and grandfather?

Then there was a baby…

"My mother and father?"

"Living," he said.

"My baby brother…"

"Let us speak more about this after."

"But…"

"Athena, this was too much to ask you to think about here. Let us speak more after."

She made it through the rest of the evening feeling numb.

Cameron's presentation was amazing, but she could hardly grasp the details. She had a family.

She had a family. So had Rose, the entire time.

Had it been the man who'd adopted her who had kidnapped her? She didn't think so.

She didn't think so.

She didn't know why, only that…there was some darkness. A gap…

They got into the limo after, and she looked over at Cameron. "Will you tell me? Will you tell me everything?" For some reason the most desperate thing was about the baby in her memory.

"I am very sorry to tell you this, but your younger brother passed. A year ago."

Something in her broke. The little dark-haired boy went from pudgy baby to wicked toddler. He'd been maybe two or three the last time she'd seen him.

And she would never see him again.

"*No*," she said. "That isn't fair. Isn't fair that I would miss him like this I…"

"I know. Your twin is married. He is the father of twins himself."

She felt awash in emotion. Pain. She had a twin brother. He was a father. That made her not only a sister, a twin, but an aunt as well. And the youngest brother…

She tried to remember him.

She remembered playing on the beach with the dark-haired boy. Her age. Dark eyes. She remembered feeling connected to him. Deeply connected. As if he was another part of her.

As if she could sense what he was thinking. Feeling.

"I remember. I remember Constantine. My twin he…"

There was a bedroom. And everything in it was butterflies. She could remember jumping on the bed with him. Laughing, reaching for the little paper butterflies that hung from the bed.

"I have a family. I wonder if my mother and father still…"

"According to this file, they live still."

"I need to go to them. I need…"

"Of course you do. Of course you need to go to them. Right away."

"Cameron, you will come with me."

"I will take you to America. I will take you as far as that."

She looked up at him, her heart suddenly torn. This was what she'd wanted, come to her sooner than she could have imagined. And Cameron… who had not left Scotland or his castle other than this past week, for a decade was willing to fly to America for her as if it was no more than a ride across the moors on Aslan.

"We should call them first… Will we…"

"I'll have Apollo contact them. We will make sure that they are ready for your arrival."

"Thank you. How can I ever thank you. You made me a real person tonight, and now you're giving me back my family."

"I guess now you know. You are Athena Kamaras."

Athena who remembered nothing of who she was, that Athena would have loved that without condition, would have lived for this. It was not the family that made her ache now. It was the name. She had been Athena McKenzie.

She had been so certain she would not cling to that, and yet now she felt she was.

And Cameron was so quick to want that undone. It hurt, and it shouldn't.

Kamaras.

She was a Kamaras. She had a family. A place.

Where she was the desired daughter. Not a replacement. Not a doll.

It was all she had ever wanted.

She blinked to keep tears from falling. "Yes. Yes. Now I know."

CHAPTER SIXTEEN

ATHENA WAS VERY quiet the entire plane ride to the United States. Her family lived in Massachusetts, out in the country. He had done his due diligence on them, to make sure that they were the sort of people she should be brought to.

And he… His time with her would now be at an end. He would take her to her family, and he would leave her there. It was perhaps the most selfless thing he had ever done. Because everything inside of him wished to hold on to her. To crush her against his body and claim her for his own. To make her his in every possible way.

Yes, everything in him longed to do that. Absolutely everything.

But he could not. Because he might be a beast on the outside, but he had learned to care for someone other than himself. What he wanted was Athena's happiness. And he could never give that to her.

"I remembered something else," she said softly.

"What is that?"

"I remembered the day we were taken. It was terrifying. Constantine fought. He fought everyone. He tried to save me. They separated us. I was put in a small room, and given tea. Given cookies to eat. I was lonely, and I was afraid of what was happening to Constantine. And then… They told me my brother died. They told me that Constantine was dead. And then they took me into a small room, and everything after that is blank. I think it was the trauma of hearing that my twin had died. I think it is what stole my memories. They told me… They told me he was dead. And…"

Even now he could see that it hurt her to talk about this. Even knowing her brother was not dead. He could see the little girl she'd been, the fear, the terror. She wanted to comfort him.

"He is not. He lives."

"My younger brother. He is dead."

"Unfortunately. He died in a car accident. Your return to your family will undoubtedly bring them great joy. It will heal some of the wounds. Can you imagine. Your parents must feel as if they lost two children. And now you've returned to them."

"That is quite a lot of pressure."

"I don't have a family to return to. I don't say that to try and make you feel only good things, because of course this will be tinged with all manner of bittersweet joy and pain. Only that it is a miracle to have this. I want you to look forward. Not back."

She nodded slowly. "Of course."

He sat down next to her. And she closed the distance between them by putting her hand on his. He did not pull away.

The plane landed on a private airfield, and his

car took them to the edge of the property. Right up to the gates. They parted for them, opening wide. Just as the clouds gave way, and the rain began to fall.

And he felt like something had given way inside of him as well.

This is why you can never let anyone too close.

This was why.

He had never wished to care, not again. He had never wished to want, not again.

He had worked too hard to harden himself.

Far too hard to let it all be undone now.

She got out of the car, and stood there for a moment, looking up at the house. "I remember this place," she whispered.

"And what are your memories?" He needed to know that she would be safe here. He needed to know that she wanted to be here.

"I was happy. My mother... My mother loved me. My father..."

"Good. Then it is time for me to let you go."

She turned to him, slowly. There was no sound around them except for the rain, and he hated it.

"You're not coming in with me?" she asked.

He shook his head. "This is something you need to do on your own. You do not need me, Athena. I was a man who was small enough to take you captive, because I could not go out into the world, and so I tried to keep you with me. I did that with a stag. I did that with Aslan. But you are not an an-

imal. You are a woman. And you are not mine to
tame and to keep. I should have you wild, Athena.
You are the goddess of war. And you are strong."
He reached his hand out, and pressed the necklace he had bought her into her palm. "Thank
you for giving me the use of this. But I will send
it to you now."

"No... Cameron..."

The rain slid over her face, like tears, and it
took him a moment to realize that there were tears
there as well. Mingled with the raindrops.

Her sadness at leaving him was real.

She should not be sad. She was going back to
her family. She was leaving him. She was finally
getting the freedom that she wanted.

"Go," he said. "Go and do not think of me
again."

"But I will. I will every day. Cameron... You
cannot possibly... You cannot."

"Go, Athena."

She turned to look at the house one more time,
and took two steps away from him. And he felt
that piece of himself that had given way exit his
body and begin to move away with her.

He knew he would never get it back.

He did not want it back.

And suddenly she stopped. She turned toward
him, and she ran. Her body hit his with the force
of a soldier on the attack. She wrapped her arms

around his neck, stretched up on her toes, and she kissed him. Deep and hard.

She parted her lips, her tongue tangling with his. And he was powerless. Powerless in the face of this glorious tactical maneuver. This conquering.

He held her.

And he kissed her. Like he was starving. Like he would never be filled again. Like there was nothing except this moment. Except them.

Like his face wasn't ruined.

Like his soul wasn't ruined.

Like he didn't have to give her away to set her free. He clung to her. And she to him.

His skin was damp and slick, the kiss even more so.

But hot with it. Needy. Greedy.

Ten years of deprivation. And yet, he knew he had never kissed another person like this.

Kissing was not something he had indulged himself in.

It was not part of paying for sex.

And it was not part of control.

There was no control in this at all.

He had given sex away with no thought at all. For many, many years. He did indulge in all manner of depravity. And yet this was somehow new. This was like an entirely different experience. When Athena took his hand, he felt like a virgin. When Athena had pulled his dress shirt onto him, buttoned it for him, it had felt more erotic than anything he had ever experienced.

And when she kissed him, she branded his soul.

He was jaded and hardened, scarred and he had no defenses against this. This was unlike anything. She was unlike anything.

And that was why he had to release her.

He stepped away.

His heart was raging, his body begging for him to take her. Begging for him to put her back in the car and lay her across the back seat and have his way with her.

But he would not. Because the man that he was, that man would have done so. That man would've taken this moment meant for her, and he would've made it his own. That man would have kept her under lock and key simply to satisfy his own needs. He would not do that. Not to her. Because she would not be another casualty of his casual lust. Of his need for control. Of his utterly bankrupt soul.

She would not be his victim.

Because Athena was too glorious to be anyone's victim.

She would walk on. Free of him.

And she would soar.

He knew that she would. Because she had been glory and strength personified from the moment he had first seen her, even curled up in the bottom of that hovel. Even that had spoken of her strength.

"Go," he said, cupping her chin with his thumb and forefinger, brushing away the water droplets on her lips. "You have found the life that you were meant to live. You have found your freedom. Take great joy in it."

And then it was he who turned away from her.

He got in the back seat of the car, for he could no longer drive. He told his driver to take him away from there.

And he knew then that he was as much a prisoner now as he had ever been. He still couldn't drive. He still couldn't have her. He was still scarred.

And he would go back to the castle. One successful launch event did not heal wounds as deep as his own. There was only one thing in his life that he could feel remotely proud of.

He had set her free.

If he could not have changed. If he could not have healing. If he could never himself be whole, then he would have that.

It would have to be enough.

CHAPTER SEVENTEEN

ATHENA WAS SHAKING, from the inside out by the time she walked up to the door. She heard Cameron's car pull away, and something broke within her. She was about to meet her family. And she was elated to have come this far. Filled with joy at finding them, and yet… She would be leaving Cameron behind. And that felt devastating. That felt like a blow she was not certain she could recover from.

Look at everything you have lived through. This will not crush you.

But she had to kiss him. And it was…

She closed her eyes for just a moment, and relived that. The glorious crush of his mouth against hers. His heat and his strength. Her desire to be closer, closer still, the realization that she would never be able to be close enough.

She had been such a childish thing when she had first met him. Her notions of romance had been so soft.

Cameron had ruined her. He had ruined those dreams. Because she had tasted something much sharper and clearer than she had ever been able to manufacture in the mists of her mind. He had shown her that she was a warrior. And soft and simple would never do.

Good your life is soft and simple. Here you are. On the verge of meeting your family. Either the fulfillment of their dreams or the reopening of a wound.

She took a breath and squared her shoulders, and knocked.

The door opened. And she was face-to-face with a woman, two inches shorter than herself, black hair pulled back into a bun. She was beautiful. "It's you," the woman said. "Athena. Athena." And she started to cry. She reached out and wrapped her arms around Athena, and Athena new.

"Mom."

She was ushered inside, where her father was. And she suddenly just knew who they were. And she felt it. It was a reunion, as her memories came flooding back to her. They were not strangers. She was not meeting her family. She was being reunited with them.

"I can't believe this," her father said, kissing her head. "After all these years."

"Yes. I'm here."

And then she looked up, and saw at the bottom of the grand staircase, a man. Tall and dark, his intensity bright and clear. There was a woman with red hair standing next to him, holding him tight.

"Do you remember me?" he asked, his voice rough.

"Of course, Constantine." Athena smiled, and

for some reason she remembered the silliest thing. "Do you remember, we used to watch that cartoon about ponies."

And he didn't speak. He took a step forward and folded her into his arms. And for the first time she felt the completeness that she had forgotten ever existed within her.

"We have a lot of catching up to do," he said, his voice rough.

They sat together for hours. And when her parents went to bed, and Morgan gave Constantine a kiss and went upstairs, it left just her and Constantine.

"Tomorrow you'll meet the children," he said. "When I found out Morgan was having twins I…"

"Twins. That's wonderful."

"It did not feel wonderful. I felt as if I had let you down, Athena. I thought you were dead. All these years."

"They told me you were dead. And I think it broke me. I didn't remember. I didn't remember my family. I didn't remember where I came from."

"Apollo told us that you had been adopted. By a different family than the one who kidnapped us."

She nodded. "Yes. I couldn't remember anything before I came to them. I understand now it was because of what happened to us when we were with the kidnapper. When he told me that you were dead."

"I remembered. All these years, I remembered.

They tortured me by telling me they were hurting you."

"I'm sorry. No harm ever came to me. I was kept safe. Kept away from the world. I didn't know who I was. And when the man that I called Father decided to sell me off in marriage I escaped."

"When was this?"

"A month ago. I escaped and I found a castle. As fantastical as it sounds."

"Nothing sounds too far-fetched after my experience with losing you and finding you again. I heard Castor Xenakis saved you."

"Cameron McKenzie saved me."

"Cameron McKenzie? The tech genius? The one that disappeared from society ten years ago and reappeared with... With his wife."

"Yes."

"I did see something about all of that, but I hadn't looked closely because immediately after I received a phone call from Apollo telling me that you were alive. He said nothing of Cameron, and these last twenty-four hours has been a blur of us coming to terms with this... This unexpected miracle."

"I married him. To help him reenter society. He married me to keep me safe. He knew that if I was his wife my father would not simply be able to find me again and... He isn't my father. That man that I just sat with here for hours is my father."

"You were told about Alex?"

"Yes. I am very sorry to hear that."

"Me too. He was a difficult child. A selfish man. But he would've changed. Given enough time. I will never think it was fair that he lost the ability to try."

"You met and married Morgan around that time."

He laughed. "Morgan was… She was Alex's fiancée. It's a long story."

"We have all the time in the world."

It was only later the next morning that Athena got the text from Apollo. She did not know how he had gotten her information.

"I wanted to give you Cameron's information. So you can reach him. This is the access to his intercom system. So that you can speak to him at the castle."

He gave her instructions to download an app, and a code to enter to talk to him.

Her mouth went dry.

She knew that Cameron had meant to leave her here.

But he was her husband. And she did not wish to leave him.

She had what she'd set out to get. A place. And she felt like she had one here, truly. The Kamaras family had already shown her more love in this short space of time than the people she'd known as her family ever had.

But she still wanted.

She still wanted *him*.

She had told herself over and over it wasn't real, and yet she knew now that it was. Because when put back into the life she'd been stolen from, she still wanted him.

Still felt married to him.

She entered the information quickly, and she thanked Apollo, who didn't respond. And then she opened the app, and pressed the button.

"I'm fine, not that you asked."

Hearing his voice made her heart leap.

"It is evening here. And how did you get this information?"

"I think you can guess."

"Be with your family, Athena."

"I *am* with my family. And don't speak to me if you don't wish, but I'm going to share with you."

And she did. She told him about her family. About Constantine, about his wife. All the stories that she heard about her brother Alex.

She talked to Cameron every day.

He did not all always talk back, but she decided she didn't need him to.

She was not willing to break her connection with Cameron.

She was home for Christmas, and still she spoke to Cameron every day. She got to know her niece and nephew, her sister-in-law, who was a lovely woman with a brilliant smile.

She reconnected with Rose—Ismena. She went and visited her and Ares at his villa in Greece. And then went with her family after that on a vacation on Constantine's private island.

She saw the world. She could dress how she liked. She went shopping with Morgan, she played with her niece and nephew. She ran barefoot through the field behind her parents house simply because she could.

She slept in her old bedroom. Her family offered to let her stay at their home forever. But they also told her she could buy her own place.

She bought a townhouse in Beacon Hill, and had it decorated exactly how she wanted. She was an heiress, and had all the resources to do whatever she wished. She lived in the city. She got up every morning and walked. Wherever she wished. However far she wished. She kept in touch with Castor and his wife, and they talked about the issue of trafficking, and how she might contribute to helping women who were brought out of situations that were similar to hers, but much uglier.

And she talked to Cameron.

But he became more and more silent. And she could imagine him, sitting there in the north tower. Doing nothing but listening.

She watched the news for any sign that he had come out again. But it was as if he had vanished.

That one appearance, and then no more.

She on the other hand had become a sensational news story. Her return to her family had resulted in her adoptive father's arrest. And not just his, but many, many other men who were connected to him. Including Mattias.

It was like she and Rose had started an avalanche. One that she was very grateful for.

Her father had a security detail on her, and they were of course all good-looking men. She thought of what she had said to Cameron. How she had crushes on the security detail at her kidnapper's compound.

Though they were not the ones who had kidnapped her on the beach, they had held her all those years, and she had begun thinking of them that way. Yes, in spite of the fact that she had all the freedom in the world, and those men around her, she felt not even the slightest bit of interest. She could think only of Cameron.

"I need to go back," she said to Constantine, one night when he and Morgan were visiting her at her townhouse.

"To McKenzie?"

"Yes. Because no matter what, I'm Athena McKenzie."

"You are not. You are ours."

She shook her head. "I'm my own, Constantine.

Or have you not realize that yet. And my heart is with Cameron. I love him."

"You know, Stockholm syndrome…" Morgan began.

"I do not have Stockholm syndrome. I could do whatever I want, I could go wherever I want. I could have whatever man I want, and I only want him. I have experienced the freedom the world has to offer. And I love being with you. All of you. I will never abandon you. But if I didn't love him, then my life would be complete right this moment, and it isn't."

Morgan's face was filled with understanding. "I do understand that. You may not have seen it, but your brother is an absolute beast himself. And I loved him anyway. I couldn't escape that, no matter how much I wanted to."

"I don't even want to," said Athena. "I want to be with him."

"Make use of my private jet," said Constantine. "It will get you there the fastest."

CHAPTER EIGHTEEN

HE KNEW WHEN she arrived at the castle. All of his sensors went off. He had thought it strange that she had not spoken to him in twenty-four hours. And now, he knew why. She was here.

And he was… Certainly not fit for company. He knew she had noticed that he had stopped speaking to her and now she was here.

"Open the door to me, Cameron," she shouted from outside the gate.

And he did. Because he was weak.

And then he opened the doors to her as well, because he was weak. And then he was down the stairs, and waiting in the antechamber, because he was weak.

And when she came into the chamber, it was he who crossed the space. It was he who pulled her into his arms. And it was he who lowered his head and conquered her mouth. Claimed it.

He had tried to be a good man. An honorable man. He had tried not to do this. To leave her be. And yet she had not left him.

How was he supposed to forget her when she did not let him.

How was he supposed to forget her when she kept on talking to him. His goddess. How was he supposed to let her go. And now he was not. He was clinging to her tightly. Now, he was feasting upon her lips, holding her against his body, relishing in the feel of her breasts crushed against him.

She was so soft.

So strong and so perfect.

She was everything. Everything he wanted. Everything he needed.

This wasn't about whether or not he'd been with a woman in ten years. Because Athena was nothing like those other encounters. His need for her was nothing like that previous, physical need. There was no amount of self-gratification that could erase his desire for her. Because it was not the same. His need for her was everything he feared.

That well of need that he had only ever let out once before. That had been crushed and destroyed and turned against him.

And yet it was also somehow something totally unique, even sharper. Even more dangerous.

And he did not possess the will to release her. Not for his sake. Not for hers. Instead, he carried her up the stairs. To the north tower, the place that he had told her she could never go.

He carried her there and into his bedchamber.

It was Spartan. Nothing really but the bed.

And he laid her down across the bed, standing away from her and slowly removing his clothing.

He did not feel fear over letting her see his scars.

Athena had seen his every scar already. The

real ones. The deep ones. The darkest ones that were in the recesses of his very soul.

Athena knew him. For better and for very much worse. She was his wife.

And it was not supposed to mean anything, and yet it meant everything. Just as she did. She watched him, her eyes sharp as he removed all of his clothing.

And then he joined her down on the bed, moving his hands over her curves. She was wearing a coat, which he stripped quickly from her body, and he looked into her eyes as he pushed his hand beneath her skirt, closing his eyes briefly, letting his breath hiss through his teeth as his fingertips moved along her smooth skin.

She was a gift. One he had not earned. And one he surely did not deserve. One he would not turn away from. For he did not have the strength left in him. Not anymore. It was not just ten years of being alone. It was a lifetime.

And he had kept all of this, all of this need, all of this desire, locked away.

And now it was flooding from him. Hemorrhaging. And he could do nothing to stop it.

He pushed his hand between her thighs, slipped his fingertips beneath the waistband of her panties, and found her wet for him. And it was as if it was the only time it had ever happened in all the history of all of mankind. That this was for him. His.

It was what he wanted. For her to be his and only his. For this moment to be the only moment. For this breath to be the only breath. This breath where his mingled with hers and their hearts beat as one.

Where he could feel the evidence of her desire coaching his hand, and it never had the chance to turn into anything else.

It never had the chance to sour. To become a disappointment.

It never had the chance to be what it would inevitably be.

Him breaking her.

Is that really what you're afraid of?

He pushed that thought aside, and he let himself feel.

For the first time in ten years. For the first time since he was a boy.

For the first time since he had hoped that someone was showing the smallest bit of care for his safety, for his well-being, but who only wanted to use him.

There had never been any control.

And surrendering it was the last thing he would ever do. Except now, he was doing just that. Now, he was surrendering.

To this. To her.

He pushed a finger inside of her and watched her face contort with need. Desire.

She arched her hips against him. When he had let her go, he had tried to do it without ever putting his hands on her. She had kissed him. She had branded them both. She had undone all of his good intentions. This was her fault.

She had come back to him. This was her fault.

The consequences...

He had tried to spare her.

He had tried to spare her him, but she simply wasn't allowing it.

And what was to be done?

He was at his end.

He had been a man cursed these last ten years. Concealed away in stone.

He had hardly been a man at all.

And now here he was with her.

Keeping one hand between her legs, pleasuring her there, he reached his other hand around behind her back and undid the zipper on her dress, moving his hand from between her thighs only to divest her of the garment.

He took off her panties. Her bra. And he looked upon the glory that was Athena.

She was golden, glorious. Her round, firm breasts had tight dusky nipples hardened into points, and they called for his touch. For his tongue.

The dark thatch of curls between her thighs made his body ache with the need to sink inside of her.

Just the sight of those glorious curves, of her womanly glory.

She was everything.

And he needed her. More than anything. More than his next breath.

He kissed down her body, sucking one nipple deep into his mouth. She gasped, crying out as she arched against him, and he gripped her hips, pressing his hardness down against her softness there and letting her feel just what she did to him. Her hands were all over him. Moving down his back, over his chest. All over his scars. But she did not stop and single them out. Did not stop and touch them.

She did not act as if they were an independent piece, something separate to him.

She touched all of him. As if every bit was Cameron.

And every bit was whole.

Only Athena could have done this. Only Athena could have waged this war and won.

She moved her hand down between them and wrapped her fingers around his shaft, squeezing him tight, slowly licking her lips as she made eye contact with him, before wiggling out from beneath him and pushing him onto his back.

"This is my fantasy. I have been thinking about this for very long time. Remember, all those long years I was kept away in a compound."

"Yes, and you have not been there for a while. You've been free."

"That's right," she said, rubbing her palm up and down his hardness. "I have been able to do whatever I wanted. Be whoever I wanted. I have seen the world. I have tasted freedom. And here I am. Because I wanted no other man, Cameron. And I touched no other man. I need you to know that. I need you to understand."

"Athena…"

But she lowered her head and slicked her tongue from the base of him to the tip, before taking him into her mouth and swallowing any of his objections along with him. His breathing was ragged, his control at its end. He moved his fingers through her hair, caressed her face as she licked him, sucked him, and shattered all that remained of his control.

"Not like this," he growled. He moved her away from him, and then turned her onto her back, kissing down her stomach, and then curving his arms around her thighs, clasping his fingers over her stomach and holding her fast as he dragged her to his mouth and began to eat the sweet center of her.

He licked her, deep. Pushing his tongue into her honeyed depths as he extracted every scream of pleasure from her that he could.

If he was going to ruin her. If he was going to ruin them both, then it would be thorough and complete. Because he was a monster who left nothing unharmed. Who left no recognizable pieces in his wake. He burned everything to ash. And it would be the same with her. The same with them. And he would relish the journey. Hell was the destination. And so getting there had to be everything.

And yet this was not like sex as he knew it. It was something more.

It was their walk on the Seine. It was the moment when he'd talked her to orgasm in the kitchen. It was when she'd put his clothes on him and given him her necklace. It was a kiss in the rain and vows in a chapel.

It was seeing her huddled in the hut and knowing, *knowing*, that she had to be his.

It was every part of him and every part of her, mingling together. The broken and the beautiful. The monstrous and the divine.

Power and glory and all the things he'd always feared.

And everything he needed to go on breathing.

She was shaking, crying out, she shattered over and over again, her fingers woven through his hair, tugging hard, her heels digging down into the mattress.

And when he was satisfied that she had reached her peak enough times, he moved up and captured her lips. He had not kissed her enough.

It would never be enough. There would never be enough.

And that in and of itself was the most sobering, horrendous realization of them all.

There would never be enough of this. He was doomed. And he would not turn back even knowing that.

She wrapped her arms around his neck, and looked

into his eyes as he positioned himself at her slick center. He pushed inside of her slowly, and she never looked away. She was so tight. And he was lost.

"Cameron," she said, as he filled her completely.

And he began to move. And this was different. Completely different. Being inside of her was not like being inside of any other woman. The pleasure that he found here was not like any other pleasure. This was not a race to release. This was not about control. He was not solidifying his power, he was surrendering it. To her.

And with every arch of her hips against his she gave it back, but it was made something more. Just as he was.

He wanted it to go on forever, but he knew it could not. And he could feel her pleasure building within her, and then when she cried out his name, her internal muscles pulsing around him, he gave up his own.

His growl reverberated off the walls as he poured himself inside of her. As every last vestige of control dissolved.

As the goddess of war made him hers.

And when he came back to himself, to them, she was clinging to him, gazing up at him.

"Cameron," she whispered. "I love you."

CHAPTER NINETEEN

SHE FELT HIS withdrawal emotionally before he physically left her.

She had known that that might be a mistake. That saying it might be a problem. She had known.

But she had also known that she was here to take all.

To conquer all.

And there was only one thing that did that. And that was love.

It was not strength or might or power. It was not manipulation. It was only love. And she had that for him. It radiated through all of her. Through everything she was.

And even in his fear, she was strong.

She stood up, naked and completely unashamed. Stood before him proud.

"Don't run from this now."

"No, Athena. This cannot be born. This is why I did not want to touch you. This is why…"

"Yes. I know. Because you don't want me to get too close to you. Because you don't want anyone to get to close you, that is why you left me on the doorstep of my family home. That is why you didn't stay with me. It is why you didn't touch me before. Because you knew that if you did you would have no protection left."

"I kept away from you to protect you. You and your hungry virgin's eyes. How do you feel now?"

"Strong. But I already did. I knew what I wanted before I arrived at this castle. I want you, Cameron. I'm Athena McKenzie. I know who I am. I know that I got a family name when I found Constantine, but you are the family I choose. Don't you see? I went out and I saw the world. I could have had anyone. But I didn't. Because what I wanted was here. I am an heiress. I bought a house. I furnished it with all things that I loved. I saw myself living a life that I created. A life without you.

"And it was not enough. It was not enough because it was not you. I am not a prisoner. And I know what is out there. I have been to beaches and cities. I have had a glorious family Christmas. And in and amongst all of that, I felt sadness. Because I missed you. Because I want you. I kept on living out there so that you couldn't tell me I didn't understand. I talked to you every day over the intercom because I chose to. Not because I was a prisoner. I'm not. I am the goddess of war, and I will fight for you. I will fight for us. And if you resent that, then you must take your own self to task. Have courage. Take heart. You told me to find my strength. And I have. Do not join the chorus of men who have tried to tell me what I am. What I shall become. I have already proven that I am stronger than those around me have ever been willing to give me credit for. You were the one person who saw it, Cameron. Don't sell me short now."

"It is… It is impossible," he said. "It is me."

The words were broken. Ragged. "I am a monster," he continued. "And there is no fairy-tale ending waiting for us. You saw the headlines, beauty and the beast. But you cannot kiss me and make this better. Here we are, I have your virgin blood on my sheets, and I am still a monster."

"And I am Athena, goddess of war, Cameron, and I was made to fight this battle. I thought my journey was to find my place with other people, but I had to find myself, so I could make the space I needed. And I have done it. And now I know who I am. I know what I want. I want you, and you can't tell me I don't. Do not make me into an object for your trauma to hold on to, that is how you turn a person into your personal plaything, a piece of a collection and steal all their humanity. That is what I was for my mother, and I will not be that for you."

"I am scarred…"

"Your scars are the mark of who you are, not a monster. A man who survived."

"I am nothing more than a broken boy. It's all I have ever been. Wanting love sent me down a path I could not come back from. It is a twisted sort of thing to sell your body, and to learn to wall your soul away so that nothing can touch you. And at the same time to want… To want desperately for even one encounter to do something to ease the loneliness inside of you. I came here to face the loneliness. To accept it. Because I've never been very good at it.

"Stolen moments, fleeting bits of closeness where someone else might put their hands on me and I might feel like I'm not the only person in this world. I cannot separate that need from how sordid it all is. I cannot…"

"You know that what happened between us was not sordid."

"And what will happen when you are done with me? What then?"

"Have I ever given you reason to not trust me? I have crossed the world to be here with you. It's what you fear is inside of you. You fight an enemy in your own self. Do not turn me into your foe, Cameron McKenzie. I was your gift. If you believe in anything, believe in that fate that brought me here. Because I do. It brought me to you. It brought me to my family. It rescued me."

"You rescued yourself. The minute you threw yourself out of that motorcade."

"Fine then. I rescued myself. Trust me to carry on knowing exactly how to rescue us both." And she realized then that she had it wrong. Just that one thing.

"Actually, I can only rescue you just so much, can't I? You must take those next steps yourself.

You are at the crossroads, and you must find a way to decide. To step into the light. The only person who can break the curse is you. Because I can kiss you and love you, and believe that you are the man I know you are. A man worthy of those things, but unless you believe it, I cannot fix it."

"Athena…"

"Do you love me?"

And he looked like he might shatter.

He wished she had not asked that.

It was the splinter in the glass that set the whole pain fracturing.

Do you love me?

He could lie. He had lied so many times in his life about so many things. To himself, to everyone else.

Do you love me?

"Yes," he said, the word raw. It was destroying him. From the inside out. She was destroying him. He would gladly jump back into that car, and that twisted heap of metal, before facing this. But he had not been given a choice. It was killing him. Because there was nowhere to hide. There was no way to protect himself.

He had told himself, he had told her, that he needed nothing. That he did not care, that he did not love. Yes, he had told her that. And he had believed it. But here he was, confronted with the truth.

He had, all these years, wanted love more than he had ever wanted anyone other thing in all the world. He was broken with his need of it, and it was that which scared him above all else.

He'd had to close himself down to survive. And perhaps the thing that angered him most about his own part in Irina's death was that he had not even given himself a chance to care for her. Because it was there. That ability.

It was only he refused to share it because he was small and mean and terrified, like the boy he had been out on the streets.

The boy who'd had to learn how to sell his body without selling his soul.

But you can have your soul back now. And you can give it to her. That's what you want.

It was true. It was what he wanted more than anything.

And in the end of all things, if he did not do this, what did his life matter?

If he could love Athena, and she could love him in return, and he had survived that accident, and he had survived that childhood, and he had survived selling himself, over and over again, only to find the reality of intimacy and love and sex now, at thirty-eight years old, then if he turned it away, what was the point of surviving at all.

"I love you," he said again.

But it wasn't easy, and the words didn't get any easier. He pulled her to him, her naked body against his, and he kissed her. Desperately. Deeply. All over. "I love you. I love you, dammit, Athena, and it hurts."

"That's okay," she said, pushing his hair out of his face. "I don't want an easy love. And I came to that conclusion all the way back when we were walking along the river in Paris. I watched all those people with their soft gazes, the way that they held each other, and I knew that for us it could never be that. I had an idea of romance. But this... This is real. Jagged and sometimes painful, but it's worth fighting for. You and I... We are survivors. We are miraculous. But nobody ever said the miraculous was easy. In fact I think living miraculous is a very hard thing to do. And who else should be able to but us? Who else to try this wonderful, improbable love, except us?"

"I love you," he said again. "I want you. I want this."

"We can have it. Because I love you too. And this is where I choose to be. It's where I want to be. With you."

"Beauty and the beast indeed."

"No. The goddess of war and the beast. We both set about conquering each other. And I feel we did a pretty good job. And that we will keep on doing so. For the rest of our lives."

"Well that might really be how we live happily ever after," he said.

"Yes, Cameron. I believe it will be."

EPILOGUE

HE AND ATHENA had made good on the promises they'd given each other. Athena's work helping trafficking victims, and his own helping children on the streets wove easily around each other, and their foundation—which provided education in technology and the chance at a new life, had helped save nearly five hundred children from life on the street or in captivity.

They were working hard to make sure that there weren't children who felt discarded, abandoned or forgotten.

Cameron went from being a boy that nobody cared for, to a disfigured man living in isolation, to a husband, a brother-in-law, and honorary son, and a father in the space of less than a year. He could never have imagined such a thing.

As he sat in the expansive living area of the family estate in Massachusetts, and looked around at this newfound family, as he cradled his infant son in his arms, he knew one thing for certain. His own imagination had been terribly lacking. And it certainly never would have manufactured such a life of love for him. Simply because it had been too afraid.

But now he knew better. Now he knew that what lay ahead had the potential to be so much better than what was behind them. Now he knew that there was more to life than what he could see.

Now he knew Athena. He knew a goddess walking around on earth.

And so everything was possible.

With love, all things indeed, were possible.

* * * * *

If you were enchanted by
A Vow to Set the Virgin Free
then these stories by Millie Adams
are going to blow you away!

Stealing the Promised Princess
Crowning His Innocent Assistant
The Only King to Claim Her
His Secretly Pregnant Cinderella
The Billionaire's Baby Negotiation

Available now!